Trace had had enough of Martha's yowling.

He grabbed the barrel of her gun, twisted it from her hand and sent it sailing through the air. "I told you once," he growled, "I don't like guns, and having one in your hand is asking for trouble."

Though he was considerably taller than she was, Martha still took a swing at his cheek. To her aggravation, he stepped away, causing her to miss. But she had swung her arm with such force, she would have fallen if he hadn't caught her.

"Take your hands off me!"

"That's strange," Trace commented as he drew her against him. "A little while back, I got the distinct impression that you rather liked having my hands on you. If I remember correctly, we were lying on your bed."

If he remembered correctly? Of all the nerve! "I wouldn't know. It was too long ago."

The blatant lie made Trace laugh. "There are always ways to remind you."

Dear Reader,

This month we are happy to bring you *Rogue's Honor,* a new book from DeLoras Scott. Those of you who have followed DeLoras's career since her first book, *Bittersweet,* will be delighted by this tale of the Oklahoma land rush and of partners each with their own dark pasts.

With *Heaven's Gate,* the writing team of Erin Yorke has created the dramatic story of a wayward English countess and the renegade Irish lord who is determined to force her surrender.

Lindsay McKenna's *King of Swords* is a sequel to her January title, *Lord of Shadowhawk.* Abducted and held for ransom, Thorne Somerset learns to love the bitter soldier who holds her fate in his hands.

A fugitive Union officer and a troubled Rebel girl overcome seemingly insurmountable odds to find happiness in *The Prisoner.* Set at the close of the Civil War, this tender story is the first historical by popular contemporary author Cheryl Reavis.

Next month look for titles by Maura Seger, Julie Tetel, Lucy Elliot and Elizabeth August from Harlequin Historicals, and rediscover the romance of the past.

Sincerely,

The Editors

EC A+
G

Rogue's Honor

DeLoras Scott

Harlequin Books

TORONTO • NEW YORK • LONDON
AMSTERDAM • PARIS • SYDNEY • HAMBURG
STOCKHOLM • ATHENS • TOKYO • MILAN
MADRID • WARSAW • BUDAPEST • AUCKLAND

Harlequin Historicals first edition May 1992

ISBN 0-373-28723-2

ROGUE'S HONOR

Books by DeLoras Scott

Harlequin Historicals

Bittersweet #12
Fire and Ice #42
The Miss and the Maverick #52
Rogue's Honor #123

Harlequin Books

Historical Christmas Stories 1991
"Fortune's Gift"

DeLORAS SCOTT

believes her writing is derived from a love for historical novels, a strong dash of humor and an excellent support group. A full-time writer, she enjoys the freedom of being able to create characters and have them come alive in plots of her choosing.

The mother of five grown children, she and her husband have lived and traveled throughout the U.S. A native of California, she now resides in the state of her birth.

Prologue

New Mexico—May, 1888

The afternoon sun glared down, but there was a hard nip to the air, and the cold breeze was cutting. It had been a light winter, however, and only patches of snow remained on the ground.

Well hidden among the mountain spruce trees, Sam Coffee reached up and cupped his hand over the big stallion's muzzle to keep the black from nickering. Within minutes riders atop lathered mounts galloped by. The dust kicked up by the horses' hooves attacked Sam's eyes and nostrils. He knew the posse would soon realize their mistake and circle back. He could ill afford the luxury of a rest. He pulled himself back into the saddle, trying to ignore the pain in his thigh. Silently he cursed the bastard that had managed a lucky shot. Taking a bullet at the age of thirty hurt a hell of a lot more than it had when he was young and thought he was invincible. He headed his mount in the opposite direction.

Thirty minutes later Sam guided his horse down a small, twisting stream lined with thick green firs. The pace was slow, but for a while at least he'd leave no tracks to follow. Convinced the posse wouldn't pick up his trail until dusk, he moved the horse up onto the dry bank. As he nudged the stallion into a full gallop, he laughed into the wind. After three days of being chased, he had once again eluded his pursuers. The bank's gold would remain safely tucked away in his saddlebags.

As horse and rider started down through the foothills, cactus began replacing trees. Sam pondered his narrow escape. Although he'd made it a practice to never tell anyone where he'd hit next, the sheriff had somehow been tipped off. Of course, with his picture plastered on Wanted posters all over New Mexico, anyone could have recognized him. Had he waited a few minutes longer before leaving the bank, he'd now be hanging at the end of a rope. No doubt about it, the time had come to get his ass out of New Mexico.

Two hours later Sam's attention centered on his wound. The inside of his boot was sticky with blood, and dizziness plagued him. Though the air was still crisp, beads of perspiration ran down into his eyes, making them burn. "Come on, Coffee," he mumbled, "you're almost at Juanita's. As always, she'll get the bullet out and make you as good as new. Besides, you have an important appointment to keep."

In an effort to take his mind off his pain, Sam concentrated on the money he had stashed away in a Texas bank. He'd accumulated enough to live comfortably for the rest of his life. His lips twitched with amusement as he thought about how he took from one bank and deposited in another. A truly interesting way of doing business.

The giant saguaro ahead suddenly became blurred, and Sam shook his head, determined not to lose consciousness.

The remaining mile seemed to pass at a tortoise's pace. Avoiding the main road, he entered the small Indian pueblo by way of a goat path. Foliage grew thick along the narrow trail and he had to keep urging his horse onward. The badly lathered animal stumbled. Like Sam, the stallion needed water and rest.

Finally he arrived at the back of the adobe hut. Damn, he thought, I'm getting too old for this. He guided his horse to the back door, then, leaning over, knocked. He passed out before he could see the door swing open.

Texas—October, 1888

It was evening when the lean, black-haired man rode into Abilene. His years of being chased across New Mexico by every posse, vigilante and bounty hunter had finally come to an end.

Sam Cottee's lips twisted into a wry smile. By a strange quirk of fate, he was no longer a hunted man. Who would have thought the governor himself would grant amnesty to the territory's most-wanted bank robber? Apparently saving a man's life still counted for something, although he'd had to give his word that he would stay out of New Mexico.

After procuring an overnight room in a cheap hotel where he hoped he wouldn't be recognized, Sam took off in search of an out-of-the-way restaurant. He kept his wide-brimmed hat pulled low, trying to avoid any young buck who might call him out in hopes of making a name for himself. He just wanted to take care of his business before leaving town in the morning. Even though he was no longer a wanted man, he still had a reputation as a fast gun.

He found a hole-in-the-wall that proclaimed itself an eatery, and entered. The place was dirty inside, with few customers, but the food turned out to be quite tasty. As soon as he'd finished his meal, he grabbed a newspaper and returned to his hotel room.

The next morning, Sam awoke feeling cramped because of the sad excuse for a bed, but at least he felt rested after his long ride. Having dressed, he ran his hand across the bushy beard that hid the scar trailing along his jawbone. His beard needed trimming, but the barber would have to wait. First the bank. Soon he'd leave Texas and assume a different name. He'd become a respectable man, marry a respectable woman, have respectable children and never again hold a .45 or any other weapon in his hand. Nothing would point to his past. He glanced down at the paper lying on the floor. The headlines proclaimed: Free Indian Land in Oklahoma Territory. Sam grinned.

At twenty minutes till ten, Coffee strapped on his gun belt, checked to be sure the ivory-handled revolver was loaded, then shoved it into the holster. His hat on and the leather saddlebags slung across his shoulder, he left the room. It took but a few minutes to pay the hotel clerk, and a few more to get on his horse and head for the bank. After making the sizable deposit, Coffee rode out of Abilene.

By the time he reached the next small town, Sam's mouth was feeling mighty dry. Spying the saloon, he decided that a drink to his success didn't sound like a bad idea. He tied his horse to the hitching post and strolled in.

After ordering a drink from the bartender, Sam stuck the toe of a dusty black boot on the brass rail and glanced around the room. *Maybe I'll enjoy a few minutes of peace,* he mused as he took a drink, appreciating the sharp bite of whiskey.

"Coffee!" The loud voice came from outside the saloon. "I know you're in there!"

"Damn!" a man near Sam whispered excitedly. "That's Sam Coffee standing at the bar!"

An old codger sitting next to the window looked out. "Lord a' mercy!" he exclaimed. "It's Luke Short calling him!"

Inside the saloon, excitement pumped through every man's veins. Not just one, but two famous gunfighters were in town, and maybe only one of them would leave alive.

Coffee downed his drink, then slammed the glass on the bar. He ambled over to the swinging doors. "What you want, Luke?" he called in disgust.

"Why don't you come find out?"

Coffee stepped out onto the wooden walk, his spurs jingling with each step. Everyone in the saloon rushed to the door or nearest window to see what was going to happen next.

"I think it's time we settled who's the fastest gun," Luke Short said. He tucked the front of his black, long-tail coat behind his guns, then dropped his hands to his sides.

"I take it you've had too much to drink. I don't want to kill you, Luke."

"You gonna draw, or do I shoot you down on the spot?"

The men in the saloon dropped to the floor.

"Very well, but if you happen to be alive when we finish, remember, you called me out." Coffee stepped down onto the street. Even with the hot breeze kicking up dust, he had no trouble keeping his eyes on the man with the full mustache.

Cautiously, Coffee walked to the middle of the street and turned full face. The two men stared at each other. Coffee's hand moved first. He never got off a shot before Short pulled the trigger. Coffee lunged backward, holding his chest, then dropped to the ground.

The sheriff and his deputy came running out of the saloon, and after one of them threw a coat over the body, they pushed the spectators away. A puff of black smoke rose and faded into the air as a picture was taken. A monumental moment in the history of the Southwest had just been recorded. Sam Coffee was dead.

Luke Short holstered his gun and walked away.

Chapter One

The group of hard-faced women marched the petite blonde through the snow to the waiting train. After making sure Blossom's steamer trunk had been loaded, the ladies watched her step inside the Kansas Pacific Railroad car.

"Make sure you don't come back!" one woman called as the train jerked forward.

Blossom entered the coach, seated herself, then pulled her wool cape more tightly about her shoulders. She wasn't trying to hide the ostrich feathers or plunging neckline on the bright red gown that heralded her profession. Her painted face made its own declaration.

Arranging herself as comfortably as possible on the hard, wooden seat, Blossom glanced at the two men seated across the aisle.

The bald one winked. "Where you headed, sweet thing?"

"Give it up," Blossom replied heartlessly. "I'm out of business."

* * *

As the train traveled across the flat, snow-covered land, Blossom stared out the window with unseeing eyes. Her thoughts were centered on her future. The biddies that had run her out of town might have done her a favor. At twenty-four, she figured it was time to see a world outside the confines of a saloon. She was tired of living in a small town where everyone knew her by sight. She took a deep breath. For the first time in her life, she was totally on her own.

Blossom disembarked in Topeka, the cold air nipping at her face. Because of the way she dressed, she knew better than to try to secure a room in a nice hotel. She purchased a newspaper and, after a brief word with the stationmaster about accommodations, started down a street he'd pointed to.

After walking ten blocks, Blossom finally spied a hotel that she felt sure would rent her a room. There were no options. She was already half-frozen and worn-out. To say the hotel was dilapidated was being too kind. Nevertheless, she entered. A fat-cheeked man with tobacco juice running down the side of his mouth sat dozing behind the scarred registration counter.

"I'd like to rent a room for the night," Blossom announced.

The clerk looked up, his thick lips suddenly twisting into a smile. "Well, now, look what we got here." He stood slowly, his eyes greedily assessing the attractive woman. "You sure are a pretty little thing. How much do you charge? And don't try to up the price, 'cause I know what you women are asking."

"As I said, I want to rent a room."

"I'll even let you stay free—in my room."

"Are you going to rent me a room or not?"

"You don't have to go getting so damn huffy, missy," the angry clerk proclaimed.

Blossom started to walk out.

"All right. I'll let you have a room, but I want the money in advance."

Blossom handed him the ridiculous price of five dollars.

"If I hear a lot of noise, I'll kick you out. And no visitors!"

After paying a boy to fetch her trunk from the railroad station, Blossom climbed the dark stairway. The small room she entered contained only a bed and commode. Atop the commode sat a candle. The melted wax had oozed down until it formed a thick, wide base. There was also a cracked washbowl and a chipped pitcher half full of water. The floor looked as if it hadn't been scrubbed since the place was built.

Her feet aching unmercifully, Blossom collapsed fully clothed onto the bed. The smelly mattress sagged, causing her to roll to the center, but she was too exhausted to care.

The next morning Blossom was ready to tackle her problems. Opening her trunk, she took an honest look at her clothes. They were all too bright to be worn on the street, especially in a town as sophisticated as Topeka. But folded neatly beneath all the satin and lace was one simple calico dress. Lovingly, she pulled it out. She'd saved it for years to remind her of times past. Maybe she'd seen men of every description drift in and out of her saloon, but was she really so different now?

Yes. She was older, much harder, and there wasn't anything she hadn't seen. Blossom released a bitter laugh, knowing that those self-righteous women in Bickerton would never have believed her maidenhood was still intact. But why should they have? If the circumstances had been reversed, she wouldn't have believed it, either.

Realizing she was only feeling sorry for herself, Blossom forced a smile. That part of her life was over and the time had come to move on. First, she'd go to the bank and get her money transferred. Why was she moping? She'd always been a shrewd businesswoman. She'd saved her money, and by anyone's standard she was wealthy.

Once she had her money transferred to Topeka, she would purchase proper high-necked dresses instead of ones that allowed men a promising view of full breasts. She might even buy a lavish house and retire. But, having worked most of her life, she couldn't picture herself spending the rest of it sitting idle. She shuddered. She wasn't ready to lie down and die yet.

She'd be a schoolteacher! At the orphanage, she had been taught to read, write and work with numbers. Those lessons had proved invaluable in running a saloon and dealing cards. Perhaps in time she'd even find a widower to marry and become a pillar of the community. Having decided on her future, Blossom chose San Francisco as a good place to start her new life. Maybe she could also locate Lawrence there.

She raised a slender finger to her lips. From this time on, she would use her real name. Martha Jackson. It sounded strange. Had it been thirteen years? She sat on the edge of the bed, her dress clutched in her hands. Memories flooded back, as if they had happened yesterday.

It was 1875, in St. Louis, Missouri. She was eleven at the time. She and her older brother were busily scrubbing clothes over one of the big vats containing hot water. Their frayed cotton clothes clung to their bodies from the heat and their labor.

"I'm going to run away, Martha."

Martha looked at her handsome blond brother in disbelief. "That's a silly thing to say. Where would you go? How would you eat? At least here at the orphanage we have food and a place to sleep."

"As long as we work ourselves to death. Besides, I'm fourteen, and they're already talking about kicking me out 'cause I eat too much."

Martha had to admit that her brother did eat a lot, but he was already taller than any other boy at the orphanage, and built like an ox.

"I'm serious, Martha. I'm taking off tonight."

Martha was crushed. She and Lawrence had never been apart. She couldn't possibly remain without him. "You have to take me with you," she pleaded. "I'll die if you leave me here alone."

"What am I going to do with a girl tagging along?"

"Please, Lawrence. I can work just as hard as you can." She looked up at him with soulful brown eyes. "We're family."

Lawrence cleared his throat, and Martha knew he was trying to keep from showing the emotion he was feeling. She also knew he would have left a year ago if it hadn't meant leaving her behind.

"Oh, all right, but stuff everything in your knapsack and get ready to go, 'cause I'm leaving as soon as everyone has gone to bed. If you're late, I'm going on without you. I'll meet you by the front door."

That night they left the only home they'd known for nine years. Lawrence lifted Martha up so she could scramble over the iron fence that circled the orphanage, then he climbed over behind her.

For two years they had stayed in St. Louis, making just enough to provide themselves with food and a place to sleep. Lawrence continued to grow. By sixteen, he was close to six feet in height, his muscles bulged, and he looked much older than his age.

They decided to go west, and soon they arrived at the small settlement of Bickerton, a short distance from Independence. To their delight, Lawrence got a job at the Spur Saloon as a bouncer. Lawrence explained that it was his job to take care of the unmanageable customers. For the first time, they had a place of their own to live in and money in their pockets.

Martha snapped herself back to the present. Remembering what two children had accomplished restored her determination. She snatched up the torn but clean towel lying on the commode, doused it in the pitcher of water, then scrubbed her face until her skin hurt. Finally satisfied that all traces of paint had been removed, she stripped to her undergarments. After putting on two petticoats, she pulled the calico dress over her head. This was the first dress Lawrence had bought her. Though she'd been thirteen at the time, she hadn't grown but an inch or so taller. Of course her bosom was larger and pushed at the material, but her waist was smaller. All things considered, the dress fit quite well. A good hair brushing followed. Unable to style her hair without a mirror, she let it hang down her back, then tied it at the nape with a blue ribbon from one of her more colorful dresses.

Martha sat back on the bed and picked up the newspaper to see what banks were listed. The headlines immediately attracted her attention. She read an article about unassigned lands in the Oklahoma District being opened in April. The possibility of owning her own land was appealing, especially since it would be free. She would have plenty of time to purchase what she'd need before leaving Topeka. Perhaps she could open a schoolhouse in

Oklahoma. Wouldn't it be amusing to be neighbors of the same type of women that had kicked her out of Bickerton? Her mind was made up. Traveling to California would have to wait a little longer.

As Martha left the grubby hotel, she felt a surge of satisfaction when the desk clerk didn't recognize her. She stopped the first person she met on the sidewalk and asked directions to Kansas Street. With that knowledge under her belt, she took off, head held high. She had a lot to do if she was going to be in Oklahoma Territory come April. For the first time in her life, she was going to have a house. Her own house. And a garden. Yes, definitely a garden. How wonderful it would be to go outside and pick anything she wanted.

She walked across the street, passing a woman wearing spectacles. Maybe I should purchase spectacles, she thought. It would certainly make me look more respectable.

Chapter Two

Oklahoma Territory — April 22, 1889

After checking her team and rigging, Martha continued walking around the farm wagon, making sure everything was secured and ready to make the dash for land. The prairie schooner loaded with furniture and household goods was parked far in the back. She had tied the team to a line rope to keep them settled down. After seeing all the people who had collected for the run, she'd decided to drive the much lighter wagon.

It had rained heavily the previous week, but fortunately, the land that stretched out ahead appeared to be dry. Martha glanced back at the thousands of white tents, stakes and ropes that comprised the town of Guthrie. "I should have gone to California," she mumbled as she climbed onto the wagon seat. "Who would have thought there'd be so damn many people?"

Martha checked her lapel watch. She'd been up before sunrise, and she still had thirty minutes to wait. At least the day was clear and warm. She rolled up the sleeves of her gray-and-green-striped shirt and pulled down her floppy hat firmly on her head. Again she glanced at the line on either side of her. People in wagons of every description, flatbeds, buggies, bicycles and even men on foot stretched as far as the eye could see, waiting to lay claim to the free land.

"Why in God's name am I even here?" Martha uttered softly. An Army man had told her that some fifty thousand people would be converging on the two million acres, and she had no doubt that he had spoken the truth. She thought of all the twitching, anxious, hopeful faces of men and women she'd seen over the past week.

When the bugle sounded at noon, everyone would move forward, and there was a strong possibility that Martha would either be squeezed out by the multitude, or that her wagon would turn over and she'd be killed. As she stared at the flat, empty land, she tried thinking of her alternatives. Again she glanced up and down the line. A horse certainly wasn't as cumbersome as a wagon, and tied at the back of her rig was a very fast gelding. She checked her watch. Only ten minutes to go. Not enough time to dig out the saddle, put it on the horse, plus tie down the team so they wouldn't take off with the other animals when the turmoil began. Why had she waited until now to come to such an obvious conclusion?

Glancing around, Martha spied a strapping boy of about eleven standing well back, obviously not taking part in the free-for-all. Hurriedly she climbed back down and ran to him. Time was of the essence. When she promised him five dollars, the boy agreed to hold her team in check until she returned. With that problem solved, she grabbed her small white flag and a rifle, then ran to the back of the wagon. It might not be very ladylike having my skirts hiked up, she thought as she untied her mount, but I'll take the speed of a horse over a wagon any day.

A few minutes before noon, Martha sat astride the frisky gray, grateful she'd had enough forethought this morning to remove her bustle. Still, she had to look a sight. Her hands shook as she kept the gray in check. The rifle and stake were held firmly in her left hand. The other hand clutched the reins as well as a big wad of mane. One way or another, she was going to get her 160 acres. Besides her worries about being killed and the strong possibility of coming out of the rush without any land at all, she now had another major concern. It was a long time since she'd ridden bareback.

A hush fell and Martha held her breath. Even the many spectators had quieted. At exactly noon, the bugle blew and the line charged. Martha's horse surged forward as total chaos erupted. The spectators yelled their encouragement, whips cracked, wagons rushed ahead—some tipping over and throwing people to the ground—and men on horses rammed into each other. Martha held on to the gelding's mane for dear life. Everything seemed to have become one big cloud of dust, which unmercifully invaded Martha's nose, eyes and mouth. Somehow she managed to stay on the gray's back, and they actually broke through the masses. There were other riders ahead, but everyone seemed to be branching off in different directions.

She rode hard for what seemed like uncountable miles before taking a good look at her surroundings. She wasn't sure how she'd made it this far, but she liked what she saw and decided this was the place to stake her claim. Before she could stop her horse, someone else rode up and drove a stake in the ground. After the same thing happened several more times, Martha became angry and desperate. She kept going, pushing the gelding to top speed.

Then she saw it. The perfect place! It even had oak trees as well as cottonwoods. Anxious to get her stake in the ground first, she pulled back on the reins, then leaped off before the horse came to a complete halt. The momentum sent her flying forward. She tripped on her skirts, then fell facedown in a mud puddle, her stake and rifle falling close by.

"Sorry, lady, this land is taken."

Sputtering, Martha looked at a pair of boots solidly planted on dry land. Her gaze traveled up long muscular legs encased in fitted doe-colored trousers, narrow hips and broad shoulders that could not be hidden by a loose white shirt. The man's black, neatly trimmed mustache matched his hair, which was partially hidden by a Stetson. His crystal-blue eyes fringed with thick lashes drew Martha's attention. They were hard and determined. He didn't even look toward the strutting black stallion that tugged at the tightly held reins.

Martha was furious at having yet another man ready to claim the land she now considered hers. Snatching up the stake, she stabbed it into the puddle, sending mud flying. "I'm afraid you're too late, mister," she stated as she yanked down her skirt from around her waist and sat up. "I was here first." She pointed to the stake. "This land is now mine." She shoved back her hair to prevent any more mud from dripping onto her face.

"And all I have to do is pull it out. I was here first."

Martha reached for her rifle, but before she could curl her fingers around it, the stranger kicked it away.

"Never have cared for guns. I believe killing is against the Lord's will. You are a churchgoing woman, aren't you?"

Martha stared up at him, wondering if he was actually serious. "Of course," she finally replied. She made an attempt at brushing the mud from her shirt, only to end up with a worse mess.

"Ma'am," the stranger asked, "how do you plan to homestead this land by yourself?"

"It's quite simple. Just take one step at a time." Though he was big and tall, she refused to let him intimidate her. "Now, leave my land immediately."

"Your land? I think not. But I wouldn't be averse to sharing."

Martha accepted the hand he held out and let him help her to her feet. They looked each other in the eye, assessingly.

He had full lips, high cheekbones and a marvelously straight nose. An exceedingly attractive man, Martha conceded, but she didn't like his cocky self-assuredness. Realizing she had been staring, she lowered her lashes. It wasn't ladylike to look a man in the eye. "What do you mean, share?" she asked suspiciously.

"Very simple. We share everything."

"I beg your pardon!"

The man snatched his hat off, his thick black hair shining in the sunlight. "You misunderstand me, ma'am." A grin tugged at the corner of his lips. "I'm willing to let you have the land providing you sign an agreement stating that should you leave or marry, the land becomes mine. After all, I was here first. We'd sort of be partners."

It was the "sort of" that bothered Martha.

"Since you aren't wearing a wedding band, I assume you're not married?" he asked.

"No, I'm not."

"Look at it this way. How much land does one woman need, and how are you going to farm all this by yourself? I know at the moment you have every intention of staying, but this land can be mighty hard on a woman, especially a single one.''

''I see.''

''I apologize for my bad manners. My name's Trace Lockhart. And yours?''

''Martha Jackson.''

''So, do we have an agreement, Miss Jackson?''

''Whose name will the land be filed under?''

''Yours, of course.''

Martha had known a lot of men in her former profession and had always prided herself on being a good judge of character. She didn't trust this man for a minute. But what difference did it make? This was her land and she wasn't about to put her name on any piece of paper. ''Did you bring something with you for me to sign?''

''No, I'll have a lawyer draw it up. Lord knows there's enough of them around. I'll take your word as a good Christian and leave the stake right where it is. I always believe a man's... or woman's word is as good as paper.''

Martha knew she had him by the tail. Now all she had to do was get rid of him. ''Very well, Mr. Lockhart, you have a deal.''

Trace put out his hand to shake on it, but Martha turned away, pretending not to notice. She'd only agreed in order to get rid of him. Once she filed her claim, he could take his so-called agreement and eat it. Good Lord! What kind of a fool did he take her for?

''Would you like me to help you mark off your quarter section?''

''Would you?'' she asked, wide-eyed. She wasn't going to refuse a helping hand. Besides, maybe he knew what to do. She had no idea how to mark off the boundaries, or even where they were. "That would be so much help."

After the lengthy task was completed, Trace swung atop his horse, ready to leave. "You'll be happy to know I intend to work toward the building of a fine church for the community."

"Are you a preacher or something?"

"No, just a man who believes in the Lord's word. I'll be back in a few days with the agreement. Good day, ma'am." He spun his horse around and rode off.

The moment Trace was out of sight, Martha allowed her jubilation to explode. Laughing aloud, she turned wide circles, her eyes scanning the land. At last, she was now the proud owner of one hundred and sixty acres.

Trace was also laughing as he headed back to Guthrie. Things couldn't have worked out better, he thought. He'd picked out that prime land more than a week ago. Having already claimed town property, he couldn't file again. He'd even had an agreement in his pocket ready to be signed, but it now contained the wrong stipulations. He'd have to have another one drawn up to fit the situation.

In fact, this was an even better arrangement. He'd get the land even sooner than he'd planned. Martha Jackson wouldn't last long on the plains. She was probably poor, like most of the homesteaders, and when she gave up, he'd pay her a fair price for her holdings. She didn't even own a saddle, so how did she plan on developing the land as required by the government? And if she didn't want to stay the obligatory five years, how was she going to pay the buck-twenty-five an acre she would then owe on the land?

Since her face had been covered with mud, he'd had no way of knowing what the Jackson woman really looked like, except that she had blond hair and brown eyes. And she did have a most appealing, petite figure. With the front of her dress wet, he'd clearly seen her full breasts pressing against her shirt—even more so when she was angry. He wished he had seen her face. Maybe he'd even consider the possibility of sharing her bed until she became fed up with her life-style. It wasn't going to be difficult to twist her around his finger.

Trace reflected on his driving need for land. Land was the one thing that represented roots, and that was important to him. Someday he'd own a big spread with fat cattle grazing on it, and he'd be at peace with himself.

Trace tipped his hat at a family of homesteaders, who were already putting up their tent. He had to get back to Guthrie and file his claim for the town section. Tomorrow his first shipment of lumber would be arriving by train.

Fifteen minutes later, Trace pulled his horse to a halt and sat looking at the big tent city of Guthrie a mile away. Guthrie and Oklahoma City were going to shoot up overnight, and it would be his lumber that built the towns. More and more settlers would arrive over the years. Trace even envisioned Oklahoma Territory becoming a state, and he definitely planned on being a big part of Oklahoma's future.

After enjoying a breakfast of eggs, ham, biscuits and gravy, Martha left the big tent of the Palace Hotel and Restaurant and headed toward the land office. A groan escaped her lips upon seeing the long line that had already formed. Ever since she'd arrived in Guthrie, it had been wait, wait, wait. Whether it was for a bucket of water or to eat in a restaurant, you stood in line.

Taking her place at the end of the line, Martha admonished herself for not rising earlier. Since arriving in Guthrie, she'd fallen back into sleeping late and going to bed late—a problem that should be easy to rectify, since there was now nothing for her to do during the late hours.

It wasn't long before the line extended behind Martha, giving her some sense of satisfaction. The man in front of her and the man behind her began talking about "sooners" and "moonlighters," which she quickly discovered were one and the same. She became intrigued with their conversation, and soon discovered that the names applied to people who had entered the rush area early, claiming land they'd already picked out ahead of time.

"What's going to be done about it?" the big burly man asked.

"Heard tell there's gonna be an arbitration board formed," the skinny one replied. "There's already been too many double filings. If one of them sooners has already laid claim on my land, I'm gonna raise all kinds of hell."

Trace Lockhart suddenly leaped into Martha's thoughts. He hadn't seemed the least bit rushed. Now that she thought about it, his horse wasn't even lathered. But Mr. Lockhart had apparently been smarter than some of the other sooners. He planned to let some gullible person file the claim, then have them sign a separate contract!

"Excuse me, gentlemen," Martha interrupted. "This sooner problem you've been discussing—is it illegal?"

"You're damned right!" The skinny man blushed. "Sorry, ma'am. I didn't mean to use such language in front of a lady."

Martha wanted to laugh. Not just because the man had apologized for saying "damn," but also because she now knew there was absolutely nothing Trace Lockhart could do to get her land. If he tried, she'd turn him over to the marshal.

* * *

Irritated that more than a week had passed since he'd last seen Martha Jackson, Trace kept his horse at an easy lope through the tall grass and over the green, sloping hills. Unfortunately, he'd been too busy to get away. The first shipment of lumber had already arrived and been sold, and the second shipment would be arriving later this afternoon. Buildings were going up everywhere, and the town of Guthrie had already taken on a look of permanency. William Host, his young manager in Oklahoma City, had reported that the same thing was happening there. Now all Trace had to do was get Martha Jackson's signature on the contract—assuming she was still there, and assuming she had filed her claim. He'd been a damn fool. He should have found a way of seeing her sooner. All she had was a horse, which had been fine at the time because he'd planned on returning the next day. But what if she'd already decided to take off?

As Trace topped the last hill, he suddenly jerked back on the reins, bringing the stallion to a halt. Open-mouthed, he stared in disbelief at the once-quiet land, which now teemed with life. Six sleek horses tethered to the line rope stretched between two trees were lazily swishing their tails, chickens were scattered about, two men were busily drilling a water well—probably at an exorbitant price—and three more men were unloading lumber, which indicated a house was fixing to be built. As if that wasn't enough, a covered wagon that looked well loaded sat off to the far side of the area, with a small farm wagon nearby. A good-sized tent was nestled in the large stand of cottonwood.

Where the hell did the woman get everything? he wondered. Either Martha Jackson had left her belongings back in Guthrie when she made the land run, or someone else had laid claim to the land. Anxious to discover what was going on, he nudged his horse forward.

Martha stood in front of the stove, looking down at what had started out to be her breakfast. Now it was nothing more than a burned mess. She contemplated the possibility that she might have put too much coal on top of the stove for cooking. Just getting the coal to start burning had proved to be more of a problem than she'd anticipated.

She released a deep sigh as she considered the advisability of discussing this with her new neighbor, Edwina Graham—or Eddie, as the woman preferred to be called— who had graciously volunteered to teach her how to cook. Already tired of eating out of cans, Martha was convinced that at the rate things were going, she'd starve to death before her house was even completed.

Ready to go inside the tent and clean up, Martha took a moment to gaze over the land, still finding it hard to believe it was all hers. Seeing movement out of the corner of her eye, she turned and watched Trace Lockhart heading in her direction. He sat tall and handsome in the saddle, his beautiful black stallion strutting as he moved. Martha released a heavy sigh and waited. She had wondered how long it would be before Mr. Lockhart made an appearance.

"Good afternoon, Miss Jackson," Trace said after dismounting. Seeing her covered almost from head to toe with soot, he couldn't help but wonder what she'd been up to now. Or maybe the woman just didn't believe in washing.

"Good afternoon, Mr. Lockhart." Martha knew she was a mess, but pride made her square her shoulders as she looked straight into his crystal-blue eyes. She'd rather be hog-tied than apologize for her appearance. "How nice of you to pay a visit. I hadn't expected to see you again."

Trace arched a dark eyebrow at her comment. She had known damn well he was going to return. "Looks like you're getting settled in."

"Indeed I am. Tie your horse and come sit down. Would you like a glass of water? I'm sure your throat is parched after traveling all the way out here."

"As a matter of fact, I would." He tethered the stallion to the tree.

As Martha disappeared into the tent, Trace glanced at the stove off to the side, a worktable and three wooden chairs. He preferred to stand. A moment later she returned, handing him a glass of water, the sides smudged from where she'd held it. He had expected a tin cup.

"I'll be so glad when the well is completed," Martha commented. She wished he had sat down, which would at least have made her feel taller. "Mr. Hawkins, the man who witched it, assured me they wouldn't have to go down far. Since you seem to be so community minded, what with wanting to build a church, you'll be happy to know I'm planning to build a school as soon as my house is completed."

Trace choked on his water.

"Will you build your church in town?"

Trace was tired of small talk. He needed to get back to Guthrie and see to the transferring of his lumber. "I don't remember a schoolhouse being in our bargain. I've brought—"

"Bargain?" Martha asked with a perfect touch of innocence. "I know of no bargain."

Trace glared at the woman, but her brown eyes didn't waver. "We have an agreement, Miss Jackson. I've brought the contract for you to sign."

"Why would I want to sign a contract? I've filed my claim, Mr. Lockhart. The land is legally listed under my name. As I'm sure you know, I'm required to either build a house or farm the land. The house is in the process of being built." She smiled sweetly.

"What the hell are you trying to pull?" Trace asked in a low, controlled voice.

Martha placed her hand over her mouth in mock shock. "Please, Mr. Lockhart! I do not believe the use of such language is at all necessary."

Trace was furious at himself for misjudging the woman. He'd been wrong about being able to twist her around his finger. "I suggest you give your decision some serious thought, Miss Jackson."

"Oh, my. And you're supposed to be a churchgoing man. Are you threatening me? Because if that's so, I see no alternative but to report it to the marshal."

"I'll be back in a week. You'd be wise to reconsider what we've talked about. I don't take kindly to someone who backs out of a deal."

Martha was feeling quite cocky as she watched the tall man ride away. Over the years she'd been threatened by a lot harder men, and she wasn't about to let some Easterner intimidate her. At least, she thought he was an Easterner, having noticed the fine waistcoat and trousers he wore. His Stetson was the only article that didn't fit in with her impression.

She slowly shook her head. Too bad such a devilishly handsome man has to be a sidewinder, she thought as she entered her tent. She started unbuttoning her dress. Actually, his being a crook was probably for the best. She might just find him entirely too tempting. But on the other hand, he certainly couldn't be too bright if he'd really thought she would be willing to share her land.

After washing up and changing clothes, Martha felt considerably better. She decided to have a talk with her builder, Adam Keeper.

"Adam," she addressed the craggy-faced man as she walked up beside him, "is this all the lumber it's going to take to build my house?"

Adam chuckled. "No, Miss Jackson. It's gonna take quite a few loads, but this'll get us started."

Martha nodded, but her attention was centered on the lumber being unloaded. She had never been as excited about anything as she was about this house. It would be the first one she'd ever owned, and it meant everything to her. Realizing she was only in the way, she decided to see how the well was progressing.

As she strolled along, she looked up at the blue sky. Seeing several fluffy white clouds, she was reminded of when she and Lawrence were children. They used to lie on their backs looking up at the clouds, determining what the shapes resembled. Maybe a face, a horse or, one time, a castle. Strange, she hadn't thought about that in years. That had been after their mother died delivering a still-born child and their father grieved himself to death. Actually, she didn't remember any of that. Lawrence had told her the story. Dear Lawrence, I wish I knew where you are, she thought.

"Good morning, gentlemen," she said to the workers. "How is the drilling going?"

"Just fine, Miss Jackson. We should be hitting water soon."

Martha stood watching for a few minutes, then took off to work in her garden. Hoeing the red soil and pulling grass at least kept her busy, but it was also a labor of love, even if it was hard work. For years she'd dreamed of having a garden. Being able to go out and actually pick or pull one's food from the ground had to be the most wonderful thing in the world.

She smiled as she arrived at the small plot of turned dirt. What a marvelous garden she was going to have! She even had flowers to plant. As she picked up her hoe and began to work the soil, she wondered how long it would take for the vegetables to grow. Coming to Oklahoma Territory was without a doubt one of the smartest things she'd ever done. She was starting a whole new life. The house, garden and well all made her feel as if she belonged. She would become someone whom people looked up to, and she wouldn't allow Trace Lockhart or anyone else to stop her.

Chapter Three

Trace sat in his office at the lumberyard, drumming his fingers on the mahogany desk as he contemplated his plans for the future. True, he was making money hand over fist, but there was also a snag in his plans. Martha Jackson. His brow furrowed. Since his visit, his anger had continued to fester. Dammit, he wanted that land!

Maybe I've approached this from the wrong angle, he thought as he rose from the chair. There were few women he hadn't been able to charm into giving him what he wanted, so why should Martha be any different? Surely the woman had a vulnerable spot; he just had to find it. If charm didn't work, he'd use more drastic measures. He'd make sure the lumber needed to complete her house was cut off. One way or another, she was going to sign his contract.

Convinced that rising early in the morning tended to make her hungry, Martha quickly twisted her hair into a topknot, then pinned it in place. Satisfied, she went outside to cook her breakfast. As she started a fire in the stove, she broke out laughing, remembering how flabbergasted she had been when Eddie Graham had informed her that the coals went inside the stove, not on top.

With Eddie's help, even her cooking had improved. This afternoon she planned to pay her neighbor another visit. Martha's mouth watered just thinking about the food that woman prepared.

Martha cracked a couple of eggs into the heated skillet, pleased that this time there were no shells in the pan. "See," she mumbled, "you're getting better."

Once her appetite was satisfied and she'd washed the dishes, Martha tied a bandanna around her head, slipped on her gloves and headed for her garden. It had taken a lot of hard labor and sweat to hoe out the buffalo grass and plant seeds, and she wasn't nearly finished. She had it in her mind to make the garden as big as possible, whatever that meant. Each day she checked to see if anything had come up yet, but so far there was no sign of growth.

As the garden came into view, Martha was horrified at what she saw. The chickens were busily pecking at her planted rows!

"You nasty critters!" she yelled as she ran forward. Martha was outraged when the chickens scattered in all directions, only to circle behind her and continue their pecking. She made a diving grab at one of them, only to land facedown in the dirt, her hands empty. Getting back up, she grabbed the hoe and started swinging it at them. "I'll have every one of you for supper!" she yelled.

By the time Trace rode up to the tent, he'd already observed a hand pump, which meant Martha now had her water, a new corral and horses grazing peacefully on the lush prairie grass. The house appeared to be nearly half-finished, though no one was working on it at present. In fact, the area looked deserted. "Anyone home?" he called. No answer. He tried again. "Hello!"

"I'm not deaf, Mr. Lockhart," Martha stated as she rounded the side of the tent.

Trace looked down at the chicken she held upside down by the legs. It was squawking loudly, flapping its wings, and feathers were flying everywhere. He wasn't surprised to see Martha's face and the front of her clothes covered in red dirt. If he ever were to see her cleaned up he probably wouldn't recognize her. Since she now had a well, he wanted to suggest that she might try bathing.

"Are you planning on having chicken for dinner?" he asked congenially.

"I'm planning on having a lot of chicken for dinner, Mr. Lockhart, just as soon as I get a gun and shoot the little . . . devils." Why did he always have to pick such inopportune times to arrive? He probably thought she belonged in the pigpen.

"You don't shoot chickens, Miss Jackson, you wring their necks."

Martha stared at him in disbelief. "Do you expect me to believe that?"

He expressed his indifference with a shrug of his shoulders. "Would you like me to show you?"

Martha dropped the bird.

"Of course, you can also chop their head off with an ax," Trace continued, a grin tugging at the corner of his lips at her obvious shock. "You have to be careful, though, because if they get away once they're decapitated, you'll have a hell of a time catching them."

"Now I know you're teasing me."

His grin broadened. "Not at all." He dismounted and handed her a small box. "I brought you some horehound candy. It's quite good."

Dismissing what he'd said about the chicken, Martha was delighted, even though she knew the candy was probably meant as a bribe. It seemed like ages since she'd had something sweet. "How very thoughtful of you, Mr. Lockhart."

"Please, call me Trace. I see your house is coming right along. Where are the men?"

"They've gone to town for more lumber. The builder says the house will be finished soon," Martha stated proudly. "Isn't this a bit far for you to be stopping by?"

"I did tell you I'd be back, and how could I resist paying a call to a beautiful woman?"

Martha found the compliment hard to believe, especially considering the way she looked. His smile was disarming, and his even white teeth were a pleasant contrast to his bronzed skin.

"You know, Miss Jackson, we made a deal and shook on it. Where I come from, a man's word is his honor."

"Oh, yes, it seems I do remember something about that, but of course I didn't take it seriously. And if I remember correctly, we didn't shake hands. Also, in case you hadn't noticed, I'm not a man. *Had* I made such an agreement with you, as a woman I'm perfectly justified in changing my mind."

"You do have a point. I assume this means you have no intention of signing the papers."

"I've already made that quite clear."

Trace nodded, as if accepting her decision. The idea of trying to sweet-talk the dirt-covered woman held no appeal. Strangling her did. "Well, Miss Jackson, I wish you the best of luck. I'm sure we'll be seeing each other again soon."

"Goodbye," Martha said brightly.

Martha opened the box and jammed several of the luscious tidbits into her mouth, savoring the sweet taste. She felt sure she'd handled the situation perfectly. Now that

Trace knew she wasn't about to sign his contract, she doubted he'd return again. He didn't have a leg to stand on.

As she watched Trace riding off in the distance, Martha suddenly wondered how it would feel to have those mocking lips against hers. His masculinity definitely could not be denied. *Stop it, Martha! You came here to be a lady, not to flirt with danger.*

With a half-disappointed sigh, Martha walked over and sat on one of the chairs that looked out over the tall grass. It was as high as the horses' bellies and swayed in waves in the soft breeze. After living among crowds of people for the better part of her life, she cherished her solitude.

Lawrence would have liked this, she thought. Where had the time gone? Thinking about Brent Hooper brought forth a smile. Brent had been so good to both of them.

Brent was the owner of the Spur Saloon, where her brother, Lawrence, had gone to work as a bouncer. It wasn't a large saloon and was situated on the outskirts of Bickerton. Martha easily remembered how lonesome she'd felt at night while Lawrence worked. She'd worked most of her thirteen years, and sitting around idle had quickly gotten on her nerves. So one afternoon, when Lawrence said he had a plan that could possibly double their money, she had become excited.

"It's simple, Martha," Lawrence said as he paced the small shack they lived in. "I'll tell the boss that a woman card dealer would draw more customers."

"What does this have to do with me?"

"You'll be the card dealer," Lawrence stated proudly.

Martha's high spirits had plummeted. "I'm not exactly a woman, Lawrence, and I know nothing about dealing cards."

"Hell, Martha, even at your age you got a better figure than most women I've seen. They either weigh too much or they're plain skinny. You're nice and slender, but not skinny by any means. All we have to do is fix you up. I'm going to borrow a dress and some paint from one of the girls who works at the saloon. By the time I'm through, no one will be able to guess your age. Then I'll take you to meet the boss."

That first meeting with Brent Hooper had been frightening. Though she'd felt very grown-up in her outfit, her knees were shaking beneath her skirt. The red dress showed more than it hid.

To her surprise, Brent had liked Lawrence's idea. "But first, we'll see how nimble her fingers are," Brent commented.

Martha smiled, then popped another horehound candy in her mouth. Brent had been impressed by how fast she'd learned to play five-card draw and three-card monte. He'd declared her a natural.

Martha stood, ready to tackle the garden again. Maybe she'd even shoot one of those chickens for supper. Wring its neck, indeed! Whoever heard of such a thing?

When Adam Keeper arrived early the next day, Martha was surprised to see the wagon empty. "Where are your helpers?" she asked with a wide grin as Adam climbed down. "Surely it's not Sunday?"

Adam pulled his hat off and slapped it against his leg. "No, ma'am. I couldn't buy any lumber, so there wasn't any reason to bring the others along."

Her smile faded. "What do you mean you couldn't buy lumber?"

"I tried, Martha, but everything's sold." He kept twisting his hat in his big hands. "I'm afraid your house is gonna have to wait a spell before it gets finished."

"Wait? For how long?"

"Until another shipment of lumber arrives. I was told that would be in a month. I'm real sorry. I know how much this house means to you. I got enough left-over wood to build you a chicken coop, though, and I brung some wire. You pen them chickens up and you won't have to go lookin' for eggs."

"Thank you, Adam. I'd appreciate that." Martha's mind wasn't on chickens or eggs. It was on having to wait for her house. She felt as if someone had just ripped her heart out. "Why don't you let me help?"

"Naw, I can do it. I'll give you a call when I'm finished."

Martha entered the tent and collapsed onto the bed. All of a sudden, nothing seemed to be going right. The chickens had practically ruined her vegetable garden, the grass kept creeping back in, she'd broken her only hoe while chasing the chickens again, and now the house was at a standstill. With the chickens contained, she would at least be able to replant the garden, but first she'd have to drive to town and have the blacksmith repair the hoe. Maybe she would even purchase another one. She also needed to get more feed. The flowers she'd planted seemed to be doing fairly well after she'd put sheets over them yesterday to keep the chickens out.

Adam spent the larger part of the day building the chicken coop. When he had finished, he called Martha.

"It's beautiful," Martha said excitedly. "What are those shelves for?"

"That's for the hens to roost. You need to get you some straw and spread it all across there, and they'll lay their eggs. Then all you gotta do is collect them each day." He put his tools in the wagon. "When I can buy some lumber, I'll be back. You know, you oughta just keep one rooster, Martha."

"Adam," Martha said thoughtfully, "how do you kill a chicken?"

Adam wasn't surprised by the question. He'd long since come to the conclusion that the girl knew nothing about anything. "Wring its neck."

"Oh."

"Go get some feed so we can get them chickens in here."

"All right." Martha curled her lip. "Adam, could you actually wring a chicken's neck?"

"You're damn right. Stick him in a pot of water and let it boil, and in an hour or so, you got some mighty fine-tastin' meat."

"Really? Maybe you could kill one for me."

"Sure thing. Now go get the feed. I gotta be headin' back home."

The thought of eating meat made Martha's mouth water.

By the time Adam left, Martha had a fresh-killed rooster on her worktable. She had turned away when Adam killed it, and seeing the blood dripping from where there had once been a head made her want to throw up. But she was determined to finally have some meat. Eagerly, she started up the fire in the stove, then hurried off to fetch a large pot from the wagon.

After the pot had been filled with water and placed on the stove, Martha picked up the chicken by the wing. Not wanting to hold it a moment longer than necessary, she dropped it into the pot, paying scant attention to the water that splashed out over the side. Immediately she slammed the lid on the top so she wouldn't have to watch it cook. Now, according to Adam, all she had to do was let it boil. Martha silently thanked the man who had stocked her wagon, since she'd had no idea what to bring. He'd done an excellent job, because so far, she'd found everything she needed.

It was turning dark, but Martha remained seated on a chair, staring at the pot. For some time a strange, noxious odor had filled the air, but never having cooked a chicken before, she tried to ignore it. It was nearly two hours since she had put the bird in the pot. Even though Adam had said an hour, she wanted to be sure it was thoroughly cooked.

"It has to be done by now," she muttered as she rose to her feet. She was already savoring the delicious taste.

She grabbed a couple of cup towels, carefully lifted the pot from the stove and placed it on the trivet atop her table. At last, she thought as she removed the lid. Steam billowed out, carrying with it that ungodly odor. When she was finally able to look inside, her eyes became two moons. There was hardly any water but what was left was caked with a solid mass of what she assumed were feathers.

Martha wrinkled her nose and picked up the fork and butcher knife, wondering how she was supposed to cut the thing. Better yet, how was she supposed to eat it? Determined to accomplish a seemingly difficult task, she jabbed the fork in the chicken. To her surprise, it went in quite easily. Cutting it was an entirely different matter. She kept hitting bone. Seeing no other recourse, she tried lifting the chicken out and onto a plate, only to have parts of it fall off. She settled for trying just one of the pieces first. Once she had it on her plate, she began picking at it with the fork. She'd never seen feathers cling to any chicken she'd eaten in the past, so obviously there had to be a way of skinning the damn things!

Though she was loath to do it, she finally gave up on the knife and fork and tackled the task with her hands. At last she saw the meat. However, the sticky feathers continued to be a problem. Frustrated beyond words, Martha went to the water pail and washed off the chicken pieces. At last she had something that looked halfway eatable, even if it was cold now. Tentatively, she took a bite. Not bad, she thought. Not bad at all.

Martha ate little, even though she was still hungry. It involved too much work. Besides, it was getting too dark to see what she was doing. She put the lid back on the pot, then went into the tent. As she lit the lantern, she decided she wouldn't be cooking another chicken anytime soon. It just wasn't worth the effort.

When Martha drove the wagon into Guthrie, she was amazed at how much it had changed. Large wooden buildings were everywhere, and others were going up. Within a month, Guthrie had become a real town. As she turned onto South Second Street, she saw at least a hundred angry men gathered in front of the survey office, their teams and wagons blocking the street.

Curious, Martha pulled her team to a halt. "What's going on?" she called to a tall, lanky man standing in the back. As he sidled over to her, he removed his hat. His thick black hair and well-trimmed beard reminded Martha of Trace. They were both strikingly handsome men.

"Name's Josh, ma'am. Josh Whitten. I own the real estate office down the way."

"I'm Martha Jackson." She liked his beguiling smile. She waved a hand toward the men. "Is something wrong?"

"Too many multiple claims, and the men are angry. A lot of the squatters are getting rejected. The arbitration board's trying to get it all settled. I hope every one of those sooners gets kicked off the land."

"I certainly agree with that. Thank you for the information, Mr. Whitten."

"I'd prefer you to call me Josh. Are you settling around here?"

"I was one of the lucky ones. I have my land and no one else laid claim to it."

"Are you married, or will you be living with your folks?"

Martha laughed, feeling flattered that such an attractive man showed obvious interest. "No, to both your questions. I really must go." She lifted the reins.

"I hope we'll be seeing each other again, Martha." He stepped away, allowing her to move the team forward.

After acquiring everything she needed, Martha decided to take a different way out of town. She wanted to see how much the place had grown, and the various stores where she could shop. At the end of town, she passed a lumberyard. Immediately she brought the team to a halt and stared. There were all kinds of lumber, yet Adam Keeper had said everything was sold. Something wasn't right. She moved the team into the yard. After tethering the horses, she entered the office.

A young gentleman stood behind the counter, his spectacles riding low on a long, narrow nose. "What can I do for you?" he asked in a friendly tone.

"I'd like to purchase some lumber."

"I'm sure that can be arranged. How much will you be needing?"

"Quite a bit. Would I be able to get delivery right away?"

"I don't see why not, unless you plan on buying everything in stock." He laughed at his own joke.

"Good. I'll send a man to pick it up. He'll tell you what all is needed."

The clerk nodded. "And who will be paying for it?"

"I will." Martha turned to leave. She wanted to get in touch with Adam and find out just why he'd told her there was no lumber.

"Oh, ma'am," the clerk called before she walked out the door.

Martha turned. "Yes?"

"What name do I put on the order?"

"Martha Jackson." Martha was surprised at how pale the man suddenly became.

"Well . . . ah . . . you see—"

"Is something wrong?" Martha inquired.

"Yes, ma'am. I don't know what I was thinking. I forgot that we have a big order, and you sound like you're going to need a lot of wood." He shoved his glasses back up his nose.

Martha didn't fail to notice that his friendly attitude had definitely changed. She walked back to the counter. "You're going to stand there and tell me all that lumber is sold?"

"Yes, ma'am."

"This doesn't make sense. A few minutes ago you were ready to sell me anything I wanted. Now you can't even look me in the eye. I want to see the owner immediately."

"Mr. Lockhart isn't in, but he'll be back in about an hour."

Martha placed her balled hands on the counter. "Would Mr. Lockhart's first name happen to be Trace?" she asked through clenched teeth.

The clerk lowered his head. "Yes, ma'am."

"And if I'm understanding this correctly, he has left orders that there is to be no lumber sold to me. Is that correct?"

"Yes, ma'am."

"Tell Mr. Lockhart I want to see him. At his convenience, of course," she said sarcastically. She left the office, not daring to say another word. Her anger was such that if she started, she knew she wouldn't stop. Her argument wasn't with the clerk, however, it was with the owner. Once outside, she saw the Lockhart Lumber sign she'd missed earlier.

On the way home, Martha considered purchasing lumber from another yard, but as underhanded as Trace was proving to be, he'd probably manage to put a halt to that also, or find some other means to pressure her into signing that damn contract.

She pushed the team hard while conjuring up every foul word she could think of to describe *Mr. Lockhart.* Having worked in a saloon for nearly ten years, she had an extensive vocabulary to draw on. How, even in her wildest imagination, could she ever have been attracted to the man?

Once she'd unhooked the team, Martha marched straight to the tent. Without even breaking stride, she went to the bed, then pulled out a hatbox from beneath it. Lying inside was a Colt .45. Beneath that rested a gun belt and holster. When Trace arrived, she planned on being ready for him. She loaded the revolver, buckled the belt on just below her waist, then shoved the .45 in the holster.

Satisfied, she headed for her garden, needing to work off her anger. But when she looked down at the neatly worked rows, her heart sank. The new shoots were lying limp on the ground. Water, she thought. They need water.

For an hour, Martha worked steadily at hauling buckets of water and dumping them in the furrows, only to see the water soaked up by the red soil. She put her hands on her hips and glanced back at the hand pump. There has to be an easier way of doing this, she thought. She could dig another garden closer to the water, or... Her brown eyes lit up. Why hadn't she thought of it sooner? She'd do what Orvil Graham, Eddie's husband, did. She'd dig a trench from the pump to the garden. Working the pump handle up and down would mean a lot of hard work, but it certainly beat carrying buckets. She headed back to the wagon to get her repaired hoe.

Martha was sitting under a cottonwood, blessing the shade, when she saw a rider approaching in the distance. The black horse, plus the way the man sat straight in the saddle, alerted her to who her visitor was. It was almost two weeks since she'd been to the lumberyard, and now the great man had finally deemed it time to pay her a visit. He hadn't fooled her for a moment. She'd known he would eventually arrive, just as she knew he'd been letting her stew. Now he was probably convinced she would sign his contract. She stood and waited.

As Trace slowly dismounted, he noted the gun nestled in Martha's holster and wondered if she knew how to use it. But what really caught his attention were her clean clothes and face. He was completely taken aback by the woman's outstanding beauty. Her facial bones were delicately sculpted, her nose pert, her mouth full and ripe. His gaze traveled to her slender neck, her breasts, her waist. Had he known there was such a jewel waiting, he most certainly would have paid a visit sooner.

"Good afternoon, Miss Jackson," he said, tipping his hat. "I understand you wanted to see me."

Martha had witnessed his obvious examination and approval, and even as angry as she was at him, her pulse still began beating rapidly. "You certainly didn't break your neck getting here," she snapped at him in an effort to get her thoughts back to normal.

"I've been in Oklahoma City," Trace replied smoothly. "I have a business to take care of." He tied his horse, then stepped forward, ready to issue his ultimatum about the contract. To his surprise, Martha drew her gun on him. His eyes narrowed. "What's that for?"

"It's to make it clear that I intend to put a stop to your shenanigans here and now. Either I get my lumber, or I'm turning you over to the arbitration board. I don't think they'll be too happy when I tell them what you've been trying to pull."

Trace broke out laughing. "You have no proof, my dear."

"Then I guess that leaves me with no alternative but to kill you."

Her eyes turned cold, a look Trace was quite familiar with. He deliberately removed his hat, ready to fan her gun away. He didn't get the chance. A bullet landed between his feet. There was now no question as to whether she knew how to shoot. His anger grew. He didn't appreciate being held at bay by a slip of a woman, but he kept his face relaxed, allowing no sign of what he was feeling to show.

"I've seen that trick pulled before. Don't try it again," Martha warned, nodding toward his hat, "or next time I'll draw blood."

"Well, I guess you've bested me." He put his hat back on. "You win. When I get back to town, I'll release your lumber." He kept waiting for her to look away so he could grab the gun, but her eyes remained steady, just like her hand.

"You can't honestly think I believe that!" She didn't wait for his reply. "Go into the tent, and walk nice and slow. I'll be right behind you."

Not having the foggiest idea what she was up to, Trace entered the tent and waited.

"There is a pencil and paper on the chest by the bed. I want you to write that you came on this land and staked it before it was opened. Then sign it."

Trace picked up the pencil and began scribbling the note, his anger growing with each word he wrote. The woman had the upper hand, and there wasn't a damn thing he could do about it except hope that eventually she would make a mistake.

"You're nothing but a snake in the grass," Martha accused. "And you were the one talking about building a church. You go around stealing people's land, land that they worked hard for. Well, *Mr. Lockhart,* you're not getting mine. I only regret that you'll probably never go to jail for what you've tried to do to me."

Trace signed the piece of paper and held it out to her. When Martha reached for it, he saw his chance. A bullet whined through the tent, but he had already shoved the gun away. Grabbing her wrist, he squeezed until she dropped the revolver on the floor. The moment he released her, Martha reached down to retrieve it, but he gave the revolver a hard kick, sending it sliding out the tent opening. "Lady, you'd better *never* try that again. I told you I don't like guns!"

"You won't get my land," Martha seethed. She rubbed her wrist, convinced there would be bruises.

"I'm going to make this clear one more time. I'm not trying to steal your land. I just want to make damn sure that when you decide to leave, it goes to me. I have every intention of paying for it. I also need a house. I'm damn tired of living in a hotel. When I make a deal, I stick by it, and you, lady, are going to do the same thing. I don't like the idea of losing this land, but having a twit of a woman determined to outfox me makes me mad as hell. I gave you your chance to sign that contract, and when you refused, I simply took matters into my own hands."

His words were so fierce that for the first time Martha was frightened.

Seeing the fear that leaped into her brown eyes, Trace smiled coldly. "You be nice to me, and I'll be nice to you."

"I don't want anything to do with the likes of you." She had tried to sound tough, but even she could hear the tremor in her voice.

Trace pulled the contract from his vest pocket and held it out to her. "Sign it," he ordered.

"No."

"You're going to get awfully cold living in a tent come winter."

All of Martha's bravado vanished at seeing the determination written across his handsome face. She snatched the contract from his hand, tempted to tear it up. However, his eyes were still as cold as ice. It suddenly occurred to her that tearing it up was exactly what he expected her to do. Did he have another contract in his pocket? She was tempted to do it anyway, but she didn't know what the consequences would be, other than her house never being finished.

She reached down and picked up the pencil he'd left on the small table. He could do what he wanted, but she was going to read every word before she signed the blasted contract. She moved to the bed, and sat on the edge.

While Martha read, Traced looked at her flawless complexion, already kissed by the sun. Her thick blond hair had worked loose from its confinement during their brief struggle, and was spread out, giving her an angelic appearance. She was a real beauty, and a most tempting prize.

The contract was simple. They were to be partners until she left, at which time he would pay her full value for the land. Martha signed her name at the bottom and handed it to him, planning to get it back as soon as she could reach her gun.

"You made a wise choice," Trace said, after checking her signature. Satisfied, he folded the paper, then placed it in his pocket.

Martha stood and followed Trace out of the tent, ready to make a lunge for her revolver at the first opportunity. But to her disappointment, Trace leaned over and picked it up. It wasn't easy for her to keep from planting her boot right on his backside. He flicked the chamber open, letting the bullets fall to the ground, then handed it back to her. She wanted to throw it at him. "Next time you won't be so lucky," she warned through clenched teeth.

Trace was laughing as he mounted his horse. He tipped his hat. "Until we meet again, partner."

Martha marched back inside the tent, listening to the hoofbeats as he rode off. "Bastard," she mumbled, tossing the gun on the bed.

By the time Martha had her hair neatly twisted into a bun again, her anger had subsided somewhat. I should have signed the contract to begin with and been done with it, she thought as she left the tent. By now the house would have been finished. She looked toward the house, nestled between the trees. Trace was going to have a mighty long wait before she gave up her land. If for no other reason, she wouldn't give the crook the satisfaction of seeing her leave. She'd live here till she was dead!

Martha smiled. The deed was in her name, and that was one thing Trace couldn't change. "At least now he'll leave me alone," she muttered, not sure she wanted that either.

Martha decided to pay Orvil and Eddie Graham a visit. The ride to their place was always pleasurable.

Her gelding was frisky and tossing his head, enjoying the beautiful warm day as much as Martha was. Eddie was always jovial, and Martha felt the need for a friendly face. It still amazed her that Eddie was only twenty-five and already had five towheaded children. Thinking about Eddie's children threw Martha back in time.

Even after Lawrence had gone to all the trouble of dressing her up so Brent Hooper wouldn't guess her age, they hadn't fooled the saloon owner. But Brent had proved to be a good, warmhearted man, and he'd still liked the idea of having a woman card dealer.

So Brent had taken Martha under his wing, and changed her name to Blossom. Brent proved to be quite the cardsharper. He taught her every trick there was, including how to recognize a sleight of hand and a marked deck. Though he believed in an honest game, he wanted Blossom to know when a man was cheating. Because of her youth, he also became very protective. Between him and Lawrence, everyone soon learned to keep their hands off Blossom. Even the prostitutes watched over her.

As the years passed, the Spur Saloon grew…and grew. Brent had long since concluded that because so many men now knew Blossom, she would be safer living at the saloon than in a house by herself. So he had quarters built for her upstairs. He even taught her how to handle a gun. So while Lawrence grew up enjoying the women, Blossom remained cloistered.

Excitement had been written all over her handsome brother's face when he informed her that Brent had agreed to let him buy in as a partner. Lawrence became a man of means. When Brent was killed in a gunfight, Lawrence and Blossom took over as owners. Blossom took care of anything pertaining to money, and if the prostitutes had a problem, they came to her for help or advice. Lawrence made sure the customers received good service and a fair deal, and that there were as few fights as possible. Lawrence and Blossom grew wealthier.

For five years, everything went smoothly. Blossom had long ago become accustomed to being snubbed by the *ladies* of Bickerton. Then Lawrence fell in love with a rancher's daughter. Not just any rancher—he happened to be a senator, and quickly forbade his daughter, Ruth, to have anything to do with the likes of a saloon owner. But Ruth had a mind of her own, and she loved Lawrence as deeply as he loved her. They finally ran off to California.

A tear trickled down Martha's cheek as she remembered the sad parting. For twenty-three years, she and Lawrence had been together. Seeing him leave broke her heart. Never had she felt so lonely. Ruth's father had tried to get her to tell him where the couple had gone, but even she didn't know. And Lawrence had never written to say where in California they had settled down.

So for a year, Blossom was the sole owner of the Spur Saloon. For a man to own such a place was acceptable, but not a woman. The self-righteous ladies of the community balked. They finally marched into the saloon and broke everything they could get their hands on, pushed the prostitutes out onto the street and delivered Blossom to the train station. Martha had a strong hunch Ruth's father had been behind their actions, because the sheriff never lifted a hand to stop what was happening.

As Martha neared the Grahams' place, she saw Eddie waving. The two youngest children ran barefoot toward her, screeching in their young, high-pitched voices. Martha smiled and waved back.

"Where are the others?" Martha asked as she dismounted.

Eddie laughed, her cheeks pink with pleasure at seeing Martha. "They're frying ants."

"They're what?"

"They found an ant hole and have placed a piece of glass over it. Now they're waiting for the sun to heat the glass and beam down into the hole. At least it's keepin' them quiet for a while."

Martha shook her head in amazement.

Chapter Four

Martha had just finished dressing when she heard the blessed sound of approaching wagons. She rushed out of her tent and to her delight, saw Adam Keeper and his helpers heading toward the house with two loads of lumber. Laughing, she hiked up her skirts and ran after them. When the horses were brought to a halt, she was already waiting.

"Well, Martha," Adam said as he climbed down from one of the wagons, "looks like you're finally goin' to get your house finished."

"You don't know how good that sounds, Adam."

The other men jumped down and started unloading the wood.

Adam removed his floppy hat and scratched his head. "I can't figure it out. I went to every lumberyard trying to buy wood, and they all said they was sold out. Last night a boy come to my place and said Trace Lockhart had some lumber he was willing to let me have. Now there's a fine man. Have you ever met him?"

Martha's smile weakened. She decided to be up-front with the older man. "Yes, I have. We're partners."

Adam's bushy eyebrows shot up in surprise. "Oh?"

"Actually, it's a good arrangement. I can't possibly work all this land by myself."

"Well, you couldn't have a nicer man for a partner. He's already highly thought of in Guthrie." He jammed his hat back on his head. "Well, sure ain't gonna get anything accomplished by just standing around."

Martha nodded, then headed for her garden. Nice man indeed, she thought angrily. Trace certainly had pulled the wool over everyone's eyes. His nice clothes and broad smile apparently hid the fact that he was nothing but a no-account rogue.

When she reached the garden, her smile returned. Miracles of miracles. The little green plants were actually standing upright! Maybe there was hope for them after all.

Martha worked for a solid hour before dropping the hoe to take a rest. As she pulled a red bandanna from the waist of her skirt to mop her brow, her gaze suddenly came to rest on a man standing on the hill about two hundred yards away. She shadowed her eyes with her hand for a better view. It looked as if he had just driven a stake into the earth! Grabbing the gun lying on the ground, she started running forward. Just what did he think he was doing?

"You can stop right there," Martha yelled as she drew closer to the stranger.

The man turned, then stared in shock at the muzzle of the gun pointing at him.

"Get off my land!" Martha ordered as she pulled to a stop. "I wouldn't hesitate a minute to shoot a claim jumper."

"No...I mean...I'm not staking a c-claim, miss," he stammered. "You're not aiming to use that, are you?"

Martha watched the corners of his eyes twitch with fear. His face had turned almost as red as his hair. "Then what are you doing here?"

"I'm marking out Mr. Lockhart's house, ma'am. He told me this was partly his land."

Martha was dumbfounded. She suddenly remembered Trace mentioning something about a house, but she'd thought that would only happen if she moved. The nerve of the man! She spun on her heel and headed back toward her own place.

"Lady? Does this mean I can continue without any trouble?"

Martha didn't bother to answer. How dare Trace build a house! And so close! The least he could have done was pick a far corner of the property where she wouldn't have him practically in her backyard. Having to look at his crooked face every day would be more than she could tolerate. He wasn't going to get away with this!

Martha dragged a rocking chair from the wagon and placed it where she could sit and watch what the red-headed man was doing. He appeared to be measuring the perimeters, and after each measurement, he'd drive a stake into the ground. Occasionally he'd stop and study some papers he'd brought with him. As she watched, she also listened to the nails being pounded into her own house. The good and the bad, she thought angrily.

When night fell, Martha scurried to the hill, carrying a lantern in one hand and a flour sack in the other. It took her some time to locate all the stakes, but she had all night to accomplish her task. With each one she found, she smiled as she reached down, pulled it up, then tossed it into the flour sack. Not until she was convinced there were none left did she return to her tent.

The following morning, Martha was up at the first ray of dawn. After a quick breakfast, she returned to her chair and waited. Adam and his helpers arrived early, but it wasn't until a little after ten that five wagons loaded with wood appeared on the hill. She counted nine men following on horseback. She had to place a hand over her mouth to keep anyone from seeing her laughing as she watched them all climb down, then start moving back and forth, searching for the stakes. For a good hour, she sat rocking and enjoying the spectacle.

Finally one of the men mounted his horse, then headed the sorrel in her direction. As he drew closer, she could see his hat had a sweat stain around the base of the brim. Though it was pulled low, it didn't hide the smattering of freckles that ran across the bridge of his narrow nose. His brown hair was curly and hung past the collar of his shirt. He brought his horse to a halt directly in front of her.

"Howdy, ma'am," he said in a friendly voice. "Name's Curly Roberts."

It wasn't difficult to figure out how he came by his name. Martha watched the surprised look on his face turn to an appreciative glint in his green eyes as he scanned her from head to toe.

"Good morning," she replied.

"I'm sorry to bother you, ma'am, but yesterday there was a man out here marking off an area. I thought you might've seen him."

"Yes, I did." Martha gave him her best smile.

"I'd appreciate it if you'd tell me just where he put those stakes."

Martha raised a hand to her breast. "Oh, my, I haven't the foggiest notion. You see, I was busy tending to my chores. But I believe it was on the next hill over."

"Yes . . . well . . ." He twisted in the saddle and glanced back at the hill. "I'm sure we have the right hill, but we can't seem to find the right spot to unload."

"I'm afraid I can't be of any help. You see, I have no sense of direction. Why don't you climb down from your horse and have a cool drink of water?" She watched his eyes twinkle with interest.

"I'd appreciate that."

He was about to dismount when an older man rode up. "Did you find out where the stakes are?" the newcomer asked as he joined them.

"Nope."

"I was just offering your friend a drink of water," Martha said to the man with a pock-scarred face. "Perhaps you would care to join us."

It didn't take long before Martha had all of Trace's crew in her camp, drinking water, flirting and laughing. Martha was on home turf. She knew exactly how to keep a group of men at a distance while at the same time making them think she might possibly be interested in one of them. She insisted on fixing them food, then was quick to remind them that it was ungentlemanly to eat and run. She suggested they play a little poker. While she entertained her guests, it pleased Martha to know that, unlike Trace's place, her house continued to be worked on.

It was four in the afternoon when one of the men finally said they'd have to be heading back to town. Martha didn't detain them. She'd accomplished what she'd set out to do. If she had her way, Trace's house would never get built, at least not in her backyard.

Martha had just let the gelding loose to graze the next day when the men returned to the hill. The skinny one who had arrived in the buggy stepped down, then pulled off his hat, allowing the sun to shine on his red hair. Again he proceeded to mark off the area, but this time he had the men drive the stakes for him.

Because the process took so long, it was midafternoon before the men were finally able to start working on what looked like the frame for a foundation. Every now and then one would ride down to ask Martha for a drink of water, and once again she tried to detain them. Her efforts didn't work this time. She decided the redheaded man was probably overseeing everything.

It was nearly dusk by the time Adam and his helpers left. About the same time, Trace's crew also departed. Martha waited until they were all well out of sight before again making her way up the hill, a shovel and lantern in her hands. At least this time there was still a little daylight.

Martha was delighted to see all the nails, hammers and other equipment the men had left lying about. Working steadily, she moved the stakes, then hammered them back into the ground with the back of the shovel. Proud of her handiwork, she proceeded to dig a ditch, which proved to be no easy task. When that was completed, she tossed all the nails, tools and anything else she could find into it. The last of her efforts had to be done by lantern light. But finally she had everything buried and the grass properly replaced on top.

After greeting Adam and his helpers the following day, Martha went to her garden. When Trace's crew arrived, she acted as though she were busy at work when actually she was surreptitiously keeping an eye on them. As they searched for their supplies, they reminded Martha of a bunch of lost kittens. When she saw Curly Rogers headed in her direction, she began putting some muscle behind her hoe.

"Morning, Martha," Curly greeted in a not too friendly tone. He stopped at the edge of her garden.

Martha straightened up, letting the hoe fall to the ground. "Well, hello, Curly. It's nice to see you again."

Curly's face turned red with pleasure, causing his freckles to fade. But he was bound and determined not to let a pretty face sway his need for direct answers. "We have a bunch of stuff missing up at the house, and I was wondering if you'd seen anyone fooling around up there."

Martha placed her hands on her sides and stretched, deliberately indicating that she had been hoeing for a long time. "No," she said thoughtfully. "Can't say that I did."

Curly looked at her house, watching the men at work. "I thought you might have found a use for them."

"You can just stop right there, Curly Rogers. I don't like your insinuation one bit. I have receipts for everything that's been purchased to build my house. If you're having problems, don't look to me for the answers. And if you don't believe me, go ask Adam Keeper. He's an honest man."

"Sorry, Martha, but I had to find out. Trace isn't going to be at all pleased about this."

"That's Trace's problem, not mine."

Curly nodded and left.

Again the work was delayed while the men went to town for more supplies.

Martha waited two days before she again made her way up the hill. The foundation was in place, and walls had already started to be built on one side. She walked around the foundation, marveling at the size of the place. "What is he building?" she whispered. "A castle?"

As she looked around, laughter started bubbling up, then suddenly spewed out. The men had faithfully followed the guidelines of the stakes she'd moved, so the foundation jutted out and away in all directions. Thinking how long it would take to correct it and start building from scratch again made her laugh all the harder. She plopped down on a beam, holding her sides.

By the time the fit of laughter had subsided, Martha finally gave some serious consideration to what she'd done. The men had left early today, probably realizing that something was terribly amiss. She didn't regret letting anger motivate her actions, nor did she feel sorry for the men doing the work. They were probably being paid well and could use the money. Just thinking about how angry Trace would be caused her to start laughing again.

He has no proof that I've done anything, she thought as she rose to her feet. Heading back to her tent, she decided that since it would probably be at least three or four days before the men could even start rebuilding, it might be wise for her to disappear for a while. She didn't want to listen to Trace's accusations, and maybe by the time she returned he would have wisely decided to build his damn house somewhere else.

She had it all planned. She'd go to Eddie's place and spend a few nights, even if it did mean sleeping in the loft. But first, she would go to town and buy groceries, which would prevent the Grahams from having to feed her. She knew how closely they had to watch their funds. They were having a hard time making a go of it. Perhaps she could start teaching the children to read and write, and at the same time learn more about cooking and gardening.

She grinned. Trace was going to be mad as hell when he saw his house.

Martha stopped and looked at her own place. It would be finished shortly, and she could hardly wait to move in. Maybe it looked like a peanut compared to what Trace was building, but to her it was beautiful, the realization of a lifelong dream. Lawrence would have liked it.

Trace stood glaring at what was supposed to be his future home. "Would you care to explain just how this happened, Oscar?" he demanded of the redheaded man.

"I have no idea, Mr. Lockhart." Oscar mopped his suddenly damp forehead with his handkerchief.

"No idea? Dammit, man, you're supposed to be the architect! Were you drunk? This place looks like a jigsaw puzzle!"

Oscar Hummings pulled the papers from his pocket and studied them. "I staked it out just the way I drew it," he said meekly. "Both times."

Trace slowly turned and looked the thin man straight in the eye. "Both times? What do you mean, both times?"

As Oscar quickly explained about the missing stakes, Trace kept glancing toward Martha's tent, which was partially hidden by trees. A niggling suspicion was beginning to build. He'd already walked around his place to determine that the men had actually followed the line of the stakes. Had Martha dared to move them?

Overhearing the conversation between the two men, another man stepped forward. He told Trace about the missing supplies and tools.

"Next time anything like this happens," Trace said menacingly, "I want to be informed immediately. Not after it's too late and it all has to be done over again!" He turned his back to Oscar, his gaze shifting from the small white tent to Martha's house, then back to the tent.

Until today, he'd had no idea his place was so close to hers. He had been busy with his lumber business and hadn't really paid attention to where Oscar had said the house should be built. The architect had chosen this site because it was high enough to prevent any damage in case of floods, and its nearness to the small pond, stream and trees made for a scenic view. Since everything would have to be torn down now, Trace was well aware he could move to another site. He didn't want to be close to Martha any more than she wanted to be close to him, which was apparently why she'd gone to so much trouble to keep his house from being built. After what the little tiger had pulled, however, he'd be damned if he was going to move.

"I want this house built as soon as possible. Hire as many men as are needed. Tear it down and start over," he yelled over his shoulder as he started down the hill. By God, like it or not, he and Martha were going to come to an understanding! At this moment he couldn't think of anything he'd like more than to wring her neck like one of those chickens she was so damn proud of.

When Trace was informed by one of Martha's builders that she wouldn't return for several days, his temper flared. He had half a notion to retaliate by doing something to her house, but finally decided there were other ways of getting his point across should she continue to give him trouble.

The setting sun had left the sky streaked with beautiful shades of purple and pink when Martha finally stopped the team behind the tent. She was exhausted and quite happy to be home. Sleeping in the loft and having five children constantly climbing all over her had taken their toll. She'd never realized just how unruly Eddie and Orvil's children were. Eddie never said a word to them as they dismantled practically everything in sight. When they continued to try to annoy Martha's horses, Martha had had to put her foot down firmly, which the children didn't appreciate one bit. Eddie had simply laughed and said, "Children will be children."

Martha decided to wait until tomorrow to unload the fruit trees she had bought in town. All she wanted to do was climb into her bed and sleep for the next hundred days. She'd unhitched the horses and turned them loose when she suddenly sucked in her breath. With the sky as a backdrop, the sides of Trace's house looked huge sitting up on that confounded hill. Adrenaline pumped through her veins as she stared in disbelief. Her already bad mood turned into pure hatred toward Trace. Forcing her to sign his contract, thereby giving up part of her land, was bad enough. But then he had the gall to taunt her by building a castle!

Before Martha realized what she was doing, she had started marching up the hill, hell-bent on tearing the monstrosity apart. Only the fear of a grass fire spreading to her own home prevented her from burning the place down. She was convinced he'd had at least twenty men on the job, for most of the walls were already up.

The first thing she saw when she entered the structure was an ax. She slowly picked it up, then sank it into one of the walls with a vengeance, wishing it was Trace's head she was hitting. By the time she headed back to her own place, there was very little she hadn't attacked with the ax. She couldn't wait to hear Trace scream and holler. In fact, she looked forward to it. She had a few things to say to him as well.

The next day Martha watched as the men returned, looked around, then rode off. When they didn't come back, she was sure they'd gone to inform Trace of their latest problem. If Trace didn't arrive tonight, she knew he'd be here tomorrow. She spent the rest of the day planting her fruit trees, then tilling the garden, welcoming the labor to help calm her temper. She cursed the bugs that seemed to be taking over as hard as she cursed Trace.

Still half-asleep, Martha was disinclined to open her eyes, even though she knew it was already daylight. Hearing Adam and the men working on her house brought forth a smile. She stretched lazily, then suddenly her eyes flew open. Someone was lying beside her on the bed. She tried to leap off, but an arm circling her waist prevented it. She jerked her head around, only to find herself staring into a pair of crystal-blue eyes. At least Trace was fully clothed!

She opened her mouth to scream, but any sound was cut off by a large hand. Again she struggled, but his leg placed over hers successfully prevented any movement. Then his lips replaced his hand in a long, lingering kiss. When his tongue entered the sanctity of her mouth, Martha was sure she would swoon.

"If you try screaming again, I'll have to assume you enjoy having me kiss you."

His lips were so close that they brushed hers as he spoke. Martha was well aware that his clothes and her silk gown were the only things separating their bodies.

"Get off my bed!" she demanded, wanting to prove that he had no effect on her. She tried yanking up the blanket, but he wouldn't let her. "What are you doing here?" She froze when he made small circles on her neck with his tongue, then trailed a path to her earlobe where he gently nibbled at it. "I won't let you..."

The words stuck in her throat. His hand had moved up her rib cage and was now resting on her breast, igniting bolts of lightning throughout her body. She might as well have been naked, because the sheer gown was no barrier to the excruciating pleasure that assailed her. No man had ever touched her in such a manner. Fighting the desire that was quickly building as he manipulated her nipple between his fingers, she again tried to jerk away.

"Get your filthy hands off me!" She struggled with all her might, only to hear him laugh softly. She became very still, mortified to realize it was all a game to him.

"Were I of a notion, Martha," he whispered in her ear, "I could take you right now." He continued his fondling.

"Why are you doing this?" Martha asked, her breathing becoming more labored by the second. His breath was like a warm caress on her neck, and she could smell the faint, pleasing scent of his body.

"I'm just giving you an example of what could happen if you continue to wreak havoc on my house."

"I don't know what you're talking about," she whispered.

"You're lying. I know it and you know it."

"Very well, I did it. Just what right do you have to build a place on my land, right under my nose?"

"Our land."

"Not until I decide to leave, Mr. Lockhart! And you'll roast in hell before that happens." To her relief, he removed his hand from her breast. But the next thing she knew he was moving it down to her thigh!

"If you try pulling another stunt, I won't give you a warning. As for hell, I've already been there."

To Martha's surprise, he slid off the bed, smiled, tipped his hat, then left. It seemed forever before her breathing returned to normal. For the first time she'd experienced actual pangs of desire induced by a man, and she wasn't

at all sure she liked it. She'd felt so vulnerable. And how
was it possible for him to do those things to her and feel
nothing himself?

Maybe he had a problem, she thought. When she was
young and peeked through the curtains of the cribs in the
saloon, she had soon discovered that when a man started
something like that, he didn't stop until he'd derived his
satisfaction. Nevertheless, whether Trace had a problem
or not, he had indeed gotten his point across. There was
no doubt in her mind what would happen if she continued trying to destroy his house. On the other hand, was
she willing to let him get by with such a threat?

She ran a finger across her lips. Maybe Trace's kiss
meant nothing to him, but to her it had been glorious. It
was her first real kiss, something she would never forget.
Nor would the feel of his hands be forgotten.

That night, Martha noticed that three guards were
posted around Trace's house, making it impossible for her
to cause any more trouble. One way or another, Trace had
put an end to her war. At least she had the satisfaction of
knowing she had cost him an uncountable amount of
money.

When Martha's house was finished, she dismissed all
thoughts about the castle on the hill. Excitedly, she
watched Adam and his helpers move the furniture from
the big covered wagon into her home. They waited patiently while she decided where she wanted everything to
go. Boxes followed, full of china, bedding and everything else needed to turn a house into a home.

When the men had gone, Martha walked through all the
rooms, laughing with delight. Her two-bedroom house
was beautiful. She bounced up and down on her bed, sat
on the red velvet sofa and chair in the parlor, ran her hand

over the top of the beautiful mahogany dining table and oohed and aahed over the china as she placed it in the large buffet.

For two weeks, Martha kept busy arranging and re-arranging the contents of her house. She had already made several trips to town, purchasing red velvet drapes and gold tassels to match her parlor furniture and bed-spread. But out of the corner of her eye, she again began watching what was happening on the hill. Finally she just stood in her garden and stared. It seemed that with each passing day, the place grew bigger. Though it looked nothing like a castle, that was what she continued to call it. She could even picture King Lockhart seated inside on his throne.

Finally, Martha couldn't contain her curiosity another day. After the builders left, she walked up the hill.

"Surely you're not planning on tearing the house down?" Curly asked as Martha walked up to him. He smiled at the petite woman, still unable to get over how beautiful she was.

She gave him a wicked smile. She wasn't about to let him know Trace had won the battle. "Not right away," she said softly. "But who knows what I might think of next? You have to admit that I was doing a mighty good job of it."

Curly dismissed the matter with sudden good humor. "That you were."

She brushed the wisps of hair from her face as she looked upward. "How many floors are there?"

"Three." He shoved back his hat. "Martha, is there anything going on between you and . . . I mean—"

"Whatever you mean, the answer is no. Do you think I could go inside?"

"The boss would probably skin me alive, but I guess he doesn't have to know. Come on, I'll take you on a tour." He started to walk toward the long porch, then suddenly stopped. "You gotta promise me you won't do anything."

Martha laughed. "I promise not to get you in trouble."

Martha was in awe as they moved from room to room. The third floor was still being finished, though the roof was already in place. The house was so big, it made hers look the size of rat's droppings. "What in heaven's name does the man plan on doing with such a big place?" she asked, more to herself than Curly.

"You got me. He said something about doing a lot of...entertaining. That's the word he used. There isn't anything like this in the entire area."

Martha had already counted six bedrooms; her pulse beat at a fast tempo as she wondered which one Trace would claim. "Where did he get all his money?"

"Well, for one thing, he's making a fortune from lumber in Guthrie, plus what he's selling in Oklahoma City. Now that people are putting up brick buildings, he's already got his own brickyard. I figure his folks must be rich to set him up like that."

"You're probably right." Martha sighed, accepting the permanency of the rogue's house. "If he has so much money, why did he want to build on my land?"

"Hell, Martha, there is no other land," Curly stated as he guided her back toward the front door. "How come you let him build here?"

"We're partners. Do you own land, Curly?"

"Sure do. Me and my brother, Rob. He's working the land, and I took this job to make me some extra money. How did Trace become your partner?"

Martha started to tell him, but changed her mind. "Like you, I need the money. Are you married?"

"Nope. Now that you brought it up, I was wondering if someday soon I could come calling."

As they walked out of the house, Martha looked again up at the third floor. Finally, she returned her attention to Curly. He probably wasn't much older than she. "I'd consider it an honor," she replied softly. Though it was getting dark, she could see that he was beaming like a Christmas tree. "What do you think of Trace Lockhart, Curly?"

"He's a mighty fine man. He could have taken it out on us for what you did, but he took it good-naturedly."

That's what you think, Martha thought.

"Said it looked like he was just going to have to post guards," Curly continued. "He'll make you a good neighbor, Martha."

The hell he will, Martha thought. It amazed her how easily Trace could deceive everyone. Hadn't anyone seen his other side? "I don't trust him and I don't like him. I think he's a sneaky...snake."

"Oh, you're wrong. You just haven't gotten to know him."

Martha didn't want to pursue the subject. She looked up at the tall, lanky man. "Thank you, Curly, for showing me around."

He doffed his hat. "My pleasure."

When Martha entered her house, it suddenly seemed much smaller. She had half a notion to get in touch with Adam and have him make it larger to spite Trace. But what purpose would that serve? "I'm not planning on *entertaining,* unlike a certain other person I know."

Martha stood outside, waiting for the wagon to come to a halt. Five laughing, towheaded children scampered down, then took off in every direction. Martha gritted her teeth, wondering what mischief they'd get into. At least they hadn't tried entering the house. Eddie was much slower climbing down. Martha always thought of Eddie as being pretty, even if she was a bit chubby. Her sunbonnet covered rich, auburn hair, and her complexion reminded Martha of a china doll's. The rosy cheeks seemed to go with being a farmer's wife.

"I came to see your house," Eddie said when her feet were solidly on the ground. "Bringham," she called to one of the older boys, "fetch my basket from the back of the wagon."

When Eddie had her basket, the two women went inside.

"Oh, Martha, this is really something," Eddie said as they walked into the kitchen. "A real sink, and even a water pump! I don't think I'll ever have anything as fine as this. And look at the cupboards. My, oh, my." She ran her hand across the buffet and stared at the china neatly stacked behind the glass doors.

"Set down your basket and I'll take you through the house." Martha felt a bit guilty. Eddie and Orvil's place was little more than a shack. Part wood, part tent. But Eddie and her husband seemed happy with what they had, and jealousy wasn't a part of Eddie's good-natured personality.

Eddie was entranced with the plush red furniture, the pink ribbons pinned to the red velvet drapes and the gold tassels throughout the rooms. "I've never seen the likes of this," she commented excitedly. But when they went upstairs, a devilish look entered her eyes upon seeing Martha's bed.

"My, oh, my." She placed her hand on the thick velvet bedspread, then gently pushed on the feather bed, giggling the entire time. "Wouldn't Orvil and I have fun on this."

"It seems to me you've already had fun, what with those five children," Martha teased.

"Six."

"Six?" Martha could see a definite twinkle in her friend's blue eyes. "Eddie! Are you telling me you're pregnant?"

Eddie giggled again. "Isn't it wonderful?"

Martha didn't think so, but the delight on the woman's face made her laugh. "Are you and Orvil planning on starting your own cavalry?"

Eddie was surprised at the statement. "This will only be our sixth, Martha. In Kentucky we have big families. My ma had twelve children. How many were in your family?" she asked as they went back down the stairs.

"Two. I have a brother three years older than I am."

They entered the kitchen and Eddie opened the basket she'd left on the table. "I brung you an apple pie."

Martha placed her hand over her heart and rolled her eyes, even though she felt guilty about accepting the gift. But she knew Eddie would be upset if she refused. "If I ever learn to cook like you, I'll be convinced I'm in heaven."

"Set it on the windowsill. It's still hot. How is your cooking coming along?" Eddie asked as she pulled a chair up to the table. "Have you cooked any more *whole* chickens?" Her laughter caused her plump cheeks to shake.

Martha joined her guest at the table. "No. I haven't cooked another chicken, period. I can't bear the thought of killing one with my hands, although I've been tempted on more than one occasion."

"Do you have any idea how few chickens most people have? You should count your blessings. You could probably even sell the eggs in town. I saw your neighbor's house as we rode up."

Martha released a grunt. She'd told Eddie all about Trace Lockhart. "It's so big, Eddie, a person could get lost in it."

"When we was in town last week, Orvil pointed out Mr. Lockhart to me. Now, there's one fine-looking man, Martha Jackson. How come you haven't set your sights on him?"

"Eddie! You know what he's like. He's a—"

Eddie raised her hand. "I know, honey, but I kinda like a man who knows what he wants and goes after it."

"He was in my bed!"

"Well," Eddie said with a big grin, "that's a start. Too bad it was only to threaten you."

Martha broke out laughing. "Eddie, you're terrible. Do you know what the other women around here would think if they heard you say something like that?"

"They'd probably turn to stone. But in the back hills of Kentucky, you never knew when a preacher was going to come through. When two people had a strong yearning, nature just seemed to take its course. Now get that shocked look off your pretty face. You'll be getting wrinkles before your time."

Martha shook her head. "I'm not shocked, I'm just surprised that you'd come right out and say something like that."

"Believe me, other women do, too, but it's behind their pretty little fans. But we've gotten off the subject. You take a good look at your neighbor and think about what I've said."

"Are you saying I should let him bed me?" Martha asked. This time she was shocked.

"Heavens, no. It only took one look for me to know he can have just about any woman he wants, so that's not what's going to catch him. What'll catch him is *not* giving him what he wants."

"You're forgetting a couple of things, Eddie. In the first place, I'm not interested in Trace. Secondly, he's not interested in me."

Eddie rested her elbows on the kitchen table and leaned forward. "Mark my word, he will be." Grinning, she pushed back her chair.

"There's something I didn't tell you."

Eddie's curiosity was immediately piqued. "Oh? What's that?"

"I think Trace may have a problem when it comes to bedding women."

"Good Lord! Whatever gave you that impression?"

"When he touched me, he didn't become aroused!"

"Honey, I would be willing to bet my land that when that man takes a woman to bed, he knows exactly what and how to do it. You can see it in his eyes. Besides, there's something I haven't told you."

Martha also leaned forward. "What?"

"Orvil's heard rumors about Trace. He squires all the beautiful women about town. From the way Orvil put it, there isn't a lady around that hasn't set her cap for Trace, and I'm not just talking about single women."

"Oh." The pain in Martha's chest made her feel as though she'd just been stabbed. For years, men had told her that her beauty was unequaled. Yet Trace could go out with all the other women and not even pay her so much as a little compliment!

Eddie settled back in her chair. "If I was you, I'd be real careful about underestimatin' the man. If you don't play your cards right, honey, that man could burn you real easy. Now. What do you say we kill a chicken?"

Martha grimaced.

"Come on, honey, you're going to have to learn sometime. Then you're gonna learn how to clean, cut and cook it."

"Why don't I check on the children while you do it?"

"Oh, no. Now get up and come along."

Though Martha wasn't in the least enthusiastic about killing a chicken, she saw her first opportunity to give Eddie something in return for all the help she'd been. "Very well, but you'll take a chicken home for your supper as well."

"You've got a deal."

They went outside and were quickly joined by the children. Martha discovered they'd been in the chicken coop and had left the gate open.

Chapter Five

Seated on a sidesaddle atop her gray gelding, and properly dressed in a blue riding habit, Martha rode proudly down Meridian Street, feeling the epitome of fashion. She still found it difficult to believe Guthrie had actually been divided into four complete townships—Capital Hill, Guthrie proper, West Guthrie and East Guthrie because of size restrictions. Admittedly the town had grown beyond all belief, but somehow it didn't seem right to split it up.

After purchasing a bag of peanuts from a street vendor, Martha continued toward Trace's lumberyard. Trace's house was completed, but because he hadn't moved in yet, she'd decided to confront him in his office. It seemed that every time she felt her life was finally going in the right direction, he did something to make her angry. Now he'd taken it upon himself to fence in her land! Her land? He acted as if it belonged to him and he was graciously allowing her a small spot on it!

When Martha entered the lumberyard office, she again faced the spectacled string bean of a man. "I've come to see Mr. Lockhart," she stated in a no-nonsense tone of voice.

"Miss Jackson. How nice to see you again. I'm afraid Mr. Lockhart isn't in, but I'll let him know you stopped by."

With his buckteeth he reminded Martha of a horse. "When do you expect him back?"

"I have no idea. He left a week ago for Oklahoma City, ma'am. Perhaps I can be of help. I'm Mr. Lockhart's assistant."

"What's your name?"

"Colbert, ma'am. Colbert Arbuckle."

"Very well, *Mr. Arbuckle.* Have you made up the story about Trace being gone? At his instruction, of course."

"No, Miss Jackson. I swear he's not here."

Martha was tempted to call him a liar. Instead, she stomped out and climbed back onto her horse. She hadn't gone far when she heard someone call out, "Hello there, Miss Jackson."

Martha turned, recognizing the man immediately. She'd met him the day the men were in town squabbling over the sooners. Though he had a fine mustache, she suddenly realized he'd shaved off his beard. Smiling, she turned her horse in his direction. As before, his coloring reminded her of Trace. But this man's features were more refined.

"Hello, Mr.— I'm sorry, I've forgotten your name."

"Josh, Josh Whitten," he replied when she'd brought her horse to a halt. "I don't see you in town often, so I hope you don't think I'm being too forward."

"Not at all."

He stroked the gelding's satiny neck. "I was just going to get some lunch. I'd consider it an honor if you'd join me."

"I'd be delighted." At least there was one nice gentleman in town, Martha thought.

"I'll be right back," Josh said with a wide smile.

While Josh went to get his horse, Martha suddenly wondered if accepting so quickly was something a lady would do. Maybe she should have refused or at least postponed. Well, she told herself when she saw him riding toward her, it's too late now.

Martha was surprised that the restaurant Josh took her to turned out to be every bit as elegant as some she'd eaten at in Topeka. As the headwaiter seated her at the table, she was grateful for that time spent in Topeka. It had allowed her to familiarize herself with etiquette and the behavior of ladies, as well as to mingle with the sophisticated. She glanced at the menu, then placed it on the table. "I'll let you order for me," she told Josh. The statement was one she'd overheard a woman make in Topeka.

"I don't know what you like, so why don't you go ahead and pick out what you want?" Josh answered.

That was not the reply the man had made to the woman in Topeka. Martha returned Josh's smile and picked up the menu again. She finally selected the roast beef, something she seldom had.

"Are you getting settled in?" Josh asked after the waiter had taken their order.

"Yes, I'm quite comfortable." Martha placed the napkin properly in her lap. She found it interesting that Josh didn't do the same.

"I understand Trace Lockhart in also living on your property."

"Word gets around fast."

"I'm in the real estate business. I hear a lot of gossip."

His crooked smile and the suggestive tone of his voice alarmed Martha. There was no doubt in her mind that Josh thought there was something going on between her and Trace. "It was strictly a business arrangement. He wanted a place to build his house and I needed the money. Are you suggesting anything else?''

"No... not at all.''

Martha was pleased to see his smug grin disappear.

"What do you think of Trace?'' he asked her.

A shyster, a user of women, a snake, Martha thought. "I don't understand the question.''

"He's well thought of in town, but because I sell land, I don't like the way he's buying up property for more than I can offer if I'm to turn a profit.''

"I have no idea what Mr. Lockhart does or doesn't do. I seldom see him. I didn't realize you had asked me to dine because you wanted to ply me with questions about Trace.''

"I'm sorry, how ungentlemanly of me. That wasn't why I asked you here. I think you're a very beautiful woman, and I wanted to get to know you.''

"How nice.'' At the Spur Saloon, Martha had received enough compliments to last a lifetime, plus proposals of marriage. Some had even come loaded with money. She'd learned to handle men well, and Josh wasn't any different.

Still, with Trace continually being a thorn in her backside, Josh's compliment seemed to come at just the right time. She'd needed something to give her a boost. Trace certainly never seemed to notice any of her good qualities. Not that she'd had an opportunity to prove to him that she didn't spend her entire life angry. At least Josh was a gentleman, and quite attractive with his black hair and mustache, albeit not quite as devastating as Trace. Where Trace was more masculine with strong, almost sculptured face and lips, Josh's features were finer, his lips thin. He was almost pretty. Actually, now that she had a chance to really compare the two men, they looked nothing alike except for their hair coloring.

The waiter interrupted her thoughts, placing their food on the table. It looked and smelled delicious.

During the meal, Josh talked about the town, throwing in compliments about Martha's beauty. She gave him her full attention, making it clear that she was interested in what he had to say.

"Where were you living before coming here?" Josh asked when they finished their meal. He shoved his plate away, filling the spot with his cup of coffee.

"Topeka. And you?"

"Missouri. You remind me of a woman I once met in a town called Bickerton. Do you by chance play poker?"

Martha's spine stiffened. "Not hardly," she replied in a haughty manner.

Josh smiled apologetically. "Here I go again, talking about things that would be of little interest to you."

Martha silently blessed the waiter for clearing the table at that moment and placing the slice of cherry pie she'd ordered in front of her. It allowed her some time to collect her wits. Josh had seen her at the saloon! Luckily, he didn't seem sure about her actually being Blossom. Silence was her best ammunition.

"Have you ever been to Missouri, Martha?"

Martha shook her head, trying to remain calm beneath his steady gaze. Having finished the pie, she dabbed her mouth with the linen napkin, then smiled sweetly. "The meal was excellent, Josh. Thank you for bringing me here."

"My pleasure. I insist that the next time you're in town you let me do it again."

Minutes later, as Josh stood watching Martha ride down the street, he was having a hard time making up his mind about the woman. The first time he'd laid eyes on her, he'd thought for sure she was the famous Blossom from the Spur Saloon. Blossom's beauty and grace were renowned throughout Missouri and Kansas. A lot of men had lost a bundle of money while sitting in on one of her poker games, including him. But he'd only seen Blossom a few times, and that was more than five years ago, so he couldn't be sure. Nor had she done or said anything that would lead him to believe he was right.

He watched her disappear from view, then untied his horse. Well, he thought as he mounted, time will tell. No matter who she was, he definitely planned on pursuing the lovely lady.

As had become a morning habit, Martha stood in her blue silk nightgown, looking out the kitchen window at the castle. It was more than two weeks since she'd seen Trace. She was tempted to try the lumberyard again. Maybe she would even dine with Josh. She finished washing her breakfast dishes, then went upstairs to her bedroom.

Sitting at the dressing table, Martha loosened the thick braid she plaited every night to keep her hair from getting tangled. Bending her head, she let the thick mane fall forward, then started her hundred strokes with the brush. As one stroke followed another, she smiled, not minding at all that her life had returned to normal. Her corn was finally starting to grow tall, and the carrots, peas, potatoes and green beans were even managing to survive. Straightening back up, she smoothed her hair with the brush, then twisted it into a knot at the nape of her long neck and pinned it in place. She pulled her faded cotton work dress from the mahogany chiffonier, then hurriedly finished her toilet. She wanted to get to her chores before the day became unbearably hot.

Taking her small wicker basket to collect eggs, Martha headed for the chicken coop, thinking about when she had first started gathering the eggs. The hens had seemed intimidating, and more than once she had jerked her hand away without an egg because some hen tried pecking her. But it didn't bother her anymore. In fact, a lot of things didn't bother her, like killing a rooster occasionally, she thought proudly. While loose, the chickens had multiplied unbelievably fast, and she already had more than she knew what to do with.

By the time she'd finished with the chickens, Martha could already feel the hot sun on her face and shoulders. She looked up at the clear blue sky, knowing she wasn't going to be able to spend as much time in her garden as she had planned. Even though Eddie had tried on many occasions to get her to wear a sunbonnet, she had steadfastly refused. It made her head too hot.

As she cleared the stand of cottonwoods, Martha glanced toward her garden, anxious to see her growing plants. Her steps faltered. At first she thought the sun was playing tricks with her eyes. But as she drew closer her fury began to build. Five big cows were standing among the rows, chomping away at her plants.

"Damn!" she yelled as she started running forward, the eggs falling from the basket. But when one of the cows lifted its big head, bawling, and she saw its long, sharp horns, she came to an abrupt halt. She tried yelling and waving her arms, but the beasts weren't about to leave such a lush meal.

Martha plopped down on the ground, heartsick. Helplessly she watched the cattle either trample or eat up all her hours of hard work. There was no doubt in her mind who was responsible for this. Trace Lockhart. Never once had he consulted her about a single thing he'd used *her* land for. He'd gone too far this time. Tomorrow she was going to see the marshal and put an end to Mr. Lockhart's shenanigans once and for all. It was something she should have done a long time ago.

Realizing she was nervously twisting her handkerchief, Martha stilled her hands and rested them in her lap. She didn't like the way the marshal was staring at her from behind his desk.

He brushed his wide mustache with his finger. "What you've told me, Miss Jackson, is hard to believe. A sooner? I know Trace, and as far as I'm concerned, you couldn't ask for a nicer fellow. He's well respected in Guthrie."

"Believe me, Marshal Huggens, he's not the fine, upstanding man everyone thinks he is. I know what he's really like." Martha started twisting her handkerchief again.

"You say he made you sign a contract. How did he do that?"

"Well, he…he…he told me he'd shoot me if I didn't."

"I see. I guess I'm having trouble understanding why he'd even want a contract. You see, he's already bought up a bunch of town sites, and I hear tell some of the settlers that haven't been able to make a go of it are already talking about selling their land to him. Now, if he has all that, why would he want your place?"

Martha could see she was getting nowhere. She couldn't answer the marshal's questions because she didn't know the answers. "I see I've wasted my time," she quietly stated as she stood.

Ben Huggens also stood. "That's not so. If you want to file a complaint, I'll look into it."

"How? By asking Trace if I'm telling the truth? Never mind, Marshal. But remember this, I know the difference between a skunk and a cat. Maybe that's something you should learn. Thank you for hearing me out."

By the time Martha returned home, the only thing she could think about was the pleasure she would receive by putting a bullet between Trace's eyes.

That night, Martha turned out the kerosene lamp and walked over to her bedroom window. Maybe I had the right idea about burning down that confounded house, she thought bitterly.

She was about to turn away when she caught sight of a faint light in the castle, moving from one window to another. Remembering how the house was laid out, she deduced it had to be in the large parlor. The reason the light looked faint was because the drapes were pulled.

Her eyes grew hard. Apparently Trace had finally decided to return home.

The sky was brushed with yellow and the big orange sun was just peeking over the horizon as Martha left the house. The dry, tall grass whipped at her dress and grasshoppers shot up into the air as she marched toward the hill. She had carefully chosen a high-necked, long-sleeved paisley cotton dress, including bustle, for just the right effect. The eyeglasses were added at the last moment. She wanted Trace to know this was strictly business. She clutched the revolver in her hand. If one of those cows gets in my way, she silently vowed, I'm going to shoot it.

Martha crossed the big porch, lifted the clapper on the door and let it fall. For good measure, she did it a few more times. When the door swung open, she sucked in her breath. Even as angry as she was, the virile man standing before her was indeed a sight that stirred her all the way down to the pit of her stomach. He was barefoot, and a pair of tight jeans rode low on narrow hips. His red shirt was open, allowing a good view of black, curly chest hair. The fact that he dared to go without wearing long underwear was even more disconcerting. Stubble covered his jaw and chin and his crystal-blue eyes were looking directly at her.

"What can I do for you, Martha?" Trace released a heavy sigh at seeing the gun in her hand. "The least you could have done was let me catch up on my sleep before killing me."

Martha squared her shoulders, trying to get her emotions back under control. Why did the man have to be so devastatingly handsome? "Aren't you going to invite me in?"

Trace stepped back, and with a gallant wave of his hand, bade her enter.

Martha followed him into the parlor, surprised to find the large room bare, except for a small, gently curved chair and the table beside it.

Trace motioned toward the chair. "Do have a seat."

"I'll stand, thank you."

"Then I'll sit."

In disbelief, Martha watched as he actually took the one chair, then looked up at her, waiting.

"Well?" Trace asked. "Obviously there's a reason for your visit."

"Just what right do you have to fence off *my* land, and—"

"Stop right there. Let's take one thing at a time. If you had paid attention, you'd have noticed that everyone is putting up fences as fast as they can." He pushed a contrary tuft of hair from his brow. "You're probably not interested in why this is being done, but I'm going to tell you anyway. Have you ever heard of the Chisholm Trail?''

"Of course."

"The cattle trail goes from San Antonio, Texas to Abilene, Kansas. Right through this area. Men are still driving their cattle through, though I doubt it will last much longer. Because of that, homesteaders are losing their cattle and milk cows because they take off to join the big herd. It doesn't seem to me that you should be squawking, 'cause I'm the one that paid the bill for that fence. Now, what is your next complaint?''

"I don't like your attitude," Martha said through clenched teeth. "You make it sound like you own this land and you're talking to some lowly tenant. How dare you make any changes without asking me! Then, as if the fence wasn't bad enough, you put those beasts on my land." She shifted to her left foot, then crossed her arms in frustration, the barrel of the revolver pointing toward the hardwood floor. "Do you have any idea how many hours I've spent working on that garden? Yet in one single afternoon, those cows trampled or ate everything. And again, you put them on my land without so much as a 'may I.' How dare you do this to me!" She unfolded her arms and started waving the gun. "If I see any more cows in my garden, so help me God, I'll shoot them."

"They're steers, not cows." Trace chuckled. "There's a big difference." He stiffened when she suddenly pointed the revolver directly at his groin. To his relief, she lowered the barrel, but before he could leap to his feet, she pulled the trigger. The chair he was sitting on suddenly tipped to the side and he landed sprawled on the floor. "Dammit, woman, you shot off the leg of my chair!"

"A gentleman never leaves a woman standing while he sits.''

By the time Trace had scrambled up from the floor, Martha had already left. He looked back at the Queen Anne chair he'd paid a healthy price for, wondering if he'd be able to get it fixed. "The damn woman's not safe to be around!"

He headed back up the stairs, two at a time. His need for sleep had vanished. "I should have known better than to go into an agreement with a woman," he grumbled as he entered his bedroom.

He yanked his socks from the drawer.

"Who would have thought that a little bit of a woman who looked so helpless and prudish could be so damn cantankerous? And eyeglasses? Where the hell did those come from?"

He pulled on his boots.

She didn't even know a steer from a cow, he thought as he buttoned his shirt. Had she spent her life in a convent? Hardly. Not with that temper. Besides, nuns don't teach girls how to shoot like that!

After his boots were on, he shoved on his gray, wide-brimmed hat and headed back downstairs. He had a lot of things to do, and that now included satisfying his persnickety neighbor. Unfortunately, the woman gave no indication of wanting to move back where she came from. Wherever that was.

As he left the house, Trace heard two shots fired. He started running toward Martha's house, convinced she'd just shot one or possibly two of his steers. Breathing heavily, he came to an abrupt halt at the far side of her garden. He stared in disbelief at Martha calmly rocking in a chair, looking as pious as a white dove, her revolver resting in her lap. At least there were no dead cattle lying about.

"What the hell were you shooting at?" he called angrily.

"Nothing," Martha replied. "I knew it would make you come running. Now that you're here, I want you to take a look at what those cows...steers...have done. Just what do you plan to do about it?"

Trace took a long, deep breath to calm his nerves. He had to admit the garden was a shambles. "Just what do you expect me to do?" He started making his way down the rows toward her. "I can't very well put it back like it was. From the looks of it, there wasn't much here to begin with."

Martha raised her pert chin in defiance. How dare he make such a statement! "I worked long and hard on that garden, but of course what would you know about work? You have everyone else do it for you."

"Dammit, Martha, I'm not going to get rid of the steers. They'll supply meat for the winter. As for your precious garden, we'll consider it an even trade for that chair you destroyed."

Martha looked up at the man standing over her. Surely he was the devil incarnate. "Then you leave me no choice but to shoot them. Just remember, I warned you."

Trace's eyes narrowed. "I have a contract stating half of this land is mine."

"Fine. You take your half and I'll take mine. I want a fence right down the middle."

"You're not being fair, lady. If you'd stop getting so all-fired angry, I'm sure we could work out an agreeable solution." He had to step back to keep from getting banged into when Martha bounded out of the chair.

"*I'm* not being fair?" Martha demanded. She poked him hard on the chest with the end of the revolver. "Let me remind you that you're the one who has taken over everything!''

Trace had had enough of her yowling. He grabbed the barrel of the gun, twisted it from Martha's hand and sent it sailing through the air. ''I told you once,'' he growled, ''I don't like guns, and one in your hands is asking for trouble.''

Though he was considerably taller than she, Martha still took a swing at his cheek. To her annoyance, he stepped away, causing her to miss. But she had swung her arm with such force, she would have fallen if he hadn't caught her.

''Take your hands off me!''

''Strange,'' he commented as he drew her against him. ''A little while back I got the distinct impression that you rather liked having my hands on you. If I remember correctly, we were lying on your bed.''

If he remembered correctly? Martha thought. *Of all the nerve!* ''I wouldn't know. It was too long ago.''

The blatant lie made Trace laugh. ''There are ways to remind you.''

He had her arms pinned to her sides, so Martha didn't struggle. She was well aware that a woman moving about this close to a man only served to increase his desire. At the same time she knew better than to look up. It would appear she was inviting his kiss. Though her face was turned, her cheek was against his broad chest, and she could feel the heat emanating from his body. Knowing she was in a precarious position, she picked her words carefully, making sure her inflection was cold. ''Go ahead, but I can assure you that I find nothing of interest in a man who uses women to get what he wants.''

''You know, I could take that several different ways.''

His hand cupped her buttocks, and he lifted her up, forcing her against his swollen manhood. It was all Martha could do to keep from gasping aloud.

"Mr. Lockhart! I am not used to being treated like a...woman of pleasure! Obviously you're no gentleman!" Trace's deep baritone laughter took her completely by surprise. But at least he put her down, then released her.

She quickly stepped away, and immediately realized that the hard knot she'd felt was actually a large, protruding greenish-blue stone on his belt buckle! She was convinced she had to be a complete ninny. Yet she wanted him to kiss her, hold her, speak soft words that would melt away the barriers in her head and let her go to him freely. But apparently, as before, he wasn't the least aroused. He was toying with her again. "I hope I don't have to put up with this every time we meet." She practically choked out the words. Needing to compose herself, she reached up and smoothed back her hair, though it was still neatly tucked into a topknot.

"Where do you come from, Martha?"

In the throes of both anger and desire, Martha was dumbstruck by the question. What did that have to do with anything? "Missouri," she blurted out before stopping to think. She was tempted to bite off her tongue. What if he repeated that bit of information to Josh Whitten?

"I've never been there, so tell me, do all women in Missouri act like you?"

"I don't know all the women in Missouri." She didn't like his broad smile, but at the same time, she didn't want to turn away. "Just what are you referring to? My temper? Contrary to what you may think, I'm not normally of such a disposition. With all you've pulled, you continue to bring out the very worst in me. Can you blame me? I came here hoping to own land and settle down. Maybe even marry. I rode with fifty thousand others to get this land, which is more than I can say for you. And once I got this land, you made me sign a contract, then proceeded to take over the place. I understand you've bought land in town. Why don't you build a house there and leave me alone?" She sat back down on her chair. To her consternation, Trace moved forward. Why couldn't the man keep his distance?

Trace reached up and grabbed hold of a low tree branch. "How did you learn to shoot a gun so well?"

He kept asking questions Martha wasn't prepared to answer. "My father taught me," she lied. "Before he died, we were planning to go West. He felt that I needed to know how to protect myself."

"How did he die?"

"That's my business." Needing to change this line of thinking, she said, "I would have thought a man from the East would prefer living in the city."

"What makes you think I'm from the East?"

Martha cast her eyes toward the sky. "The way you dress, I suppose. However, I'm quickly changing my mind. Gentlemen don't treat ladies the way you do."

"Oh? So you think because I don't kowtow to your every whim, I'm not a gentleman? Maybe you just haven't—"

"Kowtow to my every whim?" Martha wished she hadn't sat down. Now he had her blocked. "I defy you to name one thing that has gone my way since the moment we met. You've done nothing but ride roughshod over me. Why, in heaven's name, did I have to be the one to claim this land?"

"All right, Martha, maybe you have a point. On the other hand, you've done nothing to make our deal into a congenial situation, either." He turned loose the branch and walked to the edge of the garden, staring down at it.

Martha grasped the opportunity to stand. "And another thing. Why is it you never answer my questions?"

Trace turned and faced her, noting how her blond hair glistened in the sunlight, her dainty face with perfect features, her large brown eyes, her ample bosom, and her tiny waist that he could easily span with his hands. When he'd held her close to him he had smelled the faint, pleasing odor of perfume. Damn if she isn't ripe for the taking, he thought. He was sorry he'd released her and lost the opportunity to find out if he could light a fire under that normally prickly exterior. "Look, Martha, why don't we try working out an agreement of some sort?"

"Like what?" Martha asked suspiciously.

"What would it take to soothe that damn temper of yours?"

"Please refrain from using curse words. I find them to be offensive. If you're serious about soothing my temper, get rid of the cows."

"Steers."

"Whatever!"

Seeing the woebegone look on her face as she stared at her garden, Trace shoved back his hat and thought for a minute. "Did you know schools are being built in the towns?"

"No," Martha said sadly. "But I'm not surprised, what with the way everything is growing."

"So there isn't going to be a need for you to build a schoolhouse. Look, Martha, game is already starting to get scarce around here."

His serious tone made Martha look up. "What will the homesteaders do?"

"A lot of them just aren't going to make it. Many are so poor they're living off of bacon, beans and coffee."

"That's sad," Martha replied honestly. "Maybe if they get their crops in, they'll finally start seeing a profit."

"Beef is security and in time I hope to buy up land and stock it with cattle also."

Martha smirked. "So you're going to take advantage of other people the way you did me."

"Come, come, Martha. I never took advantage of you. What would you have done with 160 acres? Farmed it? I don't think so. You can't even manage a small garden. Furthermore, you didn't bring the equipment needed for farming, which leads me to believe you never intended doing anything on the land. And just to keep you properly informed, when I buy land, I pay value price. The banks snatch it up from loans, and the real estate men just want to make a healthy profit. I offer a fair deal."

Martha glanced at the covered wagon sitting off to the side, empty. A lot of settlers hadn't even had that much when they'd rushed forward to claim their land. Trace had made some valid points. She'd met several families that were really struggling. Eddie and Orvil were but a step above them.

"I think I have a solution."

"I can't wait to hear it."

"I'll have your place fenced off."

Martha stared at him in disbelief. "So, now you want to relegate me to one small area while you take the rest!"

"That's not what I meant. It will keep the cattle from getting in your yard and garden. If you want to use the land for anything, go right ahead. I noticed that you have no problem letting your horses graze." He looped a thumb in his belt. "There is one thing that I've been curious about. How do you plan on remaining here?"

Martha was feeling more defeated by the minute. "What do you mean?"

"It takes money to eat, to buy feed for your stock, and so forth. How do you plan on making that money?"

Martha wasn't about to tell him that she'd had her funds transferred to Guthrie and she didn't need any more money. "I hadn't thought about it."

"It's obvious that you had a nice little nest egg to get you this far, but it's not going to last forever."

Martha didn't like the way he kept his crystal-blue eyes focused on her. It was making her nervous. "It's really none of your business. I'll manage."

"Just to show you I want to be a good neighbor, I'll share any stock that's slaughtered with you, I'll fence off a couple of acres just for your private use, and I'll even have a man come and replant your damn garden!"

Martha flashed her brown eyes at him.

The corners of his lips tilted upward. "I'll even try to watch my language."

"And what do I have to do in payment?" *Was he going to ask her to share her bed?*

Trace's grin broadened. "You shock me, Miss Jackson. I wouldn't have believed you capable of such base thoughts."

"I don't know what you're talking about."

"You know exactly what I'm talking about. But to set your mind at ease, I ask for nothing in return. But the offer still stands. When you're ready to sell, I'll pay you a good price. In the meantime, perhaps I can come over on occasion and visit."

Martha still didn't trust him.

"Do we have a deal?"

"How do I know you'll keep your word?"

Trace chuckled. "You sure are a suspicious little thing. On my honor, my dear."

"Rogues don't have any honor."

Totally amused, Trace shook his head. "You'll just have to wait and see if this rogue is honorable or not. Well?"

"All right. We'll see how it goes."

Trace tipped his hat. "Enjoy your day, Martha. I can't say our visit hasn't been interesting."

Martha watched him walk away. He looked so different in jeans and a shirt. His shoulders seemed much broader, if that was possible, his hips narrower. When he moved she could see powerful thighs pressed against the skintight pants. She wondered what it would be like to lie next to him. Would his chest hairs tickle her face? Would he be a good lover? Would he make a good husband?

Martha smiled at the direction her thoughts were going. Why not a husband? Even Eddie had seen the possibilities. Trace was devastatingly appealing, and from various comments, she gathered he was becoming a pillar of the community. He had money, and he could give her the respectability she wanted. This was definitely something to think about. When she listened to what Trace was saying without getting upset, he was informative and interesting. The only major problem was that so far he hadn't shown any interest. Something that definitely needed to be worked on... should she decide to marry him.

Chapter Six

For two days, Martha watched wagonloads of furniture being delivered to Trace's house. The fine quality of the tables, divans, beds, brocades and tapestries, all beautifully crafted, continued to hold her attention. Though she would never admit it to a soul, she was dying to see what the inside of Trace's place looked like.

As each load arrived, Martha couldn't help glancing around at her own decor, which until now she'd been quite proud of. As she continued to make comparisons, however, the gaudier her place looked. She'd diligently tried to duplicate her rooms at the Spur Saloon. Only now did she take into consideration that the decorating there had all been done by the prostitutes. She soon came to realize that her lack of expertise in such matters was as obvious as a plague of grasshoppers.

Determined to right an obvious wrong, Martha took off for Guthrie, to the premises of William Rhodes, furniture dealer. If she was going to be a respected member of the community, she needed a respectable house. Before long, the exclusive Albatross Club would be meeting at her house to determine whether to accept her as a member. They'd never do so once they saw what her house looked like inside.

As she rode to town, Martha blessed the fact that she'd never invited Trace into her house. It might have alerted him to her past, which she could ill afford him to find out about. His house, furnishings and clothes were all strong indications that respectability was very important to him. He would never be interested in marrying her unless she could prove she was indeed a lady. An accomplishment that so far, she'd failed miserably to achieve. But that was going to change. No longer would she allow her temper to turn her into a shrew, no matter how right she was.

Trace finished his breakfast, then leaned back in his chair, sipping coffee and contemplating his success. Now comfortably established in his new home, he was content. He had adequate servants, his business was going well, he'd already purchased a considerable amount of surrounding acreage, and he'd even managed to make peace with his volatile neighbor. The last part he considered to be the most remarkable accomplishment.

At least, he assumed they were at peace. Come to think of it, he hadn't seen Martha in several weeks. As promised, he'd had a couple of acres fenced off for her privacy and the garden replanted. If all that hadn't made her happy, he was sure she would have let him know about it.

Suddenly curious about what his neighbor had been doing lately, he quietly set his china cup on its saucer, stood, then strolled over to the dining room window. Thoughtfully, he rubbed his chin as he looked toward her house. Though he had decided to take his time, he still planned to pursue the lady right into her bed. Unfortunately, his business both in town and Oklahoma City, plus various social obligations, had prevented him from beginning his pursuit. Now, with the congressional delegation soon to arrive in town, he still couldn't do anything but think about it.

As if he'd mentally beckoned her, he watched Martha leave the house and head toward that damn garden of hers. Suddenly she took off running, and of all things, she was being chased by a nanny goat! Then he saw chickens flying in all directions. What in God's name was she up to now? There was one thing for sure. Martha Jackson knew nothing about living on a farm. He headed for the front door.

Martha dashed into the house, slammed the door shut, then leaned against it to catch her breath. "I should never have let that man in town talk me into buying a goat," she muttered. "What good is the milk going to be to me if I can't even get near the godforsaken creature? She's even eating my garden!"

The sudden knock on the door caused Martha to jump. Was someone at the door or was the goat butting it? Another knock. Wondering how anyone could possibly have gotten past that four-legged beast, she cautiously opened the door a crack.

"Good morning, Martha," Trace greeted her.

Martha grabbed his arm. "Get in the house before the goat comes back!" As soon as he stepped in, she slammed the door behind him.

Trace chuckled at seeing her hair in disarray, the smudge of dirt on her cheek and her faded dress streaked down the back from perspiration. "I hadn't expected such a hearty welcome."

Martha wanted to dive into a hole. This wasn't at all the way she'd planned their next meeting, or his first visit in her house. "Please, come sit down." She motioned Trace toward the parlor, then reached up to smooth back her

hair as best she could. As soon as he walked past her, she
tugged at the hiked-up waist of her dress.

"How nice to see you again," she said graciously, trying to exhibit an air of refinement. A seemingly impossible task, considering the way she looked.

"I happened to notice you were having a bit of trouble
with your animals and thought I might be of help. So I
took the liberty of tying up your goat."

"It won't do any good," Martha groaned. "She chews
the rope in half." Seeing him glancing around the room,
she was grateful for all the trips she'd made to town. She
still had the red sofa and chair, but the curtains, drapes
and other accessories, plus a simple comfortable chair and
small table, had completely changed the appearance of the
room. His gaze returned to her and she added, "She's
been nothing but trouble. She's even butted down the
door to the chicken coop, and now I again have chickens
running all about."

"How's your garden coming along?"

"What garden? The animals are demolishing it. At least
my fruit trees are doing well."

"Maybe this life isn't for you."

Martha studied the handsome man comfortably seated
across from her. As usual his clothes were tailored to a
perfect fit. The white shirt with a ruffle adorning the front
was spotless and well starched. The chocolate-brown silk
vest was open, and the trousers were the soft tan color of
a doe's hide. "You can give up the idea of me moving,
Trace." She felt her temper starting to rise, but at the same
time she was thinking about the dark mat of chest hair
hidden beneath the shirt and how she'd wondered what it
would feel like to run her fingers across it. "I'll learn. It's
just taking a little longer than I expected." His thick black
hair reached the collar of his shirt. He was clean-shaven,

and his mustache wasn't wide and long as was the fashion. In her estimation, it looked just right. Was it possible to be attracted to a man and still be angry with him? Of course. On more than one occasion she'd heard the girls in the saloon testify to such. Get hold of yourself, Martha, she chastised. You're supposed to be acting like a lady.

Trace remained silent, watching with interest the different emotions playing across Martha's face. Her expressions were as confusing as the woman herself. First he'd watched anger leap into her large brown eyes at the mention of moving to town, then what appeared to be interest spread across her face as she scrutinized him. Now her face had become stoic. "I wasn't suggesting you move," he finally spoke up. "I was merely stating the obvious. Living out of town hasn't been easy for you. I apologize if I sounded insulting."

"Perhaps I'm being a bit too defensive." Martha clasped her hands in her lap in perfect ladylike fashion. "The other day, Josh Whitten was telling me you're buying up land."

Hearing that name, Trace released a short, ugly laugh. "At least I give the people a fair price, which is more than I can say for Whitten."

Because Josh wasn't able, Martha felt the need to defend the gentleman. "He's in the real estate business. Naturally he has to see a profit."

Trace stretched out his long legs and peered at her. "How do you know Whitten?"

"I met him one day when there was a commotion at the arbitration office. The men were upset about claims already filed on their land by sooners. But I'm sure you're well aware of that."

"As I've said before, you have no proof of that. You're guessing, Martha."

"I don't think so. But to change the subject, why are people selling their land?"

"They're hungry and penniless. Professional hunters have moved in. They're killing game and either selling it to stores in town or shipping it off to Kansas City. Before long there isn't going to be any wildlife. Selling out is better than starving." Trace's brow wrinkled. "Tell me, Martha, what made you come here?"

"I told you. The free land."

"But you're apparently a woman of means. Why would you want to be stuck out in the middle of nowhere?"

Feeling nervous at the questions, Martha stood and walked to the window. Slowly she turned and faced Trace. "I got tired of people," she stated simply. "I love being away from town, free to do as I please. Of course I hadn't expected someone to build a house practically in my backyard. Nevertheless, you have proved to be a good neighbor, and I do want to apologize for the way I've acted in the past. I have no idea what made me act so unladylike." There, Martha thought. That's a perfect start.

The apology came as a disappointment to Trace. He'd liked the fiery woman who had dared to shoot his chair out from under him. The woman before him now was too composed, and he was quickly becoming bored. But what had he expected? For her to encourage advances? "I really must be going," he stated as he stood.

"Trace? What should I do about the goat?"

The bewildered look on her face caused Trace to laugh. "Give her away."

"How? She chases me all over the place."

"How did you get her here?"

Martha followed him toward the front door. "A man delivered her. I know who I can give her to. I just don't know how I'm going to get her there."

"All right, I'll take care of it. Who am I supposed to deliver it to?"

"The Graham family. Have you met them?"

"Yes. A couple of days ago."

He turned at the doorway, almost causing Martha to run into him. She was standing so close to him that she could feel his body heat and smell the pleasing odor of shaving lather.

"I'm not going to catch your chickens for you."

Martha looked up and smiled. "I think I can handle that."

Trace was tempted to pull her into his arms and kiss her full, tempting lips, but instead he turned and opened the door. "Do us both a favor, Martha. Don't buy any more animals." He tipped his hat, then walked out.

By the time Trace reached the nanny, the critter had already chewed the rope in two. She lowered her head, ready to charge, but Trace reached out and gave her a good cuff on top of the head. She settled right down.

As he led the nanny through the wide gate, Trace broke out laughing, unable to believe that a pair of brown eyes had caused him to go on such an errand. He wanted nothing to do with chickens or goats, but for some ungodly reason, he'd foolishly offered to get rid of the nanny.

When he reached his house, he went on to the carriage house. The groom looked at the goat, then back at Trace in disbelief. "Don't say a word, Frank," Trace warned. "Just get my horse saddled. I have a delivery to make. And while you're at it, get me another rope. This one is just about done in."

Mounted and trailing the goat behind him, Trace was soon headed for the Grahams' homestead. His thoughts quickly returned to the petite woman with honey-blond hair. Martha had acted the perfect lady during his short visit, almost aloof, even going so far as to apologize for the past, none of which he was sure he believed. Women usually tended to make it quite clear either that they were untouchable or that they were interested. Not so with Martha. She kept sending out conflicting signals. At times she seemed taken with him; at other times she acted as if she didn't want him around. Since protocol had never kept him from doing what he wanted in the past, he decided that on his next visit he'd find out for certain if she was afraid of her desires or just cold-natured. He'd noticed how she'd stayed out of his reach once he was inside, and the shocked look on her face when she'd almost bumped into him at the door. She'd moved away quickly. But he'd seen the spitfire in her too many times not to know that if she ever let her guard down, her passion would be well worth the time to develop it. So either she was hiding it, or it just hadn't been awakened. He nudged his horse into a lope. He wouldn't mind the woman sharing his bed one damn bit.

Martha giggled with delight as she stood at the window watching Trace ride away with the cantankerous goat in tow. She had expected him to let one of his servants handle the task. Mr. Lockhart was certainly nothing like the men who had frequented the Spur Saloon. He had inner strength, yet could be gentle. He was also a man who knew what he wanted and refused to let anything stand in his way. The latter quality riled her no end, especially when it was directed at her. But oddly enough, she now realized it was that very quality that she admired the most.

She watched Trace yank on the rope, moving the nanny at a faster pace. Even a goat didn't try to put up an argument with him. Trace had ignited her curiosity. What would it be like to have a man make love to her? Sharing a man's bed was not a repugnant thought, especially after being around saloon girls. In fact, she looked forward to the experience. She wanted to find out if it was as pleasurable as the girls had stated. She'd just never found the right man. She could clearly remember being at the ripe age of fourteen, peeking around curtains, cracks or anything else she could find to see what men were paying the saloon girls money for. At first she'd been shocked, but that had quickly faded.

A wry smile spread across Martha's full lips. Because the saloon girls were constantly moving on, none had known she was still a virgin. She was too embarrassed to tell them differently. By the time she'd turned twenty, the girls spoke openly in front of her about the men they'd entertained the night before, and how. They confided all their worries and sorrows to her, even more so when she became the sole owner of the Spur. Martha knew that either the girls enjoyed their chosen profession, or they didn't. The latter she soon got rid of. Once she'd thought about doing away with them altogether, but they'd cried on her shoulder, saying it was the only way they had to make money. So she'd kept them on. Besides, they were the only friends she'd had.

Martha headed for the back door, ready to tackle the gate on the chicken coop that the goat had butted. She concluded that it was a sad state of affairs when, after all she'd learned over the years, Trace was the only man who had ever laid a hand on her. And to make matters worse, she would have to keep him at a distance. Unwedded bedding wasn't something a proper woman did. ''Being a lady isn't going to be easy," she murmured as she reached the feed shed.

After grabbing a hammer and nails, Martha started for the coop. One of the hinges had been pulled loose and it proved a simple matter to nail it back in place. When the job was completed, she swung the gate back and forth, proud of her handiwork. "Amazing what a person can accomplish when necessary," she muttered with pride.

When the chickens were once again contained, Martha spent the rest of the day repairing her garden. She was grateful for the cloud cover that managed to reduce the day's temperature somewhat. The humidity, however, was sweltering. When she finally laid down her hoe for the day, she looked up at the sky. There was no doubt about it, the rain would arrive soon. She could smell it. Smiling, she headed back to the house. At least her garden and the fruit trees would benefit from the rain.

That night, Martha was sound asleep when a clap of thunder caused her to sit bolt upright in bed. She clutched the blanket to her chin as fear snaked up her spine. She'd always been afraid of storms, and suddenly her beloved house seemed very empty. Even while she tried convincing herself she was being foolish, her teeth started to chatter. When they were young, Lawrence had tried telling her that her fears stemmed from the fact that it was during a storm that they'd found their father dead in his room. Maybe so; she didn't remember. But though her head said one thing, it didn't stop her body from shaking.

As the storm intensified, the thunder became deafening, the lightning illuminating her dark bedroom, and it was all she could do to keep from climbing under the bed. If lightning struck the house, it would become a blazing inferno! She squeezed her eyes shut, listening to the rain whipping against the windows in sheets. It took a moment before she realized that rain was the only thing she now heard. Martha took several long, deliberate breaths to try to calm herself.

When she knew she was safe, she slid off the bed and forced herself to go to the window. There were still streaks of lightning in the black sky, but it was at a distance. "Are you always going to be like this?" she chastised herself. "You act like some child, you ninny!" She snatched up the blanket from the bed and wrapped it around herself. "I need a cup of hot chocolate," she muttered as she headed downstairs. "This is just great. Now I'm talking to myself."

The next morning, Martha plodded toward the garden, paying no heed to the mud that collected on the bottom of her skirts and boots. She wasn't surprised to discover that most of the garden had either been battered down or washed away. For the first time, she was sorely tempted to move on. Why was she putting herself through all this when she could be comfortably situated in California? Even her plans to run a school had fallen by the wayside. And the land? The monster in the big house had that contracted! How could I ever have thought I was attracted to him, and worse yet, I was actually trying to figure out a way to trap him into marriage! As she glared at the house sitting on the hill, she angrily brushed the tears from her cheeks. How did she know he wouldn't decide to kick her off her land? She glanced up at the clear sky. "He can't. By God, it's still in my name, and neither hell nor Trace Lockhart is going to make me move. I won't give him the satisfaction of saying he knew I wouldn't last!"

"Hello, there!" someone called from her house.

Martha turned and headed back, wondering who would be paying a call after the ravages of a storm. As she cleared the stand of trees, she saw Josh Whitten dismounting. Of the people she knew, he was the last person she wanted to talk to. She was scared to death that he'd find out she really was Blossom, then spread the information. But she'd also decided that if she acted very ladylike, his suspicions would fade. After all, everyone knew the kind of woman Blossom was. Or at least they thought they did. As she neared the house, she plastered a friendly smile on her face. She couldn't afford to let Josh know he made her nervous, and in all truthfulness, she rather liked him.

"What are you doing all the way out here?" Martha asked when she'd joined him.

"I came to see if you fared all right after the storm." He tethered his horse to the hitching pole. "Some people's houses burned last night because of the lightning. I wanted to be sure yours wasn't one of them."

"I'm flattered." He had a boyish grin, but the deep crow's-feet at the side of his eyes made it apparent that he was older than he looked. "As you can see, nothing happened."

"You have a nice place." He shoved back the black hat. "I've looked for you in town, hoping we could dine together again. I have to admit, there's not a prettier woman around."

Martha blushed properly. "I find that hard to believe." Something out of the corner of her eye caught her attention. Turning, she was surprised to see Curly Roberts and another man headed toward the house. She hadn't seen Curly since he had worked on Trace's place. The bouquet of flowers Curly was carrying softened her heart. The look on Josh Whitten's face clearly showed he wasn't at all pleased at the other man's arrival.

"Do you know those men?" Josh asked.

"One of them."

After Curly and his partner dismounted, Curly handed her the flowers.

Martha beamed with delight. "How thoughtful of you, Curly."

He tugged off his hat and grinned shyly. "Sorry I've been so long in paying a visit. When I saw the flowers, I thought about the ones you tried growing. I'm glad you like them." He turned to the other man. "This is my brother, Rob."

Rob smiled from ear to ear. "I had to come along to see for myself the woman Curly's been raving about for the past month. I gotta say, ma'am, he wasn't exaggerating about your beauty."

"What a nice compliment. Gentlemen, I'd like you to meet Josh Whitten. He sells real estate."

As the men shook hands, Martha sat on a chair to remove her muddy boots. Curly immediately offered to pull them off for her, and was rewarded with another bright smile.

"Why don't you gentlemen come in the house?" she asked when her boots had been removed. "I'll fix coffee."

The men followed her inside.

"Please, make yourselves comfortable in the parlor while I fetch some slippers."

Martha hurried upstairs. As it had been with Curly, Martha liked Rob right away. Both men were tall and lanky, straightforward, and possessed quick smiles. Suddenly the house didn't seem so lonesome.

"Did you know that we're going to have electric street-lights in town?" Josh asked after she'd joined them and served the coffee.

"How wonderful," Martha said excitedly. The first time she'd ever seen such things was in the Topeka Hotel in Kansas. They'd even had bathrooms! She suddenly wondered why Trace hadn't told her about the lights. Maybe he thought that if she knew, she'd want to stay.

Josh was quite pleased with himself. He not only had Martha's complete attention, he had also shown what rednecks these other intruders were. He thought of more informative things he could discuss. "You don't come to town often enough. We're going to have our own municipal plant. I hear tell a day will come when we won't need lanterns. The place keeps growing. Why, we already have the busiest railroad depot in the United States, and wooden water veins are going in as fast as the men can work. And since we have an icehouse now, practically everyone has an icebox in their home."

"I'll be darned," Curly said in awe. "How do those iceboxes work?"

Martha and Rob looked at Josh, both wondering the same thing.

Josh smiled. "Well, it stands about yea high—" he indicated the height with his hand "—and it's closed in with a door in front. The inside has a top part to put a block of ice, and the rest of the space is used to store food. The ice keeps food from spoiling for an unbelievable time."

Curly and Rob shook their heads in disbelief, convinced Josh was pulling their legs. They'd have to see it to believe it.

"The towns are sure getting big, all right," Curly stated warily. "I hear tell in Capitol Hill they've made it against the law for a woman to appear in town wearing men's clothes."

Rob leaned forward, a frown creasing his forehead. "How does that . . . elec . . . tricity work, Josh?"

Martha watched the pompous look on Josh's face turn to confusion.

"That I don't really understand myself. I heard that when it's installed in houses, all you gotta do is turn some knob and the light goes on or off."

Now Curly and Rob knew for sure Josh was making up stories.

By the time the men had left, it was already starting to turn dark. As Martha cleaned up the cups and saucers, she hummed a tune. She'd enjoyed her gentlemen callers' company immensely. At least they weren't as intimidating as Trace, and they were much more manageable. She had felt like a young girl when Curly shyly told her he'd be courting her. She would have to wait until they were alone to inform Curly that, though she liked him immensely, he should find someone else to court.

Martha heated up last night's stew for supper, still annoyed that she'd had to purchase the vegetables instead of getting them from her defunct garden. At least the town seemed to keep growing nearer. An icebox, she suddenly thought. Wouldn't that be wonderful? But the electricity excited her the most. She remembered the huge crystal chandelier that had gone into Trace's house. No wonder there was no place for candles. He was gearing his house for electricity!

After eating her supper, Martha headed for the outhouse, her thoughts centered on whether to do the washing tomorrow, or take it to the Chinese laundry in town. The latter would give her an excuse to see Josh again. In two days, the women's Albatross Club would be meeting at her house, so she needed to go to the bakery in town anyway. Though her cooking had improved immensely, she wasn't about to try to push her luck by baking something. Especially not for the Albatross Club.

Martha was about to open the door to the outhouse when she heard noises coming from the hill. She took care of her business, then scampered past the trees to have a better view of Trace's place. When she came to a halt, her mouth dropped open. The entire inside of the house was aflame with candlelight, and grand carriages were arriving, one after another. Martha slowly backed up to her rocking chair and sat, sorry the darkness of night restricted her view. Occasionally she did get a glimpse of the women's beautiful ball gowns as they walked past the bright lanterns at the front door. The men wore formal attire and shiny top hats and white gloves. A moment later, she heard music drifting through the open windows of the castle. "What did he do," she mumbled, "hire an entire orchestra?" But the lovely waltz they were playing was quite pleasing to her ears.

Carriages continued to arrive and were soon parked all around the wide, circular driveway. Martha kept listening to the music, now muffled with the sounds of laughter. Slowly she rose to her feet, envy tugging at her breast. How wonderful it must be to go to such a gala event, she thought as she headed for her back door.

Even after she was ready to go to bed, Martha stood for some time looking out her bedroom window toward the hill. She came to realize that living away from town would probably have worked out just fine if Trace had left her alone. But as the sounds continued to drift down, she now wanted to be part of the event. She wanted to wear lovely ball gowns and be invited to such gatherings. The only way she could do that would be through the women's club,

Trace, Josh or all of the above. At first she'd thought to confront Trace with all the noise tonight, claiming that it kept her awake. Now she changed her mind. That wouldn't accomplish a thing. On the other hand, if she graciously inquired whether the party went well, he might think about asking her to the next one.

Martha went to her bed, and after pulling the covers back, climbed on top. The night was still warm from the day's heat. Were there a lot of beautiful women at the ball? she suddenly wondered. And would they set out to win Trace? Why not? Wasn't that exactly what she'd thought about doing? How many would fall prey to his good looks and eventually end up in his bed? Annoyed at herself for even wondering such a thing, she rolled onto her side with her back to the window, trying to go to sleep.

Chapter Seven

Martha felt like the queen bee as she served punch and petits fours to the Albatross Club members. Her ear was stretched out a mile when some of the women began discussing Trace's ball.

"Such a marvelous man," Beatrice Cunningham expounded, "and such a grand soiree. I tell you, ladies, it's too bad all of you couldn't attend. It was quite a coup for Mr. Lockhart to have the congressional delegation there. Mr. Lockhart is going places in this town."

"Why is the delegation here?" an elderly woman asked.

"They say that Guthrie shouldn't have been divided into four towns," an attractive auburn-haired woman spoke up. "They are talking about changing the land requirements and making Guthrie into one town again."

Holding a plate with a small slice of cake in one hand, Martha sat on the sofa beside Iris Stewart, an older woman who she had met in town on a previous occasion. "Can they do that?" Martha asked.

"Of course they can," the auburn-headed woman stated in disgust.

"You needn't get so snippy, Hazel," Iris chastised. "Not everyone is familiar with governmental procedures."

Hazel Carpenter took a dainty sip of punch before settling her gray eyes on Martha. "I didn't see you at the ball, Martha. Since you're Trace's maid, I would have thought he'd need your services."

Several of the women turned in shock toward Martha. Having a maid in their club was quite unacceptable. They were ladies of refinement.

Martha smiled sweetly. She knew a cat when she saw one, and Hazel's fangs were definitely extended. "Why would you think I'm Trace's maid?" she asked calmly.

"Your house is so small compared to his, I just assumed it was the servant's quarters. Or maybe there is something between you and Trace that we're not aware of."

The quiet conversation that had been going on among four other women suddenly ceased.

"Hazel!" Iris snapped in her quiet, authoritative manner. "You've gone too far. I think we owe Martha an apology. Just because you're attracted to Trace Lockhart doesn't give you the right to say such things, or to chase away any other single women in the territory." She reached over and patted Martha's hand.

"If Martha is to be in our ladies' club, I think we have every right to know just what her status is, Iris." Hazel returned her gaze to Martha, waiting for an explanation.

Martha was reminded of the women who ran her out of Bickerton, and she was having a hard time keeping her temper under control. Fortunately, years of playing cards had taught her how to mask her feelings. Being in the club was too important to her plans for the future. She could ill afford to be kicked out before even being accepted.

"Although I do not feel that I should have to account for myself, apparently it's necessary. This land is mine. Should you choose not to believe that—" she looked directly at Hazel ''—you can look it up at the land office. My house is small because only one person lives in it, so I feel no need for a larger place. Unless I wanted to impress people, which I don't.''

She balanced the plate in her lap and continued. ''I have personal wealth that would probably allow me to buy and sell most of the women in this room. Nevertheless, I also have a head for business. When Trace Lockhart asked to lease my land and build his home on it, I readily agreed. After all, I'm not a farmer, and what could I possibly do with so much land? If I should decide I no longer care for this life-style, I have agreed to sell the land to him. I must admit, however, I didn't realize he would build so close.

''So to answer your unasked question, Hazel, there is nothing between Trace and myself. We are simply neighbors. I'm sure you also have neighbors in town.'' Martha was pleased to see the pink flush that spread across Hazel's cheeks.

''Is there anything else you would like to know, Hazel?'' Iris asked with a pleased look.

''I just thought we should clear the air.''

For the next hour, the women treated Martha as an equal, with the exception of Hazel, who remained aloof. But Martha didn't mind; she didn't like the woman. Hazel was everything Martha had dreamed of being when she was younger. The woman's coloring was exquisite; she had a pale complexion that was enhanced by her auburn hair and rosebud lips. If that wasn't enough, she was tall, regal and self-assured, and her apricot-colored town suit hung to perfection over a slender, graceful figure.

By the time the women had returned to their carriages and left, Martha was suffering from mixed emotions. She was pleased they had accepted her into their group, but she was worried about Trace. Why would he choose to marry her over someone like Hazel, whose ladylike breeding was obvious? How many other women were after him?

Not that she'd actually decided to marry the man, Martha told herself. After all, only a few days ago she'd wanted to see him hanging from a noose. Still, she would like to at least have the opportunity to make up her mind whether or not she wanted him as a husband. She started a fire in the stove, then set a large pail of water on top for washing and rinsing the dishes. While the water heated, she ran upstairs to change out of her pale blue day dress.

By the time Martha came back down, she'd decided she would ask Trace over for supper. Now that she could cook a decent meal, she felt considerably more confident. She'd always heard the way to a man's heart was through his stomach. She stopped in front of the stove and stared down at the water. But Trace had servants to feed him anything he wanted, so why should a meal hold any appeal to him? She lifted the pail from the stove and carried it to the sink.

Being in the ladies' club was definitely going to be to her advantage. It would allow her to keep up on current affairs as well as perfect her social graces. Martha suddenly smiled. Hazel would split her britches if she knew how Martha had earned her money!

The days passed, but unfortunately Martha saw neither hide nor hair of Trace.

Josh Whitten was feeling quite pleased with himself as he entered the small, single-room real estate office and removed the Closed sign from the window. He'd just returned from calling on Martha Jackson. Tomorrow she was coming into town and had promised to have lunch with him. He sat behind his desk, leaned back and locked his hands behind his head.

He'd never been in love with any woman the way he loved Martha, but she certainly knew how to be elusive. Never once had he found an opportunity to steal a kiss, and he had absolutely no idea how she felt toward him. The other night he'd seen Trace Lockhart escorting Hazel Carpenter to the opera and had made a point of mentioning it to Martha. He'd also informed her that the illustrious Mr. Lockhart kept a suite at the Hotel Springer. Those bits of information didn't seem to bother Martha, which served to boost his confidence that he'd eventually win her love. He'd also come to the conclusion that he'd been entirely wrong about Martha being Blossom. Martha was too much a lady.

Josh grinned as he leaned his elbows on the desk. He had definite plans for his future. With his real estate dealings, he was going to become a wealthy man, and he wanted a woman of quality by his side. That woman was going to be Martha Jackson.

Hearing the door open, Josh looked up. His smile broadened and he stood. "Welcome to Guthrie, Vern. When did you arrive?"

The short, wiry man strolled forward and shook Josh's hand. "Just rode in. I left Missouri as soon as I got your telegram. You said Pete is coming up from Texas."

"That's right, and Tuley will also be joining us. This land is ripe for the taking, Vern. It beats robbing banks and trains like we used to do. By the time you boys leave, you're going to be rich men."

Martha sat in the parlor, trying to concentrate on her embroidery work. The stitches and French knots Iris had shown her weren't all that complicated, but Martha's concentration continued to drift, causing her to pull out her stitches. Ever since Josh left a little more than an hour ago, she'd been angry at Hazel for sinking her talons into Trace...which apparently he didn't mind in the least. Did Hazel also spend the night with him in his suite at the hotel? Martha poked herself with the needle and winced. Irritated, she set the work aside and stood. She thought about starting another garden, but that idea held little appeal. Besides, Eddie had said she might as well wait until next spring.

Martha strolled to the window and looked toward the hill. Though it was difficult to see because of the trees, she thought she could make out the end of a buggy in front of Trace's house. Eagerly, she hiked up her skirts and ran upstairs for a better view from her bedroom. After confirming that it was indeed Trace's buggy, she went to the mirror to be sure her hair was in proper order. She would pay her neighbor a visit. But what if Hazel was with him? she suddenly wondered.

She had returned to the parlor, still undecided on what to do, when there was a knock on the front door. She quickly smoothed out the skirt of her blue-and-pink-striped dress, then went to answer it, pinching her cheeks for coloring. As she swung open the door, Martha stopped breathing. It seemed that every time she saw Trace, he was even more handsome than before.

"Hello," she blurted out. She stepped back and invited him in.

"You're looking particularly lovely today," Trace commented as they entered the parlor. "Things must be going right for a change, or is it that I haven't been around to pester you?"

Martha turned and saw the devilish smile that displayed even white teeth. She returned the smile. "I must admit, it has been rather peaceful. Are you in a hurry, or can you sit and visit awhile?''

"I'm in no hurry."

"Then perhaps you'd like some coffee. It's already made."

Trace nodded, and to her surprise he followed her into the kitchen and sat at the table. "Wouldn't you be more comfortable in the parlor?" she asked as she took down the cups and saucers from the buffet.

"This is fine. I came by to tell you one of my men will be delivering a shank of beef. If you'll remember, I said I'd share any steer that was killed."

Martha sat a cup of coffee in front of him, then poured her own. "Apparently you are a man of honor."

"And a rogue?" He chuckled. "Maybe one of these days I'll be able to change your opinion of me." He sipped the coffee, finding it exactly to his liking. "Would you mind if I smoke?"

"Not at all."

She grabbed an ashtray from the cupboard and proudly placed it on the table. It was a brand-new item she'd found at the mercantile store. She joined him at the table, watching him pull a thin cigar from his vest and light it. She didn't dare ask him to give her one, but she hadn't had a good cigar since leaving Missouri and the thought of being able to enjoy a smoke was most appealing. "For a man who built himself a castle, you don't seem to spend much time there."

He raised a dark eyebrow. "Don't tell me you've missed me?"

Martha was pleased by the glint in his crystal-blue eyes. Had she been wrong? Could he possibly be interested in her? "I must admit, I do grow lonesome sometimes."

"That's interesting. From what I've seen, you seem to have your share of gentlemen callers."

Martha's pulse quickened. The possibility of trying to make him jealous had never occurred to her. Jealous? That was ridiculous. He'd never indicated the least bit of interest in her. God, how she loved the smell of that cigar. "You're a fine one to talk. I understand Hazel Carpenter has been keeping you quite busy. Since we are neighbors, and assuming you don't have other plans, I wonder if you'd care to have supper here tomorrow night. It's the least I can do to prove I'm no longer angry at you. It might even compensate in some small part for the damage I did to your house."

Had any other woman made such an invitation, Trace would have assumed supper really meant a toss in bed. Women just didn't ask men over unless there was a double meaning, especially if they lived alone. But nothing about Martha had ever followed the set guidelines between a man and a woman. "I'd consider it a pleasure," he said as he stubbed out his cigar.

To Martha's delight, not even half of the cigar had been smoked. Strange, she'd never noticed how long and shapely Trace's fingers were. It immediately brought to mind his hands roaming her body, which now seemed like a lifetime ago. "Shall we make it around seven?"

"Fine. How are the Grahams getting along with the nanny you gave them?"

Martha laughed. "Eddie's children already have her pulling a cart. I think instead of charging, the goat now runs when she sees the children coming. The milk has been a godsend to them. They're having a hard time of it. Trace, do you think it would be possible to give part of the beef to them? I can take it over later this afternoon and they can salt it down."

Trace tapped his fingers on the table.

"Would you like another cup of coffee?"

"No, thank you. Martha, Orvil paid me a visit the other day when he was in town. He said they weren't sure they would be able to last through the winter. He wanted to know what I would purchase their land for if they decided to return to Kentucky."

"Oh, no," Martha groaned. "Eddie didn't say a word to me about it, and I was just over there yesterday. They are so proud. I've tried to be of help, but they won't let me."

"Maybe Orvil hasn't said anything to Eddie about it. Anyway, I'll send over extra meat that you can take to them."

Trace left a few minutes later, and shortly after that the meat was delivered by one of his servants. Feeling despondent, Martha immediately took off for Eddie's place.

As usual, Eddie was happy to see Martha, and Orvil was out working the field.

"You thank Mr. Lockhart for us," Eddie said when the children had run outside and they finally had a chance to talk. "This meat is going to come in real handy."

Martha glanced around the shack. The sofa was dilapidated and torn, with the stuffing starting to come out in places, and the table and chairs were hand-hewn. There were only two beds for everyone to sleep in. Come winter, they'd all freeze to death.

"Did Trace tell you Orvil spoke to him about selling the land?" Eddie asked.

Martha nodded.

"Don't look so sad, Martha. We got family in Kentucky, and we're going to be all right. Besides, we'll be leaving with more than we came with after Trace pays us for the land."

"Then you've made your decision?"

"Yes. We'll be leaving in a month. I'll miss you."

Tears began building in Martha's eyes. "And I'll miss you. You're the only real friend I have."

"You'll meet others. You've got a good heart, Martha. Now, what are you doing about Trace? I tell you, you should latch on to that man."

"He's been seeing another woman."

Eddie tossed her hands in the air. "What difference does that make? I haven't seen one female who can hold a candle to you. You're a smart woman—surely you can figure out a way to snag the man, unless you just aren't interested."

"You're impossible, Eddie. I can't do it by myself. He also has to show interest. I've invited him for supper tomorrow night."

"Did he accept?" Eddie asked excitedly.

"He certainly did."

"Well, I sure hope something happens before I leave. If not, I'll die of curiosity."

The children came running in, and Martha rose to leave. Maybe she was never cut out to be a schoolteacher. "Eddie, you know I have that covered wagon. I want you and Orvil to use it to get you back to Kentucky. Before you refuse, hear me out. It's just sitting there. I have absolutely no use for it. I want you and Orvil to take it as a going-away gift. I'll be truly offended if you don't. I know you can use it."

The children started shouting excitedly. "Ma," one of them yelled, "you can't turn her down. We ain't got anything as nice as that wagon."

Eddie smiled. "We'd be right proud to accept it, Martha."

"Good. You have Orvil come by tomorrow to get it. That'll give you plenty of time to pack. I wouldn't want anything to happen to that baby you're carrying."

After supper that night, Martha made herself comfortable, then lit the cigar Trace had left earlier that afternoon. After several puffs to get it started, she leaned back against the cushions, then sent two perfectly shaped smoke rings floating toward the ceiling. Now that Eddie had agreed to take the wagon and team, she felt a little better about them leaving. *Maybe I should open a pipe and tobacco shop,* she thought as she watched the rings begin to lose their shape. *I could have a good puff or two on a cigar anytime I please.*

Martha paced the parlor floor, waiting for Trace's arrival. Even though she'd gone through her wardrobe several times before finally selecting the royal-blue taffeta dress, she was now having second thoughts. Maybe the watered silk with the square neckline would have been more becoming. At least it was a little more feminine. She glanced at the clock on the fireplace mantel. She didn't have time to change now. Trace would be here in five minutes, and if she changed clothes, she'd have to redo her hair. She walked into the dining room to check the table, though she'd already made the same inspection a dozen times. Piece by piece, she picked up the silverware to be sure she hadn't missed any spots when polishing it. That alone had taken most of her morning. The knock on the door startled her.

"Don't panic, Martha," she whispered. "You're supposed to be a lady, and as such you should not feel nervous about entertaining a gentleman." She took three deep breaths, then glided forward.

When Martha opened the door, Trace was convinced that if he had had false teeth, they would have fallen out. The woman standing in the doorway was devastatingly beautiful. The blue dress was high-necked, but the long sleeves and bodice fit like a second skin. The front of the waistline dipped into a V and the skirt hung straight to the floor. Though the dress was proper in every way, it couldn't have been more seductive. The only jewelry she wore was a pair of topaz earrings.

Martha was having similar thoughts. Trace looked so handsome in his white shirt, gray waistcoat and gray-and-brown-striped trousers. Then she saw the bottle of whiskey he was carrying in his left hand. She hadn't had a drink since leaving Missouri, but she reminded herself that she was supposed to act like a lady. Did ladies drink whiskey? Should she act pleased or be insulted? "Please, come in."

"I thought we could have a drink before supper," Trace said as he stepped inside.

By the time Martha closed the door behind him, she'd made up her mind to act offended. Blossom would have enjoyed a drink before eating, but Blossom was dead. "I don't drink," she told Trace. "I believe such beverages are the devil's temptation. If you'll give me the bottle, I'll set it in the kitchen."

Trace was completely taken aback by the statement. Obviously she wasn't going to allow him to have a drink, either. Annoyed, he handed her the bottle.

"Please be seated in the parlor. I'll join you in a minute."

As Trace made himself as comfortable as possible on the small red sofa, he was mulling over Martha's statement. The devil's temptation? He'd seen hellfire-and-brimstone preachers drink liquor. Was there nothing consistent about the woman? Now she was acting like a pious Madonna. Hearing the swishing sound of her skirts, he looked up and watched her enter the room. As she gracefully took her place on a chair, his eyes narrowed. When they'd first gotten to know each other, he'd kicked over the idea of drawing Martha into his bed, but because of her temper and obvious lack of interest, he'd changed his mind. But that was back then. He had never forced a woman to his bed, but seeing Martha made it awfully tempting.

"I talked to Eddie. She told me they were selling their land to you and returning home."

Trace nodded.

"I'll miss them." Martha was uncomfortable at the way he just sat there studying her with those crystal-blue eyes, as if he was trying to make his mind up about something. "How is your business doing?"

"Fine."

Was she going to have to do all the talking? "I understand you have a lady friend."

"Oh? Who would that be?"

"Well, I assumed...I mean...Hazel Carpenter," Martha finally managed to say. She decided that while she was at it, she might as well find out the status of her competition. "Will there be wedding bells soon?"

"Did Hazel say that?"

Martha wasn't sure she liked the crooked grin that slowly spread across his lips. His gaze hadn't left her for a moment. "There you go again. Why can't you just answer a question instead of asking another one?"

"No, I have no plans to marry Hazel."

"Oh?" Martha had to steel herself to keep from showing her delight at hearing that bit of news. "Josh Whitten said he'd seen you squiring her about, and I just assumed—"

"Hazel is a most attractive woman, but marriage is an entirely different matter."

"I see. But surely you plan on marrying some day and settling down?"

"Maybe. How come you've never married, Martha? You're a beautiful woman. It's hard to believe you've never been asked."

"Actually, I'm seriously considering it." *You'd probably fall off your seat if you knew who the man is.* "Supper is ready. If you'll give me a moment, I'll have it on the table."

"I'll help."

"That won't be necessary."

"I insist."

Martha could feel him right behind her as she entered the kitchen. His closeness made her jittery. She could no longer deny her desire to have him make love to her, but Eddie was right. An easy conquest would make him less apt to consider marrying her. She bit her bottom lip, bound and determined to keep her need for him in check. She had to concentrate on showing him what a good wife and hostess she would be. *Try to remember, Martha, you're supposed to be a lady.*

Few words were exchanged as they ate their supper, but Martha was quite pleased at the amount of roast, corn and potatoes Trace ate. It was without a doubt the best meal she'd ever cooked. She ate very little herself, even though she'd felt starved earlier.

"Excellent meal," Trace commented. "You're a fine cook."

"Thank you." Suddenly, Martha couldn't figure out what she was supposed to do next. To say their conversation had been sparse was putting it mildly. Sitting across from Trace had sapped away all rational thought, with the exception that her bedroom was just up the stairs.

A game! They could play a game! "Do you play cards, Trace?" She started clearing off the table.

"Poker," he said when Martha returned from the kitchen.

"Poker? I'm afraid I don't know how to play that." She looked at him, wide-eyed. "To be honest, I know no card games. However, I saw some cards in the mercantile store, and I thought . . . that is, if it's all right with you . . . that you might teach me how to play."

I'd like nothing more than to teach you to play, but not cards. "It would be my pleasure."

Martha smiled. She soon had the table cleared, then placed the cards on it. For the next half hour, Trace explained the game of draw poker, telling Martha what cards beat what. Though Martha asked the proper questions occasionally, she hardly listened to what he was saying. Her concentration was centered on his large hands, his appealing smile, as well as his low, husky voice that had the quality of silk. She didn't like having to be a lady. She wanted to ask him to take her upstairs and teach her the joys of being a woman. She could even feel the gnawing need for him in the pit of her stomach.

Fortunately, when they began playing cards, Martha had to set her mind on the game. After years of dealing, she slipped easily into the role of the innocent learner. She let Trace win the first few games, then her competitive spirit kicked in. Trace was a good player. She was better.

"I think you missed your calling, Martha," Trace said as he gathered the cards then set the deck in the middle of the table. "I'm glad we weren't playing for money. You'd have taken me for a pretty penny. I guess I should be heading home. It's getting late."

Martha rose to her feet and followed him to the door. "Thank you for coming, Trace. I enjoyed the evening."

When he turned and looked down at her, Martha quickly stepped away. She knew he was thinking about kissing her, something she didn't dare let happen. She was quite sure she would turn into a limp rag. His deep laughter startled her.

"Martha, are you afraid of me?"

"I...I beg your pardon?" Martha clasped her hands behind her back. "That's ridiculous. If I were frightened, why would I ask you over for supper?"

"I've asked myself that same question." He stepped forward, only to see her step backward. "You certainly make a point of keeping your distance. I was simply going to the kitchen to get my bottle, but you act like I have other alternatives."

"You can't take the bottle."

"If I'm not being too bold, just why the hell can't I take the bottle? It is mine, you know."

Martha threw her hand over her heart, looking thunderstruck. "Please, Trace! I have asked you not to use such language in my presence. As for the bottle, how could I possibly let you take it? The devil would tempt you to finally have a drink. No, in all good conscience, I must insist you leave it here. I know all about the sins of drinking. Though I'm ashamed to admit it, my father had a bit of a drinking problem once, but after turning to the Bible he never took another sip."

"Are you actually suggesting I start studying the Bible?" Trace's words were slow and deliberate.

Martha quickly lowered her lashes. Though she'd learned long ago how to manipulate men as well as disguise what she was thinking, somehow it didn't work when she was around Trace. "What you do is your business. I just don't want to encourage you to go down the forbidden path."

Though he didn't particularly like it, Trace could see Martha was genuinely concerned. He nodded his agreement.

Trace left the house in deep thought. How could Martha play absolute havoc with his house when he was trying to build it, pull a gun on him to make him sign a confession, shoot the chair out from under him, plus all the other hell she had raised, then turn right around and act like a frail mouse, spouting words about the devil's work and drinking? He'd never understand the woman!

He opened the fence gate, then closed it behind him, slipping the leather loop over the top. All evening he had studied the beautiful but elusive Martha, and at times his desire had threatened to get the better of him. But with the exception of when they were playing poker, she had been as stiff as an anvil and as nervous as a quail that knew it was being stalked. Martha practically jumped every time he even came near her, as if she were terrified that he might touch her. No wonder she'd never married. She probably chased all the men away. Hell, if a man were to marry a woman like that he'd probably have to spend his nights at a house of pleasure in order to relieve his need. What a waste, he thought as he stepped onto his porch. Such a face and body, only to turn out to be a block of ice. He decided that it was time to thaw Martha.

But when he entered his bedroom, Trace was wondering if that was such a good idea. If he did bed her, she'd probably never forgive him, then quote verses from the Bible about the sins of lust, or worse yet, insist he marry her. Hell, he thought as he undressed, it wasn't worth the effort. One way or the other, Martha had the innate ability to make him back away from his decision to pursue her.

Martha climbed into bed, convinced she'd never lay eyes on Trace again. Since his departure, she'd tried telling herself the evening had gone well, but she knew differently. She could tell by the way he'd acted, and especially by the look on his face when he left. Maybe she'd gone a little overboard about the whiskey. Where had she ever come up with that story about her father having a drinking problem?

She leaned over and picked up the small glass she'd set on the night table. She sipped the drink, appreciating the mellow bite as it slid down her throat. Trace certainly had good taste, and his choice of whiskey was no exception. Her desire to have a bottle in the house so she could have a drink when she pleased had put the final touch of disaster on the evening. But what was she supposed to do? She couldn't drink in front of him. Lord knew what he would think of her had she done something like that. And she couldn't buy any. Ladies didn't do such a thing.

She took another drink, then smiled sadly. "You've really got yourself in a fix this time, Martha. You want Trace, but you have to keep away from him so he won't think you're easy. You want to be a lady, but you don't like the restrictions that it entails. Maybe if you'd just been yourself instead of trying to act so proper...no, that would have been worse."

She finished her drink. As she set down the glass on the table, she tried to think of a new way to approach Trace. She refused to give up just because of a few failures. Now that she'd set her mind to marrying him, she was going to do everything in her power to accomplish that goal. It was just going to take a little time.

She fluffed the pillows and lay down. At least the drink had helped to relax her to a degree. Now all she had to do was figure out how to get rid of her desire. Would Trace be the eager type when making love, caring little about the woman, or would he be . . .

Martha jumped out of bed. Maybe she'd have just one more little nip.

Chapter Eight

Trace took his time as he made his way down through the tall grass toward Martha's house. Though he'd thought to stay away from the woman, he felt obliged to let her know the Grahams would be leaving sooner than planned.

He knocked on Martha's front door several times, but there was no reply. Knowing she had to be nearby because her gelding was in the corral, he set out in search of her. He found her in the chicken coop, putting a fresh bed of straw on the roost. Even in her faded cotton dress and with her hair a bit askew, she was still one of the prettiest women he'd ever laid eyes on. Surprisingly, his desire for her was evident in the tightening of his groin.

"You know, most people would give a rifle for just a couple of those chickens," he called to her. "They're mighty scarce around here."

Recognizing the deep voice, Martha turned, her pleasure at seeing Trace mirrored on her face. "Maybe I should start selling eggs."

"I'd be more than happy to pay."

"You've got yourself a deal." Strange how things work out, Martha thought as she finished spreading straw. She had planned on paying him a call later, under the pretext of wanting to borrow some flour.

"I'll send Wilma down later."

"Who's Wilma?" Martha asked, wondering if there was some other woman in his life.

"My housekeeper. I came down to tell you Eddie and Orvil will be leaving next week."

"But it hasn't been a month!"

He walked beside her toward the house. "Orvil came to town yesterday saying they had everything just about packed. He said they'd be dropping by to see you before coming into town to collect their money."

"I'll visit them tomorrow," Martha said sadly. "I was planning on making the trip, anyway. Thank you for letting me know."

Something landed on Trace's arm, and without thinking, he took a swat at it. He winced, then lifted up his hand. The bee's stinger was embedded in his flesh.

Seeing what had happened, Martha took him by the arm. "Come in the house," she said worriedly as she led him toward the door, "and I'll take care of that before it swells."

Normally Trace would have pulled out the stinger himself and been done with it, but the concern shown by Martha intrigued him. This was yet another side he hadn't seen. He allowed her to take him into the kitchen, then waited patiently as she hurried upstairs to fetch tweezers. Spying the bucket of water on the counter, he opened the cupboard to fetch a glass and saw his once-full bottle of whiskey sitting inside. The *lady* was definitely not what she would have him think she was. The devil's temptation, indeed! Apparently she had a different set of rules for herself when it came to drinking. Hearing Martha coming back down the stairs, he silently closed the cupboard door.

"I have the tweezers and spirits of ammonia," Martha said, a bit out of breath.

Trace held out his hand, staring down at her as she removed the stinger. What other interesting things was she hiding? Possibly a lost virginity? If she was such a good actress about whiskey, who was to say what else was all an act?

"I got it," Martha declared proudly. She applied the spirits of ammonia. "Does it hurt terribly?" Martha looked up and discovered him staring at her. Was she mistaken, or was there a strange glint in his eyes?

"Somewhat." He reached into his shirt pocket and pulled out papers and tobacco pouch.

Martha had never seen him smoke a cigarette before, but with his injured hand, she knew he couldn't roll it. "Here," she said, taking the articles from him, "I'll do that for you."

Trace watched in disbelief as she opened the pouch, cupped the paper, then poured the tobacco inside. Holding the paper in one hand and the pouch in the other, she drew the strings closed on the pouch with her teeth, then set it on the table. A quick lick of the paper followed, then she rolled it into as tight a cigarette as he'd ever seen. It took a lot of practice to be that good. After twisting the ends, she handed it to him. She then grabbed a match from the counter, struck it and held it up. Trace inhaled deeply, then slowly let the smoke trail out from between his lips. "You do that very well," he commented dryly.

Martha suddenly realized that in her concern over the sting, she'd made a very big mistake. "Thank you," she tried saying offhandedly. "I used to roll them all the time for my brother."

"I didn't know you had a brother. How come he isn't with you?"

"He went to California about a year ago. I'll be right back. I want to take these things back upstairs."

As soon as Martha reached her bedroom, she sent the tweezers flying across the room. How could she have been so stupid? Ladies probably didn't know how to roll a cigarette! She'd tried to be so damn careful. She took several deep breaths in an effort to calm herself. Maybe Trace would believe her story.

When she returned to the kitchen, Martha was surprised to find it empty. She located Trace standing outside. "I'll see you later," he mumbled. She watched him walk away. He didn't even have the courtesy to thank her for taking care of his hand!

Martha went back inside, then plopped down on the sofa to bemoan her fate. From the way Trace had suddenly turned cold, she knew she'd ruined any chance of becoming his wife. She had told the truth—she *had* rolled Lawrence's cigarettes ... and Brent's ... and special customers'.

She could clearly remember Clorenda, one of the saloon girls, showing her how it was done. It had taken a lot of time and patience before she could roll a cigarette that the tobacco didn't fall out of, and that was actually smokable. Is this how it's always going to be? she wondered. Would she constantly be making mistakes? She slapped her hand down on the seat, determined to not let that happen. Maybe everything seemed to be going downhill instead of up, but eventually the road had to turn. And there was always the possibility that she was simply making a mountain out of a molehill.

Because it was hot inside, Martha and Eddie went for a stroll down the dirt path leading away from the house. They stopped and stared out at the tilled rows Orvil had worked so hard on. The dirt plow looked lonely sitting by itself in the middle of the field.

"Eddie, do you think you could have made it if the storm hadn't destroyed your corn crop?"

"I think so, but it would still have been rough going. We could've probably borrowed from the bank, but Orvil was never one to like owin' anybody money. He's always said it's like giving a man a hammer to hold over you."

An idea popped into Martha's head, and she wondered why she hadn't thought of it sooner. "Eddie, do you think Orvil would feel the same way about me?"

"I reckon he would. Why do you ask?"

"I realize you're just about packed and ready to go, but what if I made sure you have food and a decent place to live. Come next spring, you can plant again. It wouldn't be as if I were giving you anything. As you start bringing in crops, you could pay me back a little at a time."

"I don't know if Orvil would—"

"In the meantime," Martha persisted, "perhaps I can talk Trace into hiring Orvil, which would give you some income. Let's go talk to that husband of yours," she said excitedly.

The women returned to the shack and Martha explained her idea to Orvil.

"If Trace won't hire you," Martha continued, "you can sell my eggs. How many eggs can a person eat? I only take what I want, and the rest turn into chicks. We'll split the profit. We already have one customer."

"Who?" Eddie inquired.

"Trace."

Martha looked back at Orvil, who sat stroking his beard in thought as little Edwina, the two-year-old, bounced up and down on his lap. Orvil was a big barrel of a man with a ruddy complexion, brown hair and sunken blue eyes that looked almost black. But as big as he was, Martha knew him to be a gentle man, and as honest as the sky was blue.

"I don't know, Martha. We'd done made up our minds to leave, and I don't like bein' beholden to no one."

"Beholden? I don't look at it that way, Orvil. I know you'll pay me back when you can, and I don't charge interest. At least give it a try until next fall. If you still want to leave then, I'll buy your place and take out my cost. By then, the land should be worth even more."

Edwina suddenly let out a shrill scream that made Martha feel as if she'd been sliced up the middle with a knife. It was followed by two more screams.

"What's the matter, darlin'?" Eddie asked patiently.

The screaming stopped immediately, making it clear to Martha that the child was simply demanding attention.

"I go play outside!"

Orvil gently lifted her off his lap. "Go find your brothers and sisters."

"You come wiff me!"

"I'll take you," Martha spoke up. "I'm sure your ma and pa want to talk privately." She held out her hand to the child, but Edwina crossed her arms over her chest, refusing to budge.

Edwina stomped her foot on the dirt floor. "Pa take me."

Seeing no alternative, and refusing to let the child get the better of her, Martha walked over, circled her arm around the girl's waist, then lifted her off the floor. "There is one other stipulation," she said calmly as Edwina renewed her screaming. "The older children will go to school daily, and it's time they all started learning how to be civil!"

* * *

By the time Martha was traveling back down the road, she felt like dancing a jig, even though her nerves were frayed. How was it possible for five children to constantly deplete her? She flicked the reins, moving the gelding into an easy lope. On the brighter side, Orvil and Eddie had agreed to stay. Martha was already looking forward to getting them properly situated, including a log house, which Eddie and Orvil had insisted would suit them fine. Martha had told them she would inform Trace that he wasn't getting their property after all. It would give her an excuse to see him again, though he might not be pleased to hear the news about the Grahams. At the same time, she'd see about getting Orvil a job. It might take a little coaxing, but she had to give it a try. She suddenly broke out laughing. She had seen the nanny goat tied to a stake, and she'd looked as docile as an old hound.

Martha headed straight for Trace's house, but a servant informed her that Mr. Lockhart had gone to town and wasn't expected back for several days. Disappointed, Martha led the gray down the hill. Since she had to go to town tomorrow to make arrangements with Adam Keeper about the Grahams' cabin, she'd stop and pay Trace a visit at the lumberyard. Maybe this time she'd be lucky enough to find him in his office.

Talking to Adam Keeper took longer than Martha had anticipated. By the time she left his small shop, it was nearly noon.

When Martha arrived at the lumberyard, she wasn't surprised when Colbert, the bucktoothed clerk, informed her that Trace had just left with his manager from Oklahoma City. But he assured Martha that Trace would be back in an hour or so.

Using a log to mount her gray, Martha adjusted herself on the sidesaddle, then sat trying to decide what she was going to do until Trace returned. Turning the gelding back onto the street, she headed toward Josh's office. She felt guilty about having him again take her to lunch, especially since she'd refused his invitation to the theater last time. Another concern was that he would think she was pursuing him. She did like Josh immensely, but her pick for a husband was still Trace.

When Martha entered the real estate office, Josh was seated behind his desk looking very important as he talked to a couple.

"Excuse me a moment," he said to the man. He rose from his chair and walked to where Martha was standing.

"I'm sorry," she whispered. "I didn't mean to interrupt you."

"My dear Martha, I would never consider you an interruption under any circumstances. Have you eaten?"

Martha smiled. "No, have you?"

Josh slowly shook his head. "I'll only be a few minutes longer. Will you wait?"

"I don't want to rush you." Martha glanced at the couple. Their clothes were badly worn, and they looked as though they hadn't a penny saved. "Why don't I go on to Alfonso's Restaurant and you can meet me when you're finished?"

"I won't be longer than fifteen minutes."

The moment Martha stepped inside the restaurant, a small man rushed forward. "Good afternoon, Miss Jackson. Will Mr. Whitten be joining you today?"

"Yes, Alfonso. Could we have a table next to the window?"

"Right this way."

When they reached the table, Alfonso pulled out the chair and Martha took her seat. "I'll order when Mr. Whitten arrives, but I would like a glass of wine."

Sitting at the back of the restaurant, Trace had watched Martha enter. Her large, fashionable hat was pinned atop a pile of blond curls. The dark blue bolero jacket with white embroidery work on the front and sleeves partially covered her white blouse. The full riding skirt was the same color as the jacket, and made her waist look even smaller than it was, if that was possible. The owner, Alfonso, never escorted customers to their table unless they were regulars. Normally he left that job to the man acting as host. So why would Martha have been eating here so often?

"... and that shipment never arrived," William said to his boss. "Naturally I sent them a wire stating that I expected the next train to deliver the lumber we'd already paid for."

Trace returned his gaze to the man seated in front of him. "Naturally," he commented. Though William hardly looked dry behind the ears, Trace had found him to be honest and hardworking, and he'd done an excellent job of establishing the Lockhart Lumber Company in Oklahoma City. Sales were every bit as high there as they were in Guthrie. William, however, was boring company. He possessed absolutely no sense of humor and apparently saw no reason to pursue the ladies. Trace had soon found out the man's standards were based strictly on money, and he believed in taking one step at a time. First William would make sure he had an adequate income, then he'd methodically pick out a proper bride to go with his position in life.

Taking another bite of his lunch, Trace turned his attention back to Martha. His eyes became slits as he watched her sip her wine without the least concern about its being the devil's temptation.

As Trace tried concentrating on the delicious pasta smothered with tomato sauce, William's one-sided conversation became a drone in the back of his mind. He'd forced himself to stay away from the beautiful Miss Jackson until his temper had at least settled down to a slow boil. He'd never taken kindly to someone who tried playing him for a fool, and that was exactly what she had done, with the exception of the many times she'd been angry. He believed those to have been honest, gut reactions. The half-drunk bottle of *his* whiskey and her rolling the cigarette had put all his confusion about the woman in proper perspective. His protective feeling toward his neighbor was gone. The shyness she'd shown at times, the coyness, the sweet smiles, the supposed concern about his drinking or being stung by the bee, certainly the religious muttering, had all been an act.

What made him so damn angry was that he'd actually believed her. True, there were times when he had become curious about why she would suddenly change faces, become friendly, or apologize for her past actions. He didn't have to wonder about that anymore, though. She was looking for a husband, and he was the target. He even wondered if she were one of those women who made a living by marrying then killing off their husbands. She was certainly handy with a gun.

On a good many occasions, Trace had started to pull her into his arms, convinced he could coax forth any hidden passions, but because of something she would say or do, he had always backed off. She'd been playing games with him all along. Not anymore.

"I must say, Mr. Lockhart, the food is excellent," William stated, fork held in readiness for the next bite. "You haven't said what you think about my idea of having a construction business in conjunction with the lumberyard."

Trace had no idea what William was talking about. "Since you're leaving in the morning, why don't you put it all down on paper and send it to me," he stated as he watched Alfonso escort Josh Whitten to Martha's table. "It'll give me time to go over it. I'll let you know my decision." Trace could plainly see the disappointment on the younger man's face, but wasn't about to admit he hadn't heard a word William said. "I have an engagement tonight. How would you like to join me? I've always felt that hard work should be joined with hard play."

William smiled sheepishly. "No offense, Mr. Lockhart, but if I return to my hotel room now, I can probably have the paper ready for you in the morning."

Trace had anticipated his reply. He suddenly wondered if William had ever bedded a woman, but it wasn't any of his business. Besides, if he came right out and asked, William's cheeks would probably still be red by the time he returned to Oklahoma City.

Having completed his meal, Trace waited for William. To top off everything else, William was a slow eater. Nevertheless, Trace had to acknowledge that his manager had spent most of his time talking about business.

Trace glanced around the room, his eyes again coming to rest at Martha's table. It didn't sit well with him to see Josh holding her hand as the two laughed, apparently enjoying each other's company. Was Josh another of Martha's candidates for marriage? It infuriated him even to be placed in the same stall.

William said something, and Trace automatically nodded, his thoughts still centered on the couple by the window. Josh already had a reputation about town with the women, and the town elite were speculating as to which wealthy woman he'd choose to wed. Of course Trace knew he could hardly throw stones. He'd gained a reputation of his own. But if it was true that Josh was looking for wealth, there was only one reason why he'd be taking Martha out to dine. Admittedly she was a beautiful woman, but Josh wasn't the type to let something like that get in the way of future plans. He either wanted Martha in his bed, or she was already there. Trace was enraged to think it might have been Josh drinking *his* whiskey all along.

Trace hadn't been back in his office more than twenty minutes before a light tap sounded on the door. "Come in," he called.

He hadn't expected to see Martha standing on the other side of the door. His lips twisted into a crooked smile. "What a pleasant surprise. Please, come in."

Martha felt her knees shaking. She wasn't sure just how Trace was going to take her news. "I came by earlier, but you'd already left." She stepped into the large room.

Trace glanced down at his desk and for the first time saw the note Colbert had left saying Miss Jackson would be by later. "I saw you and Josh at Alfonso's. You seemed deep in conversation, so I didn't bother to stop by your table."

Martha grasped the opportunity to try to make Trace jealous. "Yes, he's taken me there quite a few times," she said in a nonchalant manner. "Such a nice gentleman. He's taking me to the theater tomorrow night to see Lily Langtry perform."

"Will this be your first time to attend the theater?"

"Yes, it will."

"You should go more often. Stock companies from Chicago and St. Louis come here to perform." Trace walked around the desk, then propped his hip against it. He motioned toward a chair. "Have a seat."

Damn! He didn't appear to be the least bit jealous. "No, thank you. I'll only be staying a minute."

"As your neighbor, Martha, I think I should warn you about Josh Whitten. Word is he's looking for a wealthy woman to marry."

"Well . . . I'm not wealthy!"

"Exactly my point. On the other hand, maybe that isn't what you find attractive about him." He raised a meaningful eyebrow.

Martha chose to ignore the insinuation. "I came by to talk to you about the Grahams." Martha noticed how the sun shining through the window made Trace's hair look almost blue-black.

"What about the Grahams? I had expected Orvil to come see me by now. I have the papers ready for his signature."

"Well, that's what I wanted to talk to you about. You see . . ." Martha was suddenly having a hard time getting the words out. "They've decided not to leave."

"What made them change their mind?"

"Me. I mean, I made them change their mind. Oh, Trace, don't be angry with me. I couldn't bear to see them give up all their hopes and dreams, only to return to Kentucky. If they hadn't wanted to get away they would never have come here."

The pleading look in her brown eyes had no effect on Trace. However, he did wonder what Martha was up to now. "How are they going to make it through the winter?"

"I've figured it all out," she said excitedly. She moved forward. "I'm having a cabin built for them, they're going to sell my eggs for extra money, and when they bring in a crop next year, they can pay me back. If by the end of next fall they still want to leave, I've agreed to buy their land at actual value."

Now Trace had his answer. Martha didn't want him to have the land. She wanted it all for herself. Either she planned on going into competition with him, or she wanted to sell it to him at a higher price. That could also explain why she and Josh had become so friendly.

"Trace, I thought you might find a job for Orvil at either your brickyard or lumberyard. Orvil is a big strong man, and he'll work as hard as you want him to."

Trace hadn't missed how soft her voice had become, her pleading look, or the batting of her long lashes. She certainly knew the art of twisting a man around her finger. "And what is in it for me?"

He's angry, Martha thought, he just isn't showing it. "I know you're not pleased about this, Trace, but think about Eddie, Orvil and the children. Surely you have enough land that you don't need theirs, too."

"I wasn't talking about the land, Martha." He slowly stood. "I'm talking about how you plan on repaying me if I give Orvil a job."

Martha didn't like the way his eyes had become darker blue. She took several steps backward. He followed, making her feel she was being stalked. She squared her shoulders. "I . . . I guess I could have you over for supper again." She took two more steps backward.

"Then what?"

"I don't know what you mean," Martha whispered. His voice was so soft, she was sure she was becoming mesmerized. Again she stepped back, this time bumping into the wall behind her. She started to move away, but the hands he placed on either side of her prevented it. She couldn't seem to take her eyes from his.

Trace lowered his head, his lips inches from hers. "Must I explain it to you?"

"No," Martha said weakly.

"I would be a liar if I said that I hadn't noticed how beautiful you are, or that I haven't thought about the pleasures we could share." He kissed each side of her mouth, drawing satisfaction from her soft moan of pleasure. "I could ignite a fire in you the likes of which you've never known. Shall I come over tonight?"

The question set off all kinds of warning signals in Martha's head. At this moment, she couldn't think of anything she wanted more than to say yes. Instead, she said, "No." To her relief, he removed his hands, allowing her to move away. But she didn't trust his smile, or the twinkle in his eyes. Even more, she didn't trust herself. How could she be so weak every time Trace came near her? "I'm insulted that you would even entertain such base thoughts!" she stated, trying to hide her own feelings.

"I'm quite sure I'm not the only man who's ever asked for your favors, my dear." He walked behind the desk and sat in the chair.

Martha's temper started to rise. "So I take it you're not going to hire Orvil."

Trace leaned back, studying Martha's hat, which was now tipped to the side. "Whether I hire Orvil or not is your decision."

"Of all the ... Why, you—you can go to hell, Trace Lockhart!"

"Please. That sort of language offends me," he mocked.

Martha moved to the desk, placed her hands on the top and, leaning forward, looked him straight in the eye. "No man buys me. I don't ever want to see you on my part of the land again. If I do, I'll shoot you. If we should meet, I would prefer you act like you don't even know me. Have I made myself clear?"

"I'm having a ball at my house in two weeks. I'd like you to come. It will be quite a social event."

Martha straightened and marched toward the door.

"Remember," Trace called after her. "Two weeks from tonight."

Martha was so furious that by the time she entered her house, she couldn't even remember the ride home. "How could I ever have thought I wanted to marry that man!" she yelled as she went upstairs to undress. A few minutes later, her clothes were flying in every direction. "Of all the conceited . . . He can just rot in hell! I wouldn't set a foot in his house, let alone go to his ball!"

Trace wasn't in the best of moods, either, when he returned home that night. The more he had thought about Martha's entertaining Josh at her house and serving Josh his liquor, the more determined he became to find out exactly who was doing the drinking. He was already beginning to wonder if he'd come to the wrong conclusion about Martha. He wanted some definite answers. If Martha was enjoying an occasional drink, then he had proof that everything she had told him was a damn lie.

The next day he stayed home, watching to see if Martha had any visitors. Curly Roberts came by, but they remained outside talking. Trace liked Curly, and he wondered if he should warn the man that he'd probably end up with a broken heart if he set his mind to marrying Martha.

It was dusk when Josh arrived to take Martha to the theater. After they left, Trace headed for Martha's house. He had no trouble locating the bottle. It was in the kitchen cupboard where he'd found it before. He marked the level of its contents on the label with his thumbnail.

Martha was walking on a cloud when Josh brought her home. She had never dreamed that the theater could be so wonderful. Josh helped her down from the carriage and escorted her to the door.

"Wasn't Miss Langtry beautiful?" Martha asked wistfully.

"Not nearly as beautiful as you are."

"Oh, Josh. You're pulling my leg."

"Not at all." He leaned over and kissed her soft desirable lips. "I've been wanting to do that for a long time."

His voice had become husky, but Martha didn't mind in the least. She rather liked his kiss. It wasn't as leg-trembling and mind-shattering as Trace's, but at least Josh was predictable. "It's late," she whispered, "and I'd better be going in."

"Next Saturday, I want to take you to the Brooks Opera House."

"I'd like that."

He kissed her again. "I'll pick you up around six." He climbed back into the carriage. "I'm already looking forward to seeing you again, Martha." He flicked the reins.

Martha stood watching him drive away. Josh was such a wonderful man. Why couldn't Trace be more like him? She went into the house. Now that all possibilities of Trace marrying her had been dissolved, perhaps she should consider Josh as a candidate.

* * *

The next morning, Trace sent for the stable boy. When the fourteen-year-old boy entered the study, Trace told him to close the door behind him.

"Jeremiah, how would you like to make a little extra money?"

The boy grinned, showing two front teeth missing. "I'd like that real well, Mr. Lockhart."

"I don't want another person to know about this."

"I swear I won't tell a soul."

"I want you to watch Miss Jackson's house each night and tell me if she's had any visitors."

"That's all?"

"That's all."

After a week, Trace had proof of what he'd suspected all along. Martha didn't drink much, but she was definitely enjoying an occasional shot of the devil's temptation.

After listening to how excited most of the Albatross Club ladies were about Trace's ball, and how they were looking forward to attending it, Martha began to change her mind about going. She also heard at club meetings about the lovely women Trace had been squiring about town. The only pleasure she derived from that was to watch Hazel Carpenter shifting uncomfortably in her chair and constantly trying to change the subject when Trace's name was mentioned. Apparently Hazel had failed in her attempt to keep Trace all to herself.

After asking Josh to escort her to Trace's party, Martha headed for the New York Clothiers. She was bound and determined to have the prettiest gown at the ball.

Chapter Nine

Josh glanced at the two deeds to make sure they were signed. Satisfied, he tossed them in the desk drawer. He never registered *these* deeds at the land office. It was safer to let the buyers do it. The Roberts deed he'd hang on to for a while until it was safe to sell it.

In the short time it took to lock his office and head his horse toward Spring's Bordello, Josh had made up his mind to tell Pete, Vern and Tuley to step up the claim jumping. Getting the poor settlers to sign the papers and running them off the land had been even easier than he'd thought. And he needed the money. Squiring wealthy women about town and taking Martha to dinner had put a considerable crimp in his pocketbook. The real estate business didn't make that much money. He wanted to be looked up to by the people in Guthrie, build a big mansion and give Martha all the things a lady like her deserved. He wanted every woman in town to be jealous that he'd chosen her to be his wife.

As he turned onto Oklahoma Avenue, his stallion shied away from the horse-drawn trolley car that passed by. Josh patted the bay's neck, and when the stallion calmed down, Josh reflected on how his attitude had changed since he'd arrived in Guthrie.

He'd come up from Texas to start a new life and become an honest man. But with all the other real estate offices scattered about, he hadn't been able to make enough money to live in the high style he'd become accustomed to. Robbing banks and trains was dangerous, but it had offered excitement and a hell of a lot of money. He'd even decided he didn't like being settled down and came up with the idea of forcing families to sign their land over, then driving them away. But he couldn't do it by himself, so he'd sent wires to old acquaintances. With them doing the work, no one would suspect him.

That was when Martha had stepped into his life. He'd wanted her from that first day he saw her so many months ago. At first he had thought he was going to have to do away with Lockhart. He wasn't about to let any man lay claim on his woman. He'd changed his mind once he was convinced there was nothing going on between Martha and Trace. Last night he'd gotten Curly Roberts out of his way. His men had ridden out to Curly's place and beaten the hell out of him and his brother. Once Curly had signed over the land, the boys set fire to the shack and killed him. Somehow his brother had managed to escape. He was probably long gone by now. Theirs was one of the deeds he'd put in his drawer.

When Josh arrived at Harrison and Second streets, he dismounted and tethered his horse. Just thinking about Martha had increased his need for a woman. Maybe even two. He climbed the small staircase to the second floor of the building. The covered catwalk that went from this building to the Elk Hotel had always amused him. It allowed the men to come from the hotel to the small, perfectly aligned rooms and back to the hotel without being seen, keeping their respectability intact. Josh talked to the madam, who in turn directed him to a room. He pulled back the curtain and smiled at the lovely piece of flesh waiting for him.

"Be still, Martha, or I'll never get this dress fastened in the back!"

"Oh, Eddie, I'm so excited. This is the first ball I've ever been to."

Eddie laughed. "And you're not going to get to it if you don't stand still."

"What time is it?"

Eddie glanced at the clock on the night table. "You still have half an hour before Josh is due to arrive."

"Eddie, I can't thank you enough for coming over and helping me. I could never have done it by myself."

"It's the least I could do after all you've done for us. There. It's done. Now let me take a look at you." When Martha dropped the long train and turned, Eddie stared openmouthed.

"Aren't you going to say something?" Martha asked.

"Lord a'mercy, girl, are you trying to set every man's loins on fire? The rise of your breasts even shows."

"It's a Jacques Doucet design out of Paris, and perfectly respectable," Martha defended.

"I never heard of the man, but he sure must like to show off a woman's body. And what are you supposed to do with that long thing hanging in the back? How are you going to be able to dance?"

"It's called a train. There's a hoop," Martha showed it to her. "You place your hand through it, and as you can see, it lifts the train so you can dance. Or you can just drape it over your arm. Eddie, I'm quite disappointed that you don't like my dress."

Eddie's frown immediately turned into a smile. "Martha, your dress is the most gorgeous thing I've ever laid my eyes on, and you're goin' to be the most beautiful woman at the ball. You just gotta remember, I've never seen a dress that's got no sleeves and a neckline scooped so low in the front and back. Why if I had put on something like that at home, Pa or Orvil would have taken me behind the woodshed and blistered my butt.'' Eddie took Martha's slender hand in her chubby one. "Come look in the mirror. There's not a woman at that ball who's gonna be able to hold a candle to you.''

Martha studied herself critically in the full-length mirror, and slowly her lips curved into a smile. "My arms aren't completely bare, Eddie,'' she teased. "My gloves come up to my elbows.''

"After tonight, Trace is going to be knocking on your door every time you turn around.''

"I'm not going with Trace, Eddie. I'm going with Josh.''

"But I know it's Trace you're trying to impress.''

"That's ridiculous. How can you say that after the things he said to me at the lumberyard?'' Martha picked up her lace fan from the bed and practiced opening and closing it the way she'd been shown by the dressmaker.

Eddie broke out laughing.

"What's so funny?''

"I suddenly remembered your thinking Trace might have a problem when it came to women. Well, he's certainly proved that isn't so.''

Martha moved her train aside, making sure she didn't damage the yards of beautiful lace that surrounded the edge, then sat on the bed. "Eddie, what am I going to do about Trace? I haven't moved a single step toward getting him to marry me. In fact, I think I've gone backward. He doesn't want to marry me, he wants to bed me! I've never known a man who makes me so furious and yet makes me feel like weak jam when I'm near him.''

"That is your problem, Martha." Eddie lowered her full hips onto the small chair. "You haven't known men," she said softly.

Martha stared in shock at her friend. "How can you say that? I told you what I did before I came here."

"Martha, think about it. You dealt with men, but you were never really with men. You were always protected by Lawrence, Brent or the people who worked in your saloon. Now you're on your own and you're starting to feel desires. You're still innocent, but this time you have no protection. The problem is that the first real man you met was one who would turn any woman's head. He's seasoned, Martha, and I'm sure he knows exactly what it takes to draw a woman to his bed. I'm glad I never met someone like that when I was younger. I would have missed out on a wonderful life with Orvil. The only advice I can give you is to try to stay away from Trace and see if in time, he'll start looking at you as something other than a means to satisfy his lust. Maybe he just isn't the marrying type."

"Josh is. I don't know why we're even discussing Trace. When I saw him in his office, I made it quite clear that I wanted nothing more to do with him. He'll leave me alone now."

"Martha, only marry a man who you love, or a man who has money."

Martha laughed and rose to her feet. "You haven't told Orvil about my past, have you?" she asked as they headed for the stairs.

"Not a word. I think men talk more than women do. Besides, men don't have to know everything."

Hearing a buggy pull up in front, Eddie picked up Martha's white cape and placed it around her shoulders. "Don't plan on coming home and going right to bed tonight. I want to hear every single thing that happens."

* * *

When the butler allowed Josh and Martha into the large foyer and took Martha's cape, her eyes darted in all directions. A thick, flowered rug covered the center of the highly polished hardwood floor. Against one wall was a huge bouquet of roses atop a cherry wood table with long, graceful legs, and behind it, the flowers were reflected in an oval diamond glass mirror, framed in cherry wood. Martha looked at the doorway ahead and saw Trace standing there, dressed to perfection in his black tailcoat and light-colored waistcoat. She quickly looked away. She hadn't missed Hazel standing by his side, looking as though she had grabbed the biggest pumpkin from the field. Was Hazel sleeping with Trace?

Martha felt Josh take her by the arm, and the next thing she knew they were standing in front of Trace and Hazel.

"I'm so glad to see you could make it, Martha," Trace said.

Martha refused to look at him, but she definitely heard humor in his voice.

"Josh, Martha, I'm sure you both know Hazel Carpenter. She kindly agreed to be my hostess tonight."

It must have been a late arrangement, Martha thought. At the last Albatross Club meeting, Hazel had said she wasn't coming.

"Please, go on into the ballroom," Hazel said graciously. "The orchestra is just about to start playing. Help yourselves to the food and drinks in the adjoining room."

Josh again took Martha's arm, but before they moved on, Martha made the mistake of glancing at Trace. He had Lucifer's smile, and of all things, he actually winked at her!

Trace properly greeted the other guests as they arrived, but his mind was on Martha. He'd thought about asking her to be his hostess, then had changed his mind, knowing she would turn him down. He hadn't expected her to come. She was truly a vision of loveliness in her white silk crepe and lace dress, which brought out every feminine quality she possessed. The fact that Josh Whitten was her escort galled Trace more than he would have thought. But there was an entire evening ahead, and he had every intention of taking advantage of it.

Hazel was also thinking about Martha. The woman was absolutely stunning and without a doubt would be the belle of the ball—a role Hazel had planned for herself. She hadn't liked that Trace had waited until the last minute to ask her to be his hostess. It hadn't allowed her enough time to get a special dress for the occasion. But she wasn't about to turn down the opportunity to be by his side. What she especially didn't like was the way he'd looked at Martha when she entered. There had already been too much competition from other women, and she decided she wasn't going to let Martha Jackson be added to Trace's list of conquests.

Martha heard the music before they stepped into the ballroom. Her heart started beating faster. The room was large and grand, with a polished floor to dance on and comfortable-looking chairs close to the wall. The walls were a pale green with red cornices, and pulled-back drapes surrounded the many windows, with pale green lace curtains behind them. Overhead were two enormous chandeliers, their hundreds of crystals reflecting the colors of the walls and the women's dresses. Several open French doors led out to a terrace. The way the house was situated, Martha hadn't even known there was a terrace! The full orchestra was situated in a corner. *I didn't know there were such wonderful things to behold,* Martha thought. Suddenly she wondered if there was an icebox in the kitchen.

As Josh moved her around the room, Martha was surprised at the number of people she knew. She hadn't realized how many acquaintances she'd made since moving here. When she saw Iris Stewart waving to her, Martha smiled. She had become very fond of the president of the Albatross Club.

"How absolutely stunning you look tonight, Martha."

"Thank you, Iris," Martha said to the attractive gray-haired woman. "Permit me to return the compliment."

"Reginal, I'd like to introduce Martha Jackson, the young lady you've heard me speak so much about."

"My pleasure, my dear." He took Martha's hand and kissed her knuckles. "You're right, my dear. She truly is a beauty."

Martha found Reginal to be a strikingly handsome gentleman, even with the bald spot at the back of his head. What a beautiful couple they must have been when they were young, she thought. "Have you met Josh Whitten?"

When all the introductions were made, Josh struck up a conversation with Reginal about real estate, asking if Reginal thought the value of land would go up. Josh was quite pleased to have the opportunity to meet the older man. Stewart owned two banks as well as a large hardware store. The name Stewart made heads turn. Josh knew that if he could cultivate a friendship with Stewart, he would raise his own position in the town of Guthrie.

"I guess you know you're going to make Hazel pea green with jealousy," Iris said quietly, knowing the men wouldn't hear.

"I don't know why."

"Hazel considers herself to be Guthrie's most attractive and eligible woman. You, my dear, are going to usurp her position."

Martha saw the twinkle in Iris's eyes. "Iris! I do believe you would enjoy that."

"With every bone in my body. I can't stand her snootiness, and it's past time for someone to knock her down a peg or two."

"I've never heard you talk like that."

"Martha, I may be wealthy now, but believe me, I wasn't born that way. It was something I had to cultivate. I am proud to say I have never placed myself above others, which is something I can't say about Hazel."

"You're wicked," Martha teased.

"Possibly." Iris smiled. "Normally I find these occasions quite boring, but I think you are going to make this evening most enjoyable for me. See, you've already attracted attention. Two men are headed over here to ask you to dance."

Martha had planned to dance with Josh, but since he seemed so interested in his conversation with Reginal, she didn't hesitate to accept the first man's invitation.

As Martha was twirled around the room, she managed to get a glimpse of Reginal introducing Josh to other gentlemen. She had never known Josh to ignore her so.

Martha danced four dances straight, each with a different man. She saw Trace on several occasions. His first dance was with Hazel, but she didn't know the other women he took onto the floor.

When her fourth partner led her to the side, Martha felt a possessive hand on her arm. Thinking it was Josh, and still annoyed at his lack of attention, she didn't bother to look around. "I was wondering when you'd finally get around to dancing with me." She knew she sounded testy, but didn't care. If he found talking to men of more interest, there were plenty of other gentlemen who wanted to share her company. She let him lead her back to the dance floor. When she turned and looked up, she sucked in her breath. It wasn't Josh she was looking at.

Trace smiled, then pulled her into his arms, gently moving with the music. "Had I known you were so anxious to dance with me I would have asked sooner."

"I thought you were Josh." That Trace was light of foot came as no surprise to Martha.

"What a shame. I liked thinking you desired my company. Surely you're not still angry with me?"

He was holding her so close she was having a hard time thinking. "It's hot in here."

"Then by all means, let me take you out on the terrace so you can cool off."

"No," Martha blurted out.

"Are you afraid to go outside with me?"

"Of course not. It's just that I felt a breeze when we passed the French doors and I'm more comfortable now."

"Strange, I didn't notice the breeze."

Martha could hear that damn humor in his voice again.

"I've decided to give Orvil a job, after all."

Was she mistaken, or was his arm around her back drawing her closer? "I'm sure he'll be glad to hear that."

"I'm more interested in how you feel about it."

Martha missed a step, causing the sole of her shoe to land on top of Trace's foot. It occurred to her that she hadn't even been listening to the music. Trace competently guided her around so she was following his lead again.

"Well?" he asked.

"Well what?"

"How do you feel about my hiring Orvil?"

"I think he will make you a good employee." Martha wondered just how long this dance was going to last.

"Don't you think I deserve a reward for my good deed? After all, I did lose out on getting the Graham land."

In an effort to clear her mind, Martha tried concentrating on the people standing at the edge of the dance floor. "It was your decision to hire Orvil, not mine. What are you trying to say, Trace?"

"I want to take you home tonight."

"I came with Josh and I will leave with Josh. At least his intentions are honorable." Martha suddenly noticed Hazel watching them, her face clearly mirroring her anger. "What about Hazel? Do you plan to just let her go home by herself?"

"Hazel has nothing to do with us."

"Us? You have made it quite clear there is only one thing you're interested in, and I'm not prepared to let you use my body for your personal satisfaction!"

"What if I said that marriage could be a strong possibility?"

It only took a quick look at his face for Martha to know he was again toying with her. Had her desire to marry him been that obvious? Pure pride made her say, "There is just one problem with that. I don't want to marry you. I might, however, consider marrying Josh."

The music finally stopped, but to her mortification, Trace didn't release his hold. His arm still remained firmly around her back. "People are starting to stare," she whispered.

"Let them. Maybe even Josh will see that I don't give up easily when I want something," Trace said, his voice suddenly hard.

Martha didn't dare try to struggle, for it would draw even more attention. "Turn me loose, Trace, or I swear I'll scream!"

"No, you won't. You're too concerned about what people think. On the other hand, if it will make you feel better, go right ahead."

Martha didn't know what to do. Everyone was walking off the dance floor while she and Trace still stood in the middle, probably looking like lovers!

"Let me take you to the opera tomorrow."

"Fine." Martha was willing to agree to anything until she could at least get away. Out of the corner of her eye, she saw Josh headed in their direction, a thunderous look on his face. She'd never be able to live this down if Josh picked a fight.

"You'll be ready at six?"

"Yes, I'll be ready. Now please release me while I still have a least a smidgen of dignity left." Josh was almost upon them.

The moment Trace removed his arm, Martha took the two feet needed to reach Josh. "Have you finally decided to dance with me?" Martha pouted sweetly. "I was beginning to think you were going to spend the evening discussing business."

Though Josh had stopped, his blue eyes were focused over her shoulder. Martha turned. Trace hadn't moved. He was staring back at Josh with a knowing grin on his face. "Come along, Josh," Martha urged. "After all the dancing, I'm quite thirsty."

She took Josh's arm, and her breathing returned to normal when he allowed her to lead him away. Thank God he hadn't pushed the matter, because she knew as sure as the moon rose every night that Trace wouldn't back down from a fight. Not only would she have died of embarrassment had that happened, Josh wouldn't have stood a chance of whipping Trace, who was taller and broader.

"Why was Lockhart holding you like that for so long?" Josh demanded when they were out of hearing distance.

"Holding me? I hadn't noticed. We were talking about some neighbors of mine. Trace was telling me that he'd hired the man to work at the lumberyard. They can certainly use the money. I've grown very fond of the family and their children." Martha stopped and turned. "Why are you asking?"

"I didn't like the way he was holding you."

"I resent that," she said crossly. "Trace and I are good friends. You don't own me, Josh. I can see and talk to whomever I please. If you don't like that, perhaps we shouldn't see each other anymore."

Listening to Martha convinced Josh that perhaps he had misinterpreted what had been going on between her and Lockhart. Lockhart didn't know how close he had come to being a dead man. There was no doubt that Lockhart could beat him in a fight, but Josh knew Lockhart sure as hell couldn't outdraw him.

When they entered the other room, Martha wasn't even tempted to try the delicious-looking food, most of which she didn't even recognize. Because she didn't want Josh to know she'd been lying, she did accept the glass of wine he handed her. As she turned away, someone bumped into her. As if in slow motion, Martha watched the person's glass of wine tip over and pour down the front of her dress. She looked up in disbelief, and saw Hazel standing there.

"Oh!" Hazel gasped. "I'm so sorry. How could I have been so thoughtless as to not look where I was going? I hope I haven't ruined your dress."

Martha decided to set her untouched drink on the table before she threw it in Hazel's face. The look of pleasure in Hazel's eyes made it quite clear that the spill hadn't been accidental.

"Take me home, Josh," Martha demanded as she marched out of the room, her head held high.

Iris, who was standing nearby, had seen Hazel move in front of Martha and deliberately tip the glass over. She stepped up to the auburn-haired woman, who still maintained a shocked look on her face. "Don't come to any more of the club meetings, Hazel," she said in her soft voice.

As Iris moved away, Hazel quickly followed. "Iris? Wait a moment."

Iris stopped and slowly turned.

"What did you mean by that?" Hazel demanded.

"I mean you're no longer wanted in the Albatross Club. I'm sure when I tell the other ladies what you just did, they will be in complete agreement with me. Oh, and you might like to know that Trace saw it, too." Iris continued on her way.

Josh went to help Martha into the buggy, but she shook her head. "I'm going to walk home, Josh."

"You can't walk through the grass in that dress. I'll drive you home." Josh took hold of Martha's arm, but she jerked away. "Are you mad at me about something?" he asked. He was irritated by the way she was acting. "I'm sorry about your dress, but it wasn't my fault."

"I don't think we should see each other anymore."

"Why in God's name not? Now, come on and get in the buggy. I know you're upset about the dress."

"It has nothing to do with the dress, Josh!"

"Then, dammit, what are you so mad about?"

"I'm angry about the way you acted inside. You had no right to even question what Trace and I were talking about or insinuate that something was going on between us. I'm angry at the way you were just ordering me to get in the buggy. I'm angry because you're beginning to act so possessive."

He tried pulling her in his arms.

"Don't you dare touch me," Martha warned between clenched teeth. "That's all men think about! I don't want to see you anymore, Josh."

Before he could say a word, Martha took off down the hill. "To hell with you," Josh growled as he climbed into the buggy.

Martha stomped across the field, listening to the soft material of her dress ripping. She didn't care, it was ruined anyway. She didn't know whom she was the maddest at— Josh, Trace or Hazel.

When Martha entered the house, Eddie's smile immediately disappeared. "What happened to you? Your beautiful dress is ruined!" She followed Martha into the kitchen. "Is that mulberry wine spilled on the front? You'll never be able to get it out."

"Eddie, the night was a complete disaster."

Martha grabbed the whiskey bottle and two glasses from the cupboard. She poured a drink in each of them, then handed Eddie one.

"It couldn't have been that bad," Eddie said as she trailed Martha into the parlor.

Martha expelled a bitter laugh, then flopped on the sofa. "You weren't there." She proceeded to tell Eddie what had happened. By the time she'd finished, her glass was empty and she was a bit tipsy. "How come liquor never has an effect on you, Eddie?" she asked in wonderment.

"This is mild compared to the moonshine we have in Kentucky. Even my pa has a still. I'm sorry to hear what happened tonight, Martha. Are you going to the opera with Trace?"

"I don't ever want to see that man again. It was his fault all of this happened." Martha lay down on the sofa, hanging her legs over the side and letting her shoes fall to the floor. "By tomorrow every ladies' club in Guthrie will have heard about Martha Jackson's unladylike conduct. I'll be the laughingstock of the town. You know what makes me even more angry?" She didn't wait for Eddie to reply. "I think Hazel spilled that wine over me on purpose. Of course no one will believe that.'' Her eyelids felt heavy. ''Well, one good thing came out of this. If Trace keeps his word, Orvil has a job.'' She closed her eyes, just to rest them. ''You really should spend the night, Eddie.''

Eddie was about to tell her she had to get back to her family and give Orvil the good news, but she didn't bother. Martha was sound asleep. What with her stomach getting larger every day, she had to struggle to get out of the chair. She went over to Martha, then reached down and gently brushed back the strands of hair that hung across her face. ''Poor dear,'' she whispered.

Martha is such a good person, Eddie thought as she quietly closed the door behind her. The girl had tried so hard to be accepted. Surely something good had to eventually come her way. As she pulled herself up on the seat of the farm wagon, Eddie smiled. After what Martha had told her, Eddie felt sure that Martha was a long way from seeing the last of Trace Lockhart.

Hazel turned in the doorway and smiled at Trace. ''You will come in, won't you?''

''No, I can say what I have to say right here. I want to thank you for being my hostess tonight.''

''You know I would do anything for you, Trace,'' Hazel purred. She closed her eyes and tilted her chin up, waiting for his kiss.

''Why did you pour the wine on Martha, Hazel?''

Hazel's eyes flew open. ''I don't know what you're talking about. It was an accident.''

''We both know differently.''

Hazel put her arms around his neck and pressed her body against him. ''I'm sorry, Trace,'' she crooned, ''but I was jealous. I love you.''

"Hazel, you love yourself far too much to be able to ever share it with another person." He pulled her arms down and walked away.

"You love me, Trace, and you know it!" Hazel yelled after him.

Trace climbed up on the buggy. "Don't delude yourself, Hazel." He flicked the reins.

Chapter Ten

After listening to the ticket master rattle off the train schedules, Martha purchased a one-way ticket to San Francisco, California. She would leave in three days, which would give her time to pack, get the money from Trace for her land and turn it over to Eddie and Orvil, then bid them a hasty goodbye. She'd never liked long goodbyes; they were too painful. Martha knew she was running away, but there wasn't any reason left for her to stay.

When she left her horse at the livery stable and started walking toward the Guthrie National Bank, Martha told herself that the transferring of funds from bank to bank had to come to a halt. No matter what happened in California, she was not going to move again.

Deep in thought, Martha ran right into someone. Embarrassed, she looked up to apologize and saw Iris Stewart. Of all the people in Guthrie, why did she have to meet Iris again?

"You must have been daydreaming." Iris laughed. "I said hello, but you walked right into me."

"I…I'm sorry, Iris. You're right, I didn't have my mind on what I was doing."

"Think nothing of it, I do it all the time."

Martha looked toward the bank, only a block away. "I'm sorry, Iris, but I have some business to attend to and I really must be going."

"Of course, dear."

Martha started to step away.

"Before you leave, Martha, I was wondering if you could attend a small dinner party Reginal and I are having Saturday night. I'll be so disappointed if you refuse."

"I don't know, I—"

"I can assure you, Hazel Carpenter won't be there. What she did to you at Trace's party last night was absolutely unforgivable. You certainly handled it admirably, though. I don't know if I could have walked away without saying anything. I made it quite clear to her that she will no longer belong to the Albatross Club."

Suddenly Martha's world seemed a lot brighter. "I would be delighted to attend your dinner party, Iris, but I have no escort."

"Oh? Well, never mind, I'm sure I can attend to that if you don't mind sitting by some pompous old man."

Martha laughed. "Not at all."

"Then we'll expect you around seven. Well, I've detained you too long. Until Saturday."

Martha watched Iris leave with a grace and self-assuredness that Martha envied. Because she didn't want Iris to see her head back in the direction she'd come from, she continued toward the bank. Once she was sure she wouldn't bump into Iris again, she made a beeline back to the livery stable. She wanted to go straight to the train station and return her ticket. What if she'd left before finding out that things weren't nearly as bad as she'd thought. Thinking about Hazel being kicked out of the Albatross Club, Martha started laughing. She didn't care that people were staring at her.

During the ride home, Martha tried to think of an excuse for not going to the opera tonight. She was positive
Trace wouldn't let her get by with saying she'd changed
her mind. But what could he do if she just flat refused to
go? She decided she didn't want to think about that. One
way or another, he always made sure he got his way.

As she neared her house, Martha was surprised to see
Eddie sitting in front on the farm wagon, the children sitting quietly in the back. Were they all sick?

"Good morning," Martha said as she brought the gray
to a halt beside the wagon. "What are you doing? Is
something wrong? How long have you been waiting?"

Eddie giggled. "Which question do you want me to
answer first?"

"Good morning, Miss Jackson," the children said in
unison.

Not able to believe what she was seeing and hearing,
Martha raised her eyebrows at Eddie.

"Orvil and I decided you were absolutely right about
the children, so we've set down some rules. The kids don't
like it, but they don't want to be taken to the woodshed,
either. We've only been here a few minutes."

Martha was chuckling as she dismounted. This truly
was a day of miracles. "Aren't you going to get down and
come in? I'll fix us some coffee."

"No, I just stopped by to tell you that Orvil went to see
Trace early this morning."

"And?"

"Orvil starts work tomorrow."

"How wonderful," Martha said excitedly. "So why are
you looking so glum?"

"You know that nice man, Curly Roberts, you told me
about?"

Martha nodded. She'd decided that Curly hadn't come back to see her because he figured she was smitten with Josh.

"He was found dead."

"What?" Martha gasped.

The gray gelding began shying away, tugging at the reins, so Martha turned him loose. He trotted off toward the corral.

"Don't think I didn't see you throw that stone at Miss Jackson's horse, Jamie," Eddie scolded. The others started giggling. "I'm going to tell your pa about it when we get home." The towheaded children became quiet.

"What happened to Curly?" Martha asked, still shocked at the news.

"He was murdered. Had three bullet holes in him."

"Who would want to kill Curly? He was such a nice young man."

"The marshal thinks it was his brother, that they must have gotten into a fight about something. Can't find hide nor hair of the brother. I thought you'd want to know. Well, I gotta be heading back. That Mr. Keeper already has our cabin half-finished. It's lookin' real good, Martha. You gotta come by and see it."

"I'll be over in a few days. Thank you for telling me about Curly."

Martha was still in a daze as she headed toward the corral to unsaddle the gelding. It tore at her heart to think Curly had been murdered, especially by his own brother. Like Curly, Rob had seemed like such a friendly, easygoing man, and the brothers appeared to be good friends. It was hard to believe Rob would do such a thing.

Trace sat behind his desk at the lumberyard, tapping the end of a pencil on the palm of his hand, his thoughts centered on the Roberts brothers. He'd met Rob on several occasions, and he'd liked the man. Now Rob was wanted for murder. Trace glanced back down at the newspaper on top of the desk. According to the article glaring up at him, the marshal considered the case closed. Josh Whitten had come forth claiming that Rob had been furious when Curly sold the land to Josh. That Curly had been beaten before he was shot fit right in with what Josh had said.

But Trace knew for a fact that the men weren't having money problems and they'd already sold a crop of wheat. He leaned back in his chair. Curly had been well aware that Trace was buying land, and on more than one occasion Curly had laughed and said that if he ever decided to sell, he'd come to Trace first. Then he'd laughed harder, saying Trace was going to have a mighty long wait, because he and Rob were already planning to build a house, settle down and get married. Trace frowned. He hadn't liked it a bit when Curly told him the woman he planned on marrying was Martha Jackson—that was, if she'd have him. Rob was smitten with one of the women working at the Hotel Springer.

Trace slowly shook his head. No matter how he looked at it, there was absolutely no reason for Curly to sell the land to Josh, even though Josh had the signed papers to prove it. Something definitely wasn't right. He rose from his chair and looked out the window. Just for the hell of it, he was going to start visiting landowners. He already owned land on three sides of Martha's acreage, plus other land around the area, and if anything crooked was going on, it could affect his holdings as well.

He pulled his watch from his vest pocket and checked the time. He had half a notion to pay Josh a call. Not to ask about Curly, but to tell Josh to keep away from Martha. He had never liked the man, and he damn well didn't like him sniffing around Martha. If it had been Curly, Trace probably would have backed off. But he'd been mad as hell when he'd seen her arm tucked beneath Josh's at the ball, and watching her move about in that beautiful dress that accentuated her tiny waist and offered a tempting peek of soft, full breasts had made him realize just how strong his desire was. Of course his intentions weren't honorable like Curly's, but he didn't believe Josh's intentions were honorable, either. Trace had wanted to escort Martha home and delight in the feel of her body pressed against his. He'd even hoped Josh would pick a fight so he could smash the man's face in. What had happened when Josh took her home? Had Josh taken what he wanted?

Trace released a grunt. One way or another, Martha continued to elude him, but tonight he intended to put a stop to the chase. He knew for a fact that she was going to try to get out of going to the opera with him, and they would probably end up fighting over it. But this time he wasn't going to walk away. This time he would turn that anger into wild bliss. Tonight, by God, he was going to bed Martha Jackson. Something he should have done months ago.

Her hands locked beneath her head and the blanket pulled up to her chin, Martha lay on her bedroll, gazing at the twinkling stars. Not a bad way to spend a birthday, she thought a bit sadly. It would be better if Lawrence were here. She reflected on how the nights were becoming colder. Soon winter would arrive. Though they were having a wonderful Indian summer, even the horses had started getting heavier coats. She watched several shooting stars, then glanced across the heavens looking for others, disappointed that there were none. When she and the teamster were driving the wagons to the Oklahoma Territory, she'd enjoyed sleeping out in the open. On hot nights, it was much cooler than sleeping in the wagon, and the total silence was awe-inspiring.

She heard the gelding snort, but though she couldn't see him in the pitch-darkness of night, she knew he was safely hobbled nearby. The rifle lying by her side also gave her a sense of security. She laughed softly, thinking about how angry Trace must have been when he came by the house ready to take her to the opera, only to discover she was nowhere around. She still hadn't forgiven him for the way he acted at the ball, and he'd almost caused her to leave town, something she'd never tell him. But maybe now he'd learn he couldn't threaten her to get what he wanted. She wondered if he'd gone to Eddie's to see if she was there. She knew he'd never think to look for her on the land, but just to be sure, she'd picked the farthest corner to bed down for the night. After all, 160 acres wasn't that big. He would never see her because she was surrounded by tall, dry grass, but he might have spotted her horse.

Feeling tired, Martha rolled onto her side. Trace Lockhart. Why did she keep running from him when she wanted to feel his arms around her again...wanted his kisses...wanted him to make love to her? Because he was so damn appealing it scared her, because she was afraid that once she fell under his spell she wouldn't be able to turn away, because he would only be using her for his own gratification, but most important, because he would have won the battle of wills and would feel he could take her to his bed anytime he felt the need. When he tired of her, he'd cast her aside as he had the other women in his life. He'd probably even gloat about his accomplishment! Yes, she'd made the right choice not to go with him tonight.

She was positive that going to the opera wasn't the only thing he'd had on his mind.

Trace was seated on the leather chair in his study, legs stretched out, his shirt open, swirling the brandy in the snifter he was holding. It annoyed him that Martha could make him so damn angry, yet he knew there wasn't anything he could do about it. That a tiny bit of a woman could continue to outfox him and constantly turn her back on him definitely wounded his male pride. Yet she could turn around, laugh and be friendly with a skunk like Josh!

He couldn't even understand why he continued to pursue her. Hell, there were plenty of other women wanting his attention. Maybe that was the answer. The fact that he couldn't have her made him all the more determined. Or maybe it was because he'd seen and felt her reaction the few times he'd touched her, and he knew that if given the opportunity, he could coax her into seeing things his way. He took an appreciative drink of the brandy. When it came to Martha Jackson, he had a one-track mind. He also wanted to know all about the woman who said one thing, yet drank whiskey behind his back and rolled cigarettes. What other talents was she keeping hidden?

Martha stood looking at her house for some time before deciding there was no one around. This morning she saw things differently. It galled her that she'd allowed Trace to drive her out of her own home. She should have locked her doors or gone ahead and had a fight with him. She mounted her horse and rode forward. Maybe she would get a maid. Surely Trace wouldn't be foolish enough to do something with someone else around.

Martha had just dismounted when she heard another horse headed her way. Positive it was Trace, she groaned and turned. It wasn't Trace, it was Josh.

"Howdy, Martha," he said when he'd climbed down. "I'm sorry about the other night. Are you still mad at me?"

"No," Martha admitted.

Josh was elated. He knew she couldn't stay angry with him. The only thing wrong with Martha was that she needed a strong hand, something he'd quickly take care of when they were married. "I'm glad to hear that. Then maybe we can—"

"Don't misunderstand me, Josh. I haven't changed my mind about us not seeing each other anymore."

"I think you owe me an explanation."

Martha was taken aback at how hard his face had become. She could see the muscles in his jaw flexing and his eyes were dark blue stones. Gripped by sudden fear, she placed her hands on the hitching post for support. "It has nothing to do with you, Josh, it's just that—"

"Is there another man?" His voice was cold and his words clipped.

"No," Martha quickly assured him. "I think you're beginning to have feelings for me, but I can't return those feelings. That's why I've decided we shouldn't see each other again. You're a fine man, Josh, and I'm sure you would make some woman a good husband. However, that woman won't be me."

"No one else is going to have you, Martha, so be careful about having other men calling, because they're as good as dead."

"You're obviously upset, so I'll pretend you didn't say that. Now I'd appreciate it if you'd leave."

"I'll leave when I'm damn well ready." He took a step forward. "Maybe it's time I—"

"The lady asked you to leave, Whitten."

The deep voice caused Martha to spin around. Trace was standing in the doorway of her house! She looked back at Josh, whose face now looked bleached out, with red spots dotting his cheeks. He climbed back on his horse.

"No other men, huh?" he said sarcastically. "Remember my warning, Martha." He gave his horse a vicious kick and rode off, leaving a trail of dust behind him.

"Just what right do you have to be in my house, Trace Lockhart?" Martha demanded. She shoved him aside and marched into the house.

"What? Not even a thank-you?"

"Get out of here!"

"It sounded to me like you were in a bit of trouble."

"I don't need your help to take care of my affairs."

"Affairs?"

Realizing he was following, Martha stopped and slowly turned. "You know what I meant."

"Where were you last night, Martha?"

"That's also none of your business. I don't owe you any explanations."

"Oh, yes, you do, lady. Remember? We were supposed to go to the opera last night. You even agreed."

"What choice did I have? I'm telling you the same thing I just got through telling Josh. I don't want to see your face again."

"Why not? I'm safe. You don't have to worry that I'll want to marry you."

"You were listening! Of all the despicable ... Trace, I warn you, don't take another step toward me."

She reached behind her and grabbed the first thing she could find. The vase fit quite comfortably in her hand. When he was close enough, she brought her arm forward, breaking the vase across his head. Trace crumpled to the floor like an accordion.

"Damn men! They're all bastards." Grabbing him by his boots, Martha started dragging him toward the door. Because of his size, it was a difficult struggle, but finally she managed to pull him outside. Satisfied, she went back in the house, locking the door behind her.

Trace slowly came to, sure he'd been hit with an iron skillet. After managing to pull himself to a sitting position, he lifted his hand and felt the goose egg on the side of his head. When his vision cleared, he was staring at Martha's closed front door. It was all he could do to keep from kicking the damn door down and taking what he wanted. But he'd never forced himself on a woman, and by God, he wasn't going to start now.

Though his legs were still a bit wobbly, Trace began walking toward the hill. Had he heard Martha say "damn" and "bastard"? It must have been the blow on the head. No, he was certain he'd heard her call him that. The woman also had an extensive vocabulary. But what difference did it make? He was through with her. Bedding Martha Jackson just wasn't worth the trouble.

"Here's three more, boss." The blond, lanky man tossed the papers on the desk, causing the candle flame to flicker.

"Where are Tuley and Vern?"

"Gambling over at the Reazes Brothers' Saloon. Why? You wantin' to see them?" Pete leaned against the wall by the door and proceeded to roll a cigarette.

"No, just curious." Josh raked his fingers through his black hair. About the only thing he'd thought about all day was Trace stealing Martha away. "There's a man I want dead, Pete."

"Who?" He lit the cigarette and pitched the match in the spittoon.

"His name is Trace Lockhart."

"You want me and the boys to take care of it?"

"No, I'm saving that treat for myself. I want to see his face turn white before I pull the trigger, but first I'm going to let him think he hasn't a problem in the world."

Pete blew out a long trail of smoke. "With being a fast gun, at least you don't have to worry he'll outdraw you."

"Hah! He doesn't even wear a gun." Josh snuffed out the candle and headed toward the door. "When I was at Trace's place the other night, I overheard him tell some bald man that where he comes from, it's considered uncivilized."

"You're jokin'!"

"Nope." Josh closed and locked the door behind them.

"The man's gotta be loco."

"Makes the plucking real easy. He's got land and I intend to end up with every bit of it. Let's head over to the saloon and join the boys. I need to tell you what places to hit next."

After visiting George Lawson, Trace kept his black stallion at a brisk gallop. He wasn't at all pleased about what he'd found out over the past week. Down-and-out families were disappearing, and the land was being taken over. So far, it was happening on the outskirts of the free land area, but the neighboring farmers were becoming mighty worried that they'd be next. Most of them said they'd heard gunshots during the night, and when they went to find out from their neighbors what it was all about, the people had up and left.

Trace had every intention of discussing the situation with the marshal, but it would have to wait until tomorrow. He was heading straight home to enjoy a well-deserved meal. He'd spent the morning and half the afternoon in the saddle.

Even though Trace figured Martha would probably come running out of the house with her revolver pointed at him, he decided that he would get home more quickly if he cut through her place. He was in the process of congratulating himself for passing her house without her knowing it when he saw her gray gelding trot through the open gate and head toward the corral. The horse was saddled, and the reins were hanging loose. Trace headed the stallion in the same direction. When he reached the corral, he dismounted.

As the gelding tried to trot around him, Trace grabbed the reins. "Whoa, boy," he said softly. The gelding settled right down, and Trace had no trouble going over him to see if the horse had been injured. Finding nothing wrong, he let the gelding trot into the corral.

As soon as Trace was settled back in the saddle, he stared in the direction Martha's horse had come from. Seeing nothing moving, he kneed his horse forward. From all indications, Martha had been thrown. If it wasn't for the possibility that she could be hurt, he could think of nothing that would give him more pleasure than knowing she had to walk all the way back.

The gelding had left a clear trail through the dry grass. As Trace followed, he kept looking ahead for any signs of Martha. After ten minutes of tracking, he started to worry in earnest. He urged the black to a faster pace.

He'd seen the large mound of rocks for some distance, but it wasn't until he drew near that he saw Martha lying beside it. At first he didn't know why his stallion suddenly started snorting and dancing off to the side. Then he took a closer look and saw a large rattler resting on Martha's stomach. Trace yanked the horse to a halt, keeping him at a safe distance. He slowly dismounted, let the reins drop to the ground so the stallion wouldn't run off, and glanced around for anything he could use as a weapon. The area was barren. He yanked off his boot, then cautiously moved forward. Martha's eyes were squeezed shut, so he knew she wasn't unconscious.

"Martha," he called softly, "continue to lie still. I'm going to knock the snake off you."

The snake raised its head and started rattling its tail.

"When I do, I want you to roll as fast as you can to your right." Trace moved closer. "Get ready...now!" he yelled as he swung the boot forward, connecting solidly with the snake's head. Martha rolled so fast, he had to jump to keep her from knocking him over. He watched the snake slither into the rocks. By the time he turned, Martha was already on her feet, running for dear life. "Martha! Stop!" he called, but she kept running.

Trace hopped around until he finally managed to pull his boot back on. He ran the short distance to his horse and landed in the saddle with a flying leap. As the horse jumped forward, he reached down, grabbing the reins. In a matter of minutes he caught up with Martha, but she wouldn't stop running. If he moved his horse to block her, she turned and ran the other way. Seeing no other recourse, he brought the stallion alongside her, then jumped from the saddle, knocking them both to the ground. In less than a flick of the eye, she was on her knees, bending over him and pounding on his chest. She kept screaming and huge tears rolled down her cheeks.

"It's all right, Martha," Trace crooned, letting her take her terror out on him as he sat up. "The snake is gone, you're safe." The blows grew softer. "You're safe, honey. Nothing is going to happen to you." She sat back on her heels, then leaned her head down, releasing one sob after another. Trace gently pulled her onto his lap. Still sobbing, she let her head fall against his chest. Trace held, soothed and rocked Martha until her shaking body started to relax.

"Trace," Martha whispered, "it was so terrible."

"I know darling." He gently pushed her damp hair back from her face. "What happened?"

"It must have been the snake that caused my horse to rear. I fell, then I don't remember anything until I started coming to and heard the snake rattling. It was already on top of me." A shudder ran through her.

"It must be the warm week we've had that brought him out."

Martha felt so safe in Trace's strong arms, but reality had returned. She straightened, and he released his arms from around her. "I feel so silly after the way I acted."

"There's nothing to feel silly about, Martha. I've seen big men who were never quite the same after something like that happened to them."

"Really?" She turned to thank him for saving her life, but the words stuck in her throat. His face was so close, and she couldn't take her eyes from his tempting lips. Then his lips were on hers; soft, wonderful lips that could steal her very soul. *I tried*, she told herself as his kiss deepened. *Lord knows, I honestly tried to prevent this from happening.*

She felt his arms closing around her, and she knew she couldn't turn back, even if she wanted to. She was lost, and she no longer cared. When his lips trailed to her neck, she arched to give him better access. Her heartbeat quickened as his hand cupped her breast and a finger moved back and forth over the already hardened nipple.

"Trace," she whispered, "please make love to me." She heard him groan with pleasure. His tongue traced the outline of her lips, and her mouth opened, allowing him access.

Trace kissed the small mole just above Martha's lip, then gently shifted her to the ground, exalted to see the fire that already danced in her eyes. Slowly he unbuttoned her shirt, pleased that she wore no corset. Her smooth creamy skin was like an invitation to heaven. To his delight, she reached up and unbuttoned his shirt, then trailed her hands across his skin as she slipped the shirt off his shoulders and down his arms. Not since he was a boy could he remember ever wanting a woman as much as he wanted this one. That she was obviously experienced added to the pleasure he was already anticipating.

When they lay naked beside each other, Martha couldn't stop moving her hands over Trace's body. She kissed his chest, enjoying the feel of the short hair against her face. Never had she seen such a magnificent man. She knew she had to be dying a glorious death as he suckled her breast, then ran a trail of fire along her body with his tongue. When he straddled her, she eagerly lifted her hips so the invasion could be made easy. Her entire being was screaming from the need for fulfillment.

It wasn't until Trace plunged deep within Martha that he realized she was a virgin. He felt her body stiffen from the pain, but not a word of complaint escaped her lips. From her actions and eagerness, he'd been positive that he was not her first lover. Though his need was pounding in his head, he started to pull away only to feel her hands on his buttocks, holding him to her. "Martha, I—"

"Shh," she said, her breathing heavy, "it's all right." She began moving her hips, drawing pleasure from the feel of him deep inside her. "You can't stop this time... you can't leave me like this," she pleaded.

Her writhing alone was driving Trace half out of his mind. He couldn't have left her if he'd wanted to. "No, not this time," he whispered before claiming her lips, his hips already moving rhythmically up and down.

Martha lay wrapped in Trace's arms, her breathing finally having returned to normal. She could smell the dry grass and feel the sun beaming down on her naked body as she relived the glorious ecstasy she had just experienced. Somehow she doubted it would have been as wonderful with anyone other than Trace. She sat up and looked down at his handsome face. His eyes were closed, but she knew he wasn't asleep. "Trace, do you think we can do this again soon? What a fool I've been to wait so long."

Trace opened one eye and stared at her. He'd been waiting for her to ignore the fact that she'd asked him to make love to her and give him hell, or for her to break into tears, bemoaning her lost maidenhood. He certainly hadn't expected such blatant elation. She wasn't even embarrassed by her nakedness. Now she wanted to know when they would do it again. "I think that can be arranged," he replied hesitantly. *Maybe when she has time to think about it, she'll feel differently.*

"When?"

Trace opened his other eye and rose on his elbow. "Don't you have any regrets?"

"No, should I? Didn't you enjoy it?"

Seeing the concerned look on her face and thinking about the absurdity of the situation made Trace break out laughing.

"What's so funny?"

"Usually the man asks the woman if she enjoyed it."

"Well, it's not as if I've had practice at this," Martha said in a huff.

Trace reached up and pulled her down on top of him. His hand cupped her buttocks, moving her against him. "Did I hurt you?" he asked in a more serious tone.

"No. Did I hurt you?"

"Not nearly enough." His voice became husky.

"Trace! You're not . . . I mean . . ."

"I assure you, my needs are every bit as strong as yours." He reached up and pulled her head down to his, stifling her laughter with a kiss.

Chapter Eleven

"Do you have any idea who's doing this?" the marshal asked lazily.

Trace looked at him with a keen eye. "No, but that doesn't change what's been happening."

The marshal leaned his shoulder against the door jamb, watching the traffic moving up and down the street. He returned his gaze to Trace, who was standing on the walk. "How come no one has told me about this?"

"You know as well as I do that those people hardly ever come to town. Certainly the people who have disappeared in the night aren't going to come calling."

"Well, I'll look into it, but it's my feeling that everyone is just getting all worked up over nothing. Those people who you say have disappeared probably just couldn't make it, so they sold their land and took off. Can't say as I'd blame them. At least they left with some money in their pockets."

"Assuming they got paid."

"You're jumping to conclusions, Trace. Besides, you know I can't do anything unless I got proof. And who am I going to arrest?"

"Who's ending up with the land? Hell, Ben, you know as well as I do that Josh Whitten has the deed to the Robertses' land."

"You claiming Whitten is in on this fool's tale? You know it was Curly's brother who shot him."

Getting more irritated by the moment, Trace stuffed his hands in his pockets. "I'm not convinced that Rob did the shooting."

"You're starting to sound like a loco coyote. Say, did I tell you some lady came by a few months back, accusing you of stealing her land? Said something about you making her sign a contract."

Trace grinned. "What did you say to her?"

"Told her I'd look into it. When she left, she was madder than a hornet. Was there any truth to what she said?"

"No, she was just angry at me. If you were to see her now, I'm sure she'd be telling a whole different story." Trace stepped down off the walk and untied his horse. "I'm telling you, Ben, you'd best be finding out who those land robbers are."

"Like I said, I'll check into it."

Trace mounted and rode off. Not until he'd mentioned to the marshal about Josh's having Curly's deed had it occurred to him that Josh could be involved with the homesteaders who'd been run off their land, or killed. Holding the prancing stallion in check as they moved down the street, Trace tried telling himself that he was only suspicious because of Josh's threats to Martha. Still, there was that old, familiar gut feeling, the same one that had saved his life on more than one occasion. It was something he never passed off lightly.

When Trace arrived at his office, he was surprised to find Iris Stewart waiting for him. "This is a pleasant surprise," he said as he circled the large leather chair she was sitting in. "Is Reginal in need of lumber?"

Iris waved her lace handkerchief at him. "Heavens, no. I'm here on an entirely different matter. I realize you have your own box at the opera, but we were wondering if you would like to join us in our box on Friday to see *La Bohème?* I understand it's a marvelous production. You haven't already seen it, have you?"

"No, as a matter of fact, I haven't. I'd consider it an honor to join you and Reginal. Would you care for a small glass of port?"

"That would be delightful." Iris was quite impressed with Trace's office. The rich mahogany walls matched the large imposing desk. A Persian rug covered part of the hardwood floor, and the leather chairs were deep and comfortable. When Trace returned from the sideboard, she graciously accepted the crystal glass he handed her. She sipped at it as he settled in one of the other chairs. Such a gentleman, she thought. Most men would have sat behind the desk. "I hope you don't mind, but I've also decided to invite Martha Jackson. She's such a lovely girl."

Trace's lips spread into a slow smile. "Would you like me to escort her, Iris?"

"Oh, I couldn't expect you to do that." Iris took another sip of her drink. "I don't want you to think that I would consider the two of you being paired off. No, I'm sure Martha can come by herself."

"Nonsense. We're neighbors. In fact, I'll extend the invitation for you."

"Are you sure it won't be an inconvenience? I know you're a very busy man."

"I'll ask her tonight on my way home and give Reginal her answer tomorrow."

"Well . . . it would save me a trip."

"Consider it done."

By the time Iris left, she was feeling quite pleased with herself. Everything had turned out exactly the way she'd planned it. She laughed inwardly, remembering the dinner party she'd invited Martha to a week or so ago. Howard Niemann, the young man she'd picked to be Martha's dinner partner, had been absolutely smitten with the woman. Though Martha had been friendly to him, it was quite obvious that she wasn't the least interested in Howard.

Iris climbed into her carriage and motioned the driver to move on. Did Trace suspect what she was up to? she wondered. But what difference did it make? He certainly wasn't averse to the idea.

"Just look at that, Martha," Eddie said gleefully as she pointed to the finished cabin. "Isn't that the prettiest home you've ever laid eyes on?"

Martha grinned and turned to Adam Keeper, who was standing beside her. "Thank you, Adam. You did a fine job."

"Don't thank me, you paid for it." Nevertheless, he smiled. "Come on, boys," he called to his helpers. "We gotta be goin'." He patted Martha's shoulder. "If you need me for anything else, you know where to find me."

As the men left, Eddie drew Martha into the house.

"Oh, Martha, I know this cost you a heap of money, but me and Orvil are goin' to pay you back."

"I know, Eddie."

Excitement flushed Eddie's round cheeks as she took Martha on a tour of the small cabin, which consisted of a large front room with a wood-burning stove, a small kitchen, two bedrooms and a loft for other beds. Not much for a soon-to-be family of eight, Martha reflected, but to Eddie it was obviously a mansion. She could remember when, not too long ago, she and Lawrence would have felt the same way. It surprised her to realize how different her values were now. Rubbing shoulders with the well-to-do had definitely made a difference in what she wanted out of life.

"We're not goin' to know how to act with the kids having a room to themselves," Eddie said as she led Martha back into the living room. "We even have a floor and an outhouse!" She stopped and looked at her friend. "Martha, are you all right?"

"Of course. I was just thinking about Lawrence."

"Think you'll ever hear from him?"

"Probably not," Martha replied sadly. "Where are the children?"

"Three of them are in school and the other two are churning butter." Eddie studied Martha, who had moved back to the doorway. Her wide-brimmed hat covered her head, the thick blond hair falling down her back with a ribbon tying it back at the nape of her slender neck. She had on a brown corduroy jacket with a plaid shirt underneath. An ankle-length split riding skirt matched the jacket, and her high-topped boots were black. No, it wasn't the clothes that made Martha seem different. It was the way she carried herself, or maybe...

"We didn't have the house built too soon," Martha said as she turned. "Winter is on its way. There's already a nip in the air."

"That's it! You've been bedded!"

"What?" Martha knew the unexpected statement had turned her cheeks pink.

"Was it Trace or Josh?"

Martha pulled on her soft leather gloves. "I don't know what you're talking about. I really must be going."

Holding her stomach, Eddie wobbled over toward the door, blocking Martha's exit. "Oh, no, you don't. Don't you lie to me, Martha Jackson, or I swear I'll tell Orvil about your past."

Martha smiled. She knew Eddie was bluffing. "Trace," she said softly.

"And?"

"And what?"

"Was it disappointing or not?"

Even though Martha had listened to the girls in the saloon discussing their romps with men, she was embarrassed to talk about herself. A smile tugged at the corner of her full lips. "You're the one who always expounds on Trace's qualities, so what do *you* think?"

Eddie clapped her hands in delight as she lowered herself onto a wooden chair. "I think it must have been heavenly."

Martha laughed. "Even better," she said, again ready to leave. "I really must be going. If you need anything, let me know." Suddenly she stopped and turned. "Eddie, I can't believe how different the children are. Nevertheless, I owe you an apology. I shouldn't have said those things about them."

"I'm glad you did. When it came from you, Orvil finally saw the light. He spent most of his time in the field and excused the kids' actions as excitement at him being in the house. I couldn't make them behave by myself, so I just gave up trying. Let me tell you, when he put his foot down it was a blessing."

Martha looked out the door and saw the two children splashing water from the trough onto her horse, making him shy away. "Well," she said, "there might still be some room for improvement." She went out the door, and the children scattered.

"John, Edwina," Eddie called from the doorway, "I want to see you two in the house, right now!"

The children lowered their heads and locked their hands behind their backs, looking the perfect picture of innocent angels. "Yes, ma'am," they said in unison.

As soon as she'd ridden out of hearing range, Martha burst into laughter. Oddly enough, she had really come to care for the five Graham children. Their antics, though annoying at times, were actually quite humorous. They were very bright, curious and ornery as the devil, but they weren't mean children.

Martha guided the gray gelding along the dirt path that was now practically a road. She looked out over the land, finding it hard to believe she'd actually been in Oklahoma Territory more than six months. She was glad she hadn't left, because now she felt she was a part of this vast country. She had watched raw prairie turn into fields of cotton, wheat and corn. She'd seen a tent town become a metropolis practically overnight. And she'd been accepted in a group that was quickly becoming the society of Guthrie proper.

And, of course, there was Trace. He made it all come together. Just thinking about what had happened yesterday made her quiver. She had never dreamed a man could make love more than once a day. The men in the saloon paid their money, took the girls upstairs, had their romp, then left. He had made love to her twice in the field, then again when he took her home. Each time had been even better than the last. He'd laughed and told her she was just getting broken in. Would he come by the house tonight? she wondered. She was already tingling with anticipation. She was also falling in love, and she wanted to tell everyone. Of course she couldn't. She had no idea how Trace felt, but so far there had been no indication that he was experiencing anything but a good romp.

As Martha turned the gelding onto the road toward home, concern began to thread her thoughts. Would Trace think about marrying her now that she'd given her body to him, or would he be content to just take what she offered? She would never regret what had happened, but maybe it was something she needed to give more thought to. Perhaps if she waited a bit before letting him make love to her again it would make him think about a permanent commitment. It wouldn't be easy; there was nothing she wanted more than to be in his arms again. Still, she couldn't let him think she was at his beck and call. He had to realize that those privileges went with marriage vows. She decided that if she was going to do this, she'd have to start tonight. If she didn't, she'd never be able to refuse his advances again. "I hope I'm doing the right thing," she whispered.

Because of a busy day of meetings with lumber suppliers and railroad officials, it was evening by the time Trace arrived home. He ate a quick supper, then went upstairs to enjoy the hot bath his manservant had prepared.

Submerged in the water and finally relaxed, Trace found his thoughts turning to Martha, and how the woman continued to flay him with contradictions. Until yesterday she had been a virgin. Yet she was devoid of any inhibitions and had moved into sexual positions no virgin could possibly know about. Last night she'd even straddled him, saying this time she was going to make love to him. Not that he was complaining. Far from it. He just damn well didn't understand it! She acted and carried herself like a lady—as long as she wasn't angry—but when making love she became a delightful tiger. A combination any man in his right mind would be more than content with.

Trace scooted down, letting the water cover his head, then sat up, shoved his hair from his face and grabbed for the soap. As he began scrubbing, he decided to let things be. There was no doubt that after yesterday, Martha would willingly share her pleasures with him anytime he chose, which was what he'd been after all along. She'd make a good mistress, and he had a strong feeling that it was going to be some time before he tired of her. Just thinking about her was already stirring his blood. He climbed out of the tub and dried off. He quickly dressed, then left the house, headed for Martha's place and the joy that awaited him there.

When Martha opened her door, Trace was surprised to see her in a perfectly proper green dress, with a high neck, long sleeves and even a bustle. Considering her lustful appetite yesterday, he had expected her to meet him in a sheer gown. As they entered the parlor, he looked around, wondering if she had company. They were alone. If she wanted to play games with him, he decided he would humor her. He sat on the sofa and she primly took her place on the chair across from him.

"Did you have an interesting day?" Martha asked.

"Yes. And you?"

"I visited the Grahams. Their cabin is finished. They should be quite comfortable for the winter. I want to thank you for hiring Orvil." Martha dabbed her nose with her handkerchief. This was proving to be more difficult than she had imagined. She couldn't even look him in the eye for fear she'd lose her resolve. Even now she was picturing him naked.

"I really didn't need anyone. I only hired Orvil because you asked me to."

"Oh. Well, it was still nice of you."

"Do you have a cold?"

"No. I mean . . . just a bit of a runny nose. I'm sure it will be gone by tomorrow."

"Iris came by my office today to invite us to the opera Friday. Would you care to go?"

"That's only two days away. I mean, yes, I'd like to go."

Trace grinned. "Can I count on you not to change your mind this time?"

Martha expelled a nervous laugh. "I'll be ready. Can I get you some coffee?"

"It isn't coffee I want."

"Perhaps a piece of pie?"

"I've already eaten."

Martha cleared her throat. "The weather's turning cold. I'm not looking forward to it."

"What's this all about, Martha?"

"I . . . I don't know what you're talking about." She dabbed her nose again.

"You know exactly what I'm talking about. You're as nervous as a drop of water on a hot skillet." He leaned forward. "Don't tell me you're having second thoughts about what we shared."

"Actually, I am. I'm sorry, Trace, but I need a little time to adjust to this change in my life. Don't get me wrong, I have no regrets, it's just that . . . it's just that I don't want to feel like I have to . . . This is very difficult for me."

"You don't want to feel you have to oblige me every time I feel a need for you. Is that what you're trying to say?"

Martha didn't like the sudden harshness in his voice. She wanted to hold him and hear him speak sweet words to her. "Yes." The word came out no more than a whisper.

"And what about when you have needs?"

"I don't understand."

"It works both ways, Martha. Now that you've experienced carnal pleasures, you're not going to be able to shut your mind to it. And when you feel that burning need, what are you going to do? Turn to another man?"

Martha gasped. "I wouldn't do such a thing. You seem to forget that I was a virgin. Just because you've changed that doesn't mean my standards are any different! I am still quite capable of fighting off such temptations!"

"When you're lying alone in your bed, and your need is so strong that you're covered with perspiration, remember what you just said. You're full of fire, Martha Jackson, I've already proved that. That kind of fire will eventually turn into a blazing inferno if it's not smothered." Trace stood and looked down at her. "I'll be here at six, Friday night."

Martha didn't bother to say goodbye. But as soon as she heard the front door open and close, she sent a slipper viciously flying through the air. She would just prove to Trace Lockhart that he was wrong! She'd show him she had complete control over *all* her emotions! She kicked the other slipper across the room.

As Trace drove the one-horse buggy toward town, Martha kept her eyes straight ahead, staring into the dusk of night. As usual, he looked devastatingly handsome in his formal attire and top hat. But she wasn't about to let that sway her determination to prove his presence didn't stimulate a bodily need, even though the bodice of her dress had seemed suddenly tight when he'd arrived at her house. And surely the ache she still felt in the pit of her stomach would eventually pass.

"Have you ever been to an opera?" Trace asked.

"No." It galled Martha that he sounded so nonchalant. Didn't sitting next to her have any effect on him?

"I think you'll enjoy it. It's like a play, but the actors **sing the** words. This particular opera is about Mimi, who is dying of tuberculosis. Her lover is an art student. I particularly like the aria he sings called 'Che Gelida Manina.' He's telling Mimi that her hands are cold and he wants to hold and warm them. Are your hands cold, Martha?"

His low, baritone voice had that silken quality to it, and Martha had to fight the urge to reach her hands out to him. "Not at all. You forget, I'm wearing gloves."

If Trace knew one thing well, it was women. Though Martha was definitely a puzzlement, he was quite aware of her discomfort at being near him. He'd seen it in her large brown eyes when he picked her up at her house. Even sitting as far away as the small seat would permit, she still continued to fidget. When he had left her house the other night, he'd been angry, but at the same time was amused at her effort to thwart him. There was no doubt in his mind that it would take very little to get her to return to his arms, but for the present he'd let her think she had the upper hand. By making love to her, he'd released a tiger. That tiger wouldn't be able to deny the demanding need for bodily satisfaction for long. When he claimed her again, she would have learned her lesson and would have no desire to pull another stunt like this.

"I suppose you saw a lot of operas when you were living back East."

Trace remembered her mentioning something about that once before. "Why do you think I come from the East?" he asked out of curiosity.

"I don't know. I guess it's the way you dress and your knowledge about social things. The opera, for instance. I never knew anyone who's... been to an opera." Martha had almost said that she never knew anyone who had even *heard* of an opera.

Trace thought about when he was a young boy living in Boston, and how his mother delighted in taking him to the opera. He'd come to love it as much as she did.

"Were your parents wealthy?"

Not accustomed to talking about such things, Trace hesitated a moment. "My mother's side of the family was," he finally said as he brought the horse to a halt in front of the opera house. He tied down the reins and climbed out. "I hope you find the evening's entertainment to your liking." He helped Martha down from the buggy.

Martha was amazed at the number of people milling in the large entry. She especially noticed the women adorned in beautiful gowns. Clusters of diamonds hung from earlobes, and necklaces worth a fortune glittered in the lamplight. Martha held her head high, but for the first time in months she felt as if she didn't belong. Her lack of jewelry didn't help matters. Though she'd mingled with aristocrats at Trace's ball and at the Albatross Club, this was entirely different. No matter how much she tried putting on airs, she was, after all, just a saloon girl.

After several introductions, Martha was relieved when Trace led her up the long, wide staircase. A long hall followed, with rows of curtained doorways on the right. Martha was reminded of the prostitute cribs, but those didn't have what looked like footmen standing outside them.

When Trace stopped, the man standing there took Trace's top hat and Martha's cape, then pulled back the curtain. Martha was relieved to see Reginal and Iris seated alone inside. At least with them she felt comfortable. Trace took her by the elbow and led her through the opening. Reginal immediately stood.

"I'm so glad you could come, my dear," Iris said to Martha. She extended a hand to Trace and he brushed a kiss on her fingers.

"Good to see you, Trace." Reginal smiled and the two men shook hands.

"Come sit beside me, Martha." Iris patted the seat of the chair. "The men will take their place behind us."

Martha started to move forward, then suddenly froze at seeing how far up they were. She felt herself sway, her eyes glued to the floor below. She was grateful when Trace placed his arm around her, steadying her.

"Are you all right?" he asked.

"We're so high," Martha managed to say.

Trace sat her down gently. The chair at least offered Martha some stability.

"I didn't realize you had such an aversion to height," Trace said teasingly.

Feeling like a ninny, Martha smiled. "I just wasn't expecting the front of the box to have such a drop-off. I'll be all right now."

Trace took his place behind her.

"You look stunning tonight," Iris commented in an effort to divert Martha. "Few people can wear black and look so attractive. I certainly can't."

"I have no jewelry." Martha could have bitten off her tongue for saying the first thing that came to mind.

"With your beauty, you don't need any, which is more than I can say for most women."

"You're being overly kind, Iris."

"If you don't believe me, look around at the other boxes." Iris nodded at someone she knew. "The women keep glancing this way and whispering among themselves, wondering who you are. They're probably pea green with envy. I'm sure all next week I'm going to be receiving female callers, each dying to know everything about you. Oh, to be young again," Iris said wistfully. "Those were the glorious days."

The men had been quietly talking, and Martha had thought they weren't listening to what she and Iris were saying. But Reginal placed a hand on Iris's shoulder and leaned forward.

"You will always be young in my eyes, dearest."

Iris reached up and patted his hand, and Martha sighed. How wonderful it would be if Trace loved her the way Reginal loved Iris. Had refusing to let Trace bed her again been a mistake? Would he now lose interest? Well, she'd made her decision and she was going to stick to it. Besides, there was still that little matter of his thinking she would soon be sick with lust. Though he hadn't said it, he had as good as insinuated he wouldn't have long to wait until she asked ... no, *begged* him to come to her bed.

As Martha practically glided out of the opera house, she was still engrossed in Mimi's world. She felt a bit ridiculous at having stated that she couldn't understand the singers' words, only to be told the opera was in Italian. Fortunately, no one made an issue of it. But the scenery, costumes, voices and music had been magical. She'd even cried. It was something she'd relive many times over. It was wonderful.

Seeing the dreamy look in Martha's eyes as he helped her into the buggy made Trace smile. It pleased him to know she enjoyed herself. Twice now they'd actually been together without getting into a damn argument.

As they traveled toward home, since Martha seemed disinclined to talk, Trace reflected on her question about his family. His grandparents on his mother's side had accepted him with open arms. They'd even asked his mother to let them raise him. They had never accepted his father, however, and threatened to disown their own daughter unless she agreed to get a divorce. But even though Quinten Lockhart was a penniless drifter, Mary loved her husband dearly.

Trace had been almost ten when his father insisted their future was in the West. So Quinten packed their few things in a wagon and took off. Mary never questioned his decision; all she wanted was to be with her husband. Trace had learned years later that his father had left to get even with Grandpa and Grandma Fisher for not giving them money. He knew that by taking Trace and Mary away, he would break their hearts.

Grandpa Fisher was right, Trace thought bitterly. *My mother should have divorced the no-account.* She'd given up everything. Trace had been thirteen when she died penniless and heartbroken. His father had long since left, and he'd never seen him again.

"How is Orvil working out?"

The question brought Trace back to the present. "The man does the work of two. In fact, I'm going to raise his salary. However, I'd like to be the one to tell him." He heard Martha laugh quietly, and was reminded of soft bells. *Damn,* he thought. *The woman just laughs and I feel my groin start to tighten.*

"I promise not to say a word. Trace, because of what I've done for them, Eddie insists she wants to start delivering my eggs." Feeling a chill from the night air, Martha pulled her cloak more tightly about her.

"Are you cold?"

"No!" Martha blurted out.

Trace chuckled. "There's no need to be so touchy, Martha. I wasn't going to suggest that I hold you. I was merely going to say there is a blanket behind the seat, and if you like, I'll get it for you."

"Oh. I'd like that."

Trace stopped the horse, then pulled the blanket forward.

Martha couldn't ignore the flame of desire that shot through her as he reached around and tucked the blanket behind her shoulders and sides. He was so close she could feel the warmth of his breath on her face. For one flashing moment, she thought he was going to kiss her. She *hoped* he would kiss her. But he settled back in his seat and started the horse forward again. *You're weak, Martha Jackson,* she chastised herself. *What happened to all those vows you made to not let him touch you? Good God! All he did was place a blanket around you!*

"Is that better?" Because of the darkness of the night, Trace couldn't get a good look at Martha's face. But it wasn't necessary. He had heard her suck in her breath when he leaned toward her. The tiger in the lady was still definitely there.

"Yes," she replied, her voice sounding hoarse. "I'm quite comfortable now."

"Good. Now what was it you were talking about?"

"Was I talking about something?"

"About Eddie and the eggs."

"Oh. Yes. The eggs." Delicious memories of Trace's hands roaming her naked body were flashing in Martha's mind.

Trace had to steel himself to keep from stopping the buggy, lifting Martha to the ground and satisfying their driving need for each other. All night he'd smelled her enticing perfume, looked at the marvelous black creation she wore and watched the lust and envy that entered men's eyes when they looked at her. All of which had made him want to cart her away, spend the next week with her wrapped in his arms listening to her moans of ecstasy, and her panting as she writhed in uninhibited desire. But he could be just as stubborn as she was. Besides, her social graces clearly indicated that she was a lady, and it was time he started treating her as such. She needed time to adjust to a situation that was not acceptable to single, upper-class women. "Isn't she due to have her baby soon?"

"Who?"

"Eddie."

"Yes." *The eggs, Martha, the eggs.* "Actually, I'm either going to have to sell chickens or their eggs, but I don't want Eddie doing it."

"Why don't you try trading?"

"What do you mean?"

"The Jordans, a couple of sections over, have a milk cow. Because there are so few chickens around, I'm sure they would be more than happy to supply you with milk for some of your chicks."

Trace brought the horse to a halt, and Martha was surprised to see they had already arrived at her house.

"And Norman," Trace continued, "that's their boy's name, would probably be more than happy to take your eggs to market daily for a small percentage. That way you'd be helping each other."

Martha watched him step down and come around to her side. "That's a wonderful idea," she said a bit too excitedly, already anticipating the pleasure of having him lift her down. She shoved the blanket aside. "Trace, thank you for taking me to the opera." At least she felt her voice was a little more normal this time. "I truly enjoyed myself." To her disappointment, he simply held out his hand for her to hold as she stepped down. He removed it as soon as her feet were solidly on the ground.

"It's been my pleasure. Perhaps we can do it again soon. Tomorrow I'll stop by the Jordan place and tell Norman to come see you." He walked Martha to the doorstep, tipped his hat, then headed back to the buggy.

Martha remained on the step until Trace was out of sight. "He has lost interest!" she whispered. "He didn't even try to kiss me."

Feeling totally dejected, Martha turned and went inside, already trying to decide what she should do next. Slowly it dawned on her that there was candlelight flickering at the entrance to the parlor. Fear gripped her as she realized someone was in her house. Her revolver was in her bedroom. If she could make it up the stairs without being seen, she'd be safe. Slowly she inched forward, the creak of a floorboard sounding as loud as thunder. She was about to take the first step when a male voice said, "Welcome home."

Refusing to allow her fear to show, Martha turned and faced the intruder seated on the brocade chair. "What are you doing in my house, Josh?" she demanded.

"I came to pay a visit. I didn't realize you were out being entertained by your *neighbor*."

"What did you do with your horse? I didn't see it," Martha asked as she deliberately strolled into the room.

"That's because I tied him on the far side of the house."

Martha casually moved toward the corner cabinet that housed her rifle. But Josh rose to his feet, and she stopped. To her annoyance, he crossed to the window, preventing her from getting to the rifle. "It's late, Josh, and I want you to leave." She didn't like his evil smile.

"Don't you want to know why I'm here?"

"Very well, tell me, then be on your way." Martha sat on the edge of the sofa, anxiously waiting for him to move.

"I came to ask you to marry me."

Martha's eyes widened in shock. "I—"

"Hear me out before you say anything." He pushed his hat to the back of his head and gazed at her. "I've got money, Martha. I'll have a big house built for us, and you'll live the life you're accustomed to. You can even entertain all your wealthy friends in style. You'll become the queen of Guthrie. You won't be sorry. I love you."

Seeing the sincerity that had washed over his hard features, Martha's heart softened. "That's the nicest compliment anyone has ever paid me, Josh," she said kindly, "but I don't love you."

"You'll learn to love me."

"No, Josh. That's something that can't be forced. You're a handsome man, and I've heard you've turned quite a few women's heads. You deserve better. Marry someone else."

He banged his fist on the windowsill, causing her to jump. "Dammit, I don't want anyone else! Is it Lockhart? Is that why you won't marry me?"

His harsh words were causing Martha's fear to return. "No. Trace has nothing to do with this," she insisted.

Josh walked over and stood in front of her. "I warned you once that I'd kill him. In Texas, there's no such thing as an idle threat."

"I thought you said you came from Missouri?" Martha could feel her own anger beginning to rise.

"I lied." His laugh was bitter. "I was in Missouri several years back, but I came here from Texas."

Anger replacing fear, Martha jumped up and gave him an unexpected shove backward. "You want me to marry you, and you can't even tell the truth?" she demanded as she stepped forward. "What else are you hiding? Next thing you'll be telling me that you're a gunslinger, or something like that! You break into my house, threaten to kill someone, then tell me you've been lying! And you expect me to marry you?"

She tried shoving him again, but he grabbed her wrists and yanked her to him. His mouth came down on hers, his hard, punishing kiss hurting her lips. To her relief, the kiss was brief. He pushed her away, causing her to fall back down on the sofa. When she looked up, she sucked in her breath. His handsome face had become twisted with cruelty.

"You're closer to the truth than you realize, Martha, my dear. I am quite handy with a gun—something you'd do well to remember." He reached down and picked up his hat from the floor. "Trace Lockhart is a dead man, unless you're smart enough to have nothing more to do with him. His future is in your hands. *No man* is going to take my woman from me!"

"I'm not your woman! You can't do this! I have a right to live my own life!"

"Your life is with me. The sooner you realize that, the better things will be. When you come to your senses, you know where to find me." He spun on the heel of his boot and left.

Martha fell against the back of the sofa, clutched with fear for Trace. She had to warn him. He didn't even know how to defend himself. She jumped up and ran to the window. Unable to see much because of the trees, she rushed upstairs and looked out her bedroom window. All the lights were out in the castle. She'd have to wait until morning to warn him.

Racked with worry, Martha changed into her night-dress and lay down on the bed, knowing sleep was impossible. She couldn't sleep until she'd talked to Trace. But her weariness became too much, and near dawn, her eyes slowly closed.

Martha awoke with a start. Seeing how bright the sun was, she knew it was nearly noon. She dressed frantically and left the house, practically running the entire distance to Trace's house. Breathing heavily, she raised the door clapper and let it fall. A moment later she was staring at a young maid. "I must see Mr. Lockhart immediately."

"I'm sorry, Miss Jackson, Mr. Lockhart isn't in. He left for Oklahoma City early this morning."

Chapter Twelve

Martha stood watching Norman Jordan ride off with the day's delivery of eggs, her breath looking like steam. Like her, the boy was bundled up in a heavy coat to ward off the cold. She bowed her head into the chill breeze and strolled across the frostbitten land past the bare-limbed cottonwoods, remembering the day the boy had arrived at her house.

It had been the same day Trace left for Oklahoma City. Concerned for Trace's safety, she'd forgotten their conversation about selling her eggs. Nevertheless, when she had opened the door two weeks ago, a tall, gangly boy, with a mass of curly brown hair covering his head stood before her, a milk bucket sitting on the step beside him. Martha smiled. It warmed her heart to know Trace had remembered.

Norman had been shy at first, but now he seemed to never stop talking. He was also an honest boy. He hadn't thought it fair for her to only take twenty percent of what they made for the eggs, but she explained that it paid for the chicken feed, and she was tired of always finding a new batch of chicks running about. She agreed that the eggs he took home would be payment for the milk he brought her. Actually, she'd been astounded by the boy's ingenuity. He refused to take any of the setting hens home, claiming he could sell as many eggs as she could furnish. In no time, Norman had a thriving business going, and to her delight, she'd noticed that today he'd been wearing a new wool coat.

Martha continued her stroll, letting out a grunt when she looked at what was once a garden. Well, almost a garden. Spying the rocking chair, she walked over and sat down. It creaked so loudly that at first she thought it was going to break. She ran her hands up and down the smooth wooden arms, admonishing herself for having left such a fine chair outside to weather the elements. Thinking about all the scheming she'd done while sitting on the rocker caused her to laugh. Her anger and frustration had gained her nothing. Every time one problem ended, another one began.

Martha wrapped her arms around her body to keep warm, but she still didn't want to go inside. Not yet. She leaned her head against the back of the chair and looked up at the clear blue sky. The sun was bright, but it bore no warmth. Just like Trace. At first she'd been hurt that he hadn't told her of his trip but his leaving had proved to be a godsend in more ways than one. Her sleepless nights of unfulfilled desire would have driven her into his arms. It had all happened just as he had predicted, even down to the perspiration that covered her body. She'd agonized over her foolishness of keeping him at arm's length when they could have shared those few glorious nights together, and she cursed the women who were probably sharing his bed in Oklahoma City. But she had finally come to realize that she'd done the right thing. If Trace had lost interest in her, Josh would leave him alone.

There was still one big problem, however. If she'd learned anything about Trace, it was that he didn't give up easily. Whether to humor his pride or satisfy his need, he'd try again to claim her body. That was when she would find out just how good an actress she was, or harder yet, how much inner strength she had. During Trace's absence, she'd also come to accept that she was madly in love with him. She couldn't let him die.

Hearing a horse galloping toward the house, Martha pushed herself from the chair and shoved her coat back so she could have easy access to the revolver she now wore at all times. She'd been waiting for Josh's return. This time he was going to be in for a big shock.

As Martha rounded the house, she was surprised to see Daniel, Eddie's oldest son, riding bareback on one of the wagon horses Martha had given the Grahams. The horse was in a hard, pounding trot, but Daniel didn't pull back on the muzzle rope until he was almost on top of her.

"Miss Jackson! You gotta come back to the house with me right away! Ma needs you!"

Seeing the boy's ashen face, Martha didn't waste time asking questions. "You head on back. My horse is faster than yours and it won't take long for me to catch up."

As the boy rode off, Martha ran to the corral. It seemed to take forever to saddle and bridle the gelding, but finally she was mounted and had the gray galloping full stride, chasing after Daniel. When she caught up with the boy, he motioned her on. Martha didn't hesitate. The cold wind whipped unmercifully against her face, but she tried to urge her horse to a faster speed. Something terrible had to have happened, or Daniel wouldn't have been sent to fetch her.

As Martha neared the house, she was horrified to see smoke coming from the lower logs at one side of the cabin. The children were running back and forth with pails of water, and it appeared they had managed to douse the fire. Martha leaped off her horse and ran inside. The first thing she saw was Orvil lying on the floor, his broad face looking as if it had been used for a battering ram. From the way the big man's leg was stretched out awkwardly in front of him, she guessed it could be broken. She started to go to him when she heard a scream from the bedroom.

"Go to Eddie," Orvil pleaded, his voice raspy. "I'll be all right. She's having the baby. I can't help her."

Martha fought to control her panic. She had never delivered a baby, and this one wasn't supposed to be due yet! Hearing Eddie scream again, she steeled herself and entered the bedroom. Eddie lay on the bed, her hair wet, her face twisted with pain, and her dress clinging to her damp body. Seeing the jolly woman in such a condition ripped at Martha's heart. She turned back into the living room.

"Orvil, I know you're hurting, but I've never done this before. You're going to have to tell me what to do."

Orvil nodded. "You need hot water... the shears and cord are in... are in the stand by the bed."

Martha threw wood into the stove and stirred the hot coals. As soon as the fire had built up, she ran outside to fetch a bucket of water. When she turned to go back inside, she saw the children standing in a group, staring at her. Their faces were smudged with smoke, their eyes questioning. Hearing Eddie scream, little Edwina threw her hands over her ears, tears leaving a trail down her dirty cheeks. Martha knew she had to help Eddie, but she couldn't leave the children thinking that the worst was happening. She set down the bucket and waved the children forward. At first they hesitated, but when Edwina ran forward the others joined her.

Martha hunched down, collecting them in her arms, stroking their thick hair. "It's going to be all right," she soothed, "but in order to help your ma and pa, I need to count on all of you to be very good and very strong. Can you do that?"

They all nodded.

She heard the hard thud of horse's hooves. "Here comes Daniel. I'm going to send him to town for the doctor. Now run to the barn, it's too cold for you to stay out here. Your ma and pa are going to be all right. I promise."

Martha picked up the bucket, then grabbed another one the children had left behind. "Daniel," she called as the boy slid off the big horse, "take my horse and ride to town as fast as you can, and bring the doctor back with you." She saw the concern on his young face. "Like I told the others, everything is going to be fine."

"But, Miss Jackson, I don't know how to ride on a sidesaddle."

Martha glanced at the gelding, which was feeding on a clump of grass. "Can you ride him bareback?"

"A heck of a lot better than I could that plow horse."

"Then pull the saddle off. Now skedaddle."

As Martha entered the house, she prayed she'd be able to keep her promise to the children about everything turning out all right. She placed one of the metal buckets on the stove and was about to return to Eddie when she realized Orvil was no longer in the room. She hurried forward. Orvil was sitting by the bed, holding Eddie's hand as she slept. Martha knew that the only way he could have gotten there was by pulling himself across the room. The pain had to be excruciating.

"I brought water to clean Eddie up," Martha whispered. "Well, Orvil, I think you and I are about to deliver a baby. What do I do first?"

Orvil shook his head. "She's not ready yet. It'll be a while. Let her rest while she can."

"What happened, Orvil?" Martha asked as she went around the bed to examine his leg. She grabbed the shears off the table, then squatted so she could cut his pant leg.

"I don't understand it, Martha." Pain shot across his face as she touched his leg.

"Try to keep talking. I know it hurts. At least this is one thing I do know how to do. My brother used to get in a lot of fights, and I was the only one he would let touch his broken limbs. Now, tell me what happened."

"Three men rode up with bandannas over their noses...."

"It's not a clean break. Go on."

"I came out of the house and they started beating me up. One of them tossed a rope around me, then drug me behind his horse in a wide circle. That's how I broke my leg. I could hear Eddie screaming, begging them to leave me alone. They just laughed. They finally cut me loose, but before leaving they lit some straw and threw it down by the side of the house. That's when Eddie started going into labor."

"Did they say anything?"

"Yes."

His soft-spoken reply made Martha look up. "What?"

"They said they was gonna return, and that I'd best be ready to sign over the land, or next time they wouldn't be so kind."

A hard knot twisted in Martha's stomach. "The snakes."

It was nightfall before the baby arrived. Martha, Orvil and Eddie all laughed with delight as the doctor placed the healthy, strapping son in Eddie's arms. Martha went to the barn and brought the children back so they could all see their new brother.

As Martha lay in the hayloft with the three youngest children cuddled next to her sound asleep, her blood boiled at what those crooks had done to this family. The doctor had set Orvil's leg, but it was going to be some time before he'd be able to do anything, including returning to work. Fortunately the baby was healthy in spite of his early arrival.

It just wasn't fair. The Grahams were good people. Martha contemplated going to the marshal, but what would she say? Three men had come to the Grahams, beat Orvil up and made threats, but no one could identify them. The marshal would scoff at her, just as he had the last time she went to him. Besides, she didn't trust any lawman. She and her brother had kept the Spur Saloon in business by paying off the sheriff. Nevertheless, he certainly turned his back when those biddies had run her out of town.

Before going to sleep, Martha decided to move the entire Graham family to her place. At least they'd be gone when the three crooks returned. She also needed to send Daniel back to town to inform the lumberyard that Orvil wouldn't be reporting to work.

As the stagecoach bounced over the land, Trace watched the first winter snow lightly falling. For three weeks he had perused ledgers and accounts and listened to William telling him how much the profits had risen after he'd combined the construction business with the lumberyard. When he wasn't with William, he had attended parties, played poker and squired beautiful women about town.

He'd gone to Oklahoma City to get Martha out of his system. The possibility of building a house and living there had even entered his mind. He'd never been jealous of a woman's attentions, nor had he ever felt such an overpowering determination to bed a woman. But Martha was driving him over a cliff, and he didn't like it one damn bit.

Unfortunately, it turned out that the women in Oklahoma City didn't appeal to him, something he never thought would happen. He wasn't even tempted to go to a whorehouse. As the days passed, all he could think about was Martha. Had she turned to Josh Whitten in his absence? The thought of that happening only served to lick the flame of fury he felt. If it hadn't been for the fact that Martha was a lady, he would have handled her a lot differently. So he'd decided to return, and this time he wasn't going to let her escape him. She was going to find out that until he tired of her, she was his.

Hearing loud snoring, Trace turned and looked down at the man slumped beside him. Trace pulled his wide-brimmed hat down over his face and leaned his head against the back of the coach. Catching some sleep seemed like a pretty good idea.

Trace arrived home late, and left for the brickyard early the next morning. Because of William's success in Oklahoma City, Trace also was going to add construction to his businesses in Guthrie. After spending the morning talking with his manager at the brickyard, he ate lunch, then went to the lumberyard. He immediately called Colbert into his office.

It wasn't until late afternoon that Trace found out Orvil had suffered a broken leg more than a week ago. Colbert said that Orvil's son had delivered the information, but the boy then hurried off, giving no details about how his father got hurt. Curious, Trace made up his mind to stop by the Graham place on his way home.

Trace stood outside the door of the Grahams' log cabin, looking up at the heavy clouds overhead. Then his gaze returned to the snow-covered land as he tried to figure out where everyone had gone. The stove inside was cold and there were no footprints in the fresh snow, which meant that the family wasn't just off visiting. Strange, considering Orvil was supposed to have a broken leg. He'd already checked the barn. He'd also seen the charred logs at the side of the cabin, which indicated trouble. Were the land robbers now moving into this area? Hoping Martha might be able to supply some answers, he mounted the black stallion and rode off.

As Trace topped a hill, he saw the smoke from Martha's chimney rising above the trees. The stallion's hooves made a crunching noise in the snow as he moved on, and the sound of wood being chopped echoed through the chilling air. Martha was probably getting stocked up before the clouds dropped their next load of snow. She would have to stop soon, because it was already dusk. But as Trace drew nearer, he discovered it wasn't Martha chopping wood, it was the oldest Graham boy. Even more confused, Trace stopped in front of the house and dismounted. He hadn't realized how concerned he was about the family until he felt the flood of relief at seeing Eddie answer his knock on the door. Her flattened stomach made it obvious that she'd had her child.

"Mr. Lockhart, how nice to see you're back," Eddie said worriedly. "Come in and warm yourself. Did you come to tell Orvil he's fired for not being able to work?"

Trace tapped the toes of his boots on the step to knock the snow off, then stepped inside. The delicious smell of food cooking permeated the room, making him realize how hungry he was. "No, Eddie. Is Orvil here?"

"He's in the parlor. You go in."

Trace pulled off his coat, hung it on the peg by the door, then placed his hat over it. "Where's Martha?"

"Upstairs with the baby. I don't mean to be inhospitable, but I must finish supper. You'll stay, won't you? There's plenty."

Trace smiled, thinking about the meal his cook probably had waiting for him. "I'd consider it a pleasure."

Relieved that Orvil might get to keep his job, Eddie scurried back to the kitchen, glad that she'd made three lemon pies instead of the usual two.

Trace stood in the doorway of the parlor, staring at four children spread out on the floor playing . . . poker?

Edwina looked up at her father, who was seated on the chair behind her, helping her hold her cards. "What cards do I want to draw, Pa?"

Hearing the back door slam shut, Trace assumed the older boy had come in. With seven extra people in the house—eight, including the baby—Trace wondered how Martha was faring. Especially since she had claimed she wanted the land so she could be by herself.

"Orvil," Trace acknowledged.

Orvil leaned back in his chair, his bruised face mirroring his pleasure. He shifted his body, moving his splinted leg so it stretched out in front of him. "Mr. Lockhart! How was your trip?"

"It went fine." Trace made his way around the children to the sofa. "Sorry to hear you broke your leg. How did it happen?"

"You kids go see if you can help Martha or your ma. Mr. Lockhart and I want to talk."

Trace watched the towheaded children scatter, leaving the cards in the middle of the floor. "Just because you work for me, Orvil, doesn't mean you can't call me Trace. I stopped by your place and was surprised to find no one home."

"Martha insisted we all come here. She said we'd be safer."

"Oh? What happened to you?"

Edwina was huffing and puffing as she entered the bedroom. "I don't like stairs," she announced to Martha.

Martha held a finger to her lips. "Shh." She rose from the rocking chair and gently put the baby in the crib, careful not to wake him.

Edwina tiptoed over and looked down. "Is he gonna be all right?" she whispered. "He sure is little."

Martha was smiling as she headed Edwina back toward the door. "He's going to be just fine. Is supper ready?"

"I don't know. Is Mr. Lockhart gonna eat with us?"

Martha's heart skipped a beat. "I didn't know we had company," she said as she closed the door behind them.

"He's down talking to Pa."

Though having so many people constantly underfoot had worn on her nerves, Martha was suddenly glad the others were here. The moment she had dreaded had finally arrived. For his own safety, she had to make Trace feel he was no longer welcome in her home.

When Martha entered the parlor, her resolve plummeted. Trace looked so strong and damnably handsome she wanted to run to him and declare her love. But when his eyes shifted toward her, she was surprised by the thunderous look on his face. She had accepted that he had lost interest, but she hadn't expected him to be angry. Hurt at his reaction toward her after having been gone for more than three weeks, she headed for the kitchen. She hadn't gone more than a few feet when a hand clamped down on her shoulder, bringing her to an immediate halt.

"I want to talk to you in private, lady."

His deep voice was gruff, and there was no doubt in Martha's mind that she'd just received an order. She steeled herself, refusing to turn and look at him. She could ill afford to become mesmerized by those crystal-blue eyes. "I'm busy. Surely you've noticed I have company."

"Supper's ready," Eddie called.

Edwina ran up and threw her arms around Martha's legs. "I get to sit by you," she proclaimed in her small voice.

"You pick where we're going to sit while I bring your pa in."

"I'll do it," Trace snapped.

To Martha's relief, Trace removed his hand. She marched into the dining room where Eddie stood waiting.

With the help of a cane, as well as an arm around Trace's shoulder, Orvil had little trouble getting to the table.

Though the food was delicious, Trace was sorry he had stayed. Martha's table could hardly accommodate nine people, plus plates and the bowls of food sitting in the center. Trace felt like a closed-up accordion. He had barely enough room to cut his meat. But apparently he was the only one bothered by the situation.

"What is it you wanted to talk to me about, Trace?" Martha asked nonchalantly as she spooned mashed potatoes onto her plate.

"It can wait."

Having had time to collect her wits, Martha was able to look him straight in the eye. "It can wait?" She put some potatoes on Edwina's plate, then passed the bowl to Daniel. "A moment ago you made it sound urgent."

Trace refused to let Martha bait him. "It is, but I didn't want to embarrass your guests."

The innuendo almost caused Martha to drop her fork. She glanced up and saw Eddie and Orvil staring at her. Nervously, she cleared her throat. "Surely it's not something you can't say in front of us ... or the *children.*"

Trace had to chuckle at seeing how large her eyes became when she said "the children." But his humor quickly faded. "Orvil tells me that you've had their land put in your name."

"That's right, though I hardly think it's any of your concern." Realizing her appetite had suddenly vanished, Martha picked at her food with her fork.

Daniel reached out and grabbed a piece of bread, but before he could get it to his plate, Eddie slapped his hand. Trace watched in disbelief as the bread fell into the peas, quickly soaking up the juice. When Daniel yanked his hand back, his elbow knocked over Edwina's glass of water, its contents splashing all over her. She started screaming and kicking the bottom of the table. One of the other boys threw his napkin at Daniel, calling him a dumb ass, then everyone began yelling at one another. Somehow Trace's glass tipped over, and because of the tight squeeze at the table, he wasn't able to move away before the water cascaded onto his lap.

The room became deathly silent. Trace slowly and deliberately scanned the children's gawking faces. The baby started crying upstairs, which to Trace seemed only fitting. He pushed back his chair and stood.

"I have to go attend to the baby," Eddie whispered. She didn't look at Orvil, she looked at Trace, waiting to be dismissed. Trace nodded, and she hurried away.

Martha was amazed at the control Trace had over everyone, especially the children.

"Daniel," Trace said quietly, "tomorrow night you will have dinner with me at my house. Each night thereafter, another child will dine with me. That is, if it's agreeable with you, Orvil."

Dumbfounded, Orvil nodded his head in agreement.

Trace's gaze shifted to Martha. "Now, I want to talk to you. Come with me to the door."

"No one gives me orders in my house!" Seeing his eyes turn dark blue and the meaningful lift of his eyebrow, Martha knew he wasn't going to take no for an answer. But it wasn't until he started around the table toward her that she jumped to her feet. "Very well," she said, trying to sound condescending, "but make it quick. I have to get this table cleaned up." She followed him to the entry. "All right," she said impatiently, "what is so important?"

"What the hell did you think you were doing by putting the Grahams' land in your name?"

"I told you, that's my business."

"Then just let me guess. You did it so that when those crooks return, Orvil can tell them the land isn't in his name."

"Those men won't return."

"And pray tell, what will keep them from returning?"

"I spoke loudly about it at the land office," she bit out at him, "and I've told everyone I know that I own the land. Whoever these men are, they're bound to find out."

Trace placed a hand on his hip, fighting the desire to give the stubborn woman a good shaking. "Did you tell everyone in all four towns? Think of the number of people you told compared to the number of people that live in this area. The chances of those crooks finding out is nil, my dear. But even if they do, then what? They come after you.''

"That's not your real worry, is it, Trace?'' she seethed. "You're worried about your house, your holdings, and that the crooks will eventually come after you! Well, unlike you, I'm not afraid of them. I wear a gun at all times, and I know how to use it.''

"So, how tall are you? Five foot three, maybe four? How much do you weigh? A hundred and five or ten pounds? And all by yourself you're going to take on three grown men who will be on horses and damn well know how to shoot, rope and apparently aren't averse to using fire!'' He grabbed his hat and shoved it on his head. "I've heard of some foolhardy things in my life, but this beats all!'' He yanked his coat off the peg. "Have you gone to the marshal about this?''

"What good will it do? We have no proof,'' she stated sarcastically.

"Orvil's place isn't the only one those varmints have attacked. Believe me, there have been many more people who they've either run off the land or killed. It looks like I'm going to have to handle this in my own way.'' He pulled on his coat and opened the door.

Martha slammed it shut. "Now you listen to me, Trace Lockhart. I don't want you interfering in my business. Furthermore, I would appreciate it if you never showed your face in my house again. As for the children eating at your place, you can just forget that, also!''

Trace flexed his jaw with determination. "A buggy will arrive at six each night for you and a child. Be ready.''

"Me?'' she gasped. "I refuse, on both accounts. You can't make me do your bidding, *Mr. Lockhart.*''

"I thought you were concerned about the Grahams."

"You know I am."

"Orvil isn't going to be the least bit happy when he finds out he's fired because of you."

"That's blackmail! You wouldn't do that to them."

"No? You're basing a lot on your assumption. Six o'clock." He opened the door and left.

After closing the door, Martha leaned against it, not sure what she should do. Was Trace bluffing? How was she going to get him out of her life if he expected her to dine with him each night? No matter which way she turned, it seemed the chips were always stacked against her. Trace's words about the crooks bore a lot of validity. He'd brought up points that she hadn't stopped to think about. She'd been so sure she had everything under control; now she was having second thoughts. Damn him!

"Are you all right?"

Martha saw Eddie standing a few paces away, holding the nursing baby in her arms.

"You heard?"

"Most of it."

"Did Orvil hear?"

"I doubt it. He's busy making the children clean up the mess they made. Martha, I'm sorry about the way the children acted."

Martha placed her arm around her friend's shoulders and guided her into the parlor. "There's no need for you to apologize, Eddie." Martha grinned sadly. "Actually, I rather enjoyed seeing Trace get water spilled in his lap."

They sat side by side on the sofa, each deep in her own thoughts. "Do you think Trace would fire Orvil?" Martha finally asked.

"I don't think this has anything to do with us," Eddie said quietly.

"What do you mean?"

"Martha, I think you were wrong about Trace losing interest. In fact, I would say he's even more determined than before to have you."

Martha cursed the excitement that charged like tidewater through her veins. "That's ridiculous. Besides, I'm no longer interested in him. I don't even want to be his wife, let alone his mistress." Seeing that the baby had fallen asleep, she took him from Eddie's plump arms and started rocking him.

Eddie placed a cloth over her nipple, then proceeded to button her dress back up. "That's something I don't quite understand."

They both winced upon hearing a plate break in the kitchen.

Eddie refused to let the distraction deter her. "Why have you suddenly lost interest? I've never met a more handsome man. He's charming, intelligent, rich, and he knows what he wants and goes after it. For heaven's sake, what more could you want?"

"A man who loves me."

"That's my point, Martha. Why would Trace be so determined if he doesn't love you? Especially since we both know he could have just about any woman he wants."

"Try to understand, Eddie, I don't love him."

"I don't believe you. There's something going on here that you haven't told me."

"Nonsense."

"Eddie!" Orvil hollered. "Would you come help me out of this blasted chair?"

Eddie was right about one thing, Martha thought as she ran a finger along the baby's tiny hand. Trace was a very determined man. But he wouldn't stand a chance against a man with a gun. She was afraid that if she told Eddie about Josh, somehow it would get back to Trace. Knowing Trace, he'd probably go straight to Josh and confront him. But certainly not with a gun! Oh, no. Trace didn't believe in using weapons, the damn fool! When would he realize that this was the West, not the East?

Chapter Thirteen

Trace stood looking out the window at the carriage driving up from Martha's house. Would she and the boy be in it, or would she refuse to come? If he had to drag her here personally, so be it. She was making it damn hard for him to treat her like a lady, but by God, he wouldn't take no for an answer. He was still furious at her for putting her life in jeopardy.

He thought about his conversation with Marshal Huggens this morning. Ben had ridden out and questioned the same people Trace had, and yes, he agreed that there was every indication land robbers had moved in. But catching them was an entirely different matter. He didn't have enough men to cover the entire area, nor did he know where they would strike next. He was sorry to hear what had happened to the Grahams, but he couldn't keep men constantly staked out at their place, especially without knowing when or if the crooks would come back.

Trace knew Ben was right, but it didn't pacify his gut feeling, which continued to persist. So he'd gone to the roughest saloons he could find and hired ten strong gun-toting men to watch over the Grahams' land as well as his own. If the crooks returned, he'd be ready for them.

He left the dining room and walked the short distance to the foyer. When the heavy front door swung open, he was waiting. He was actually surprised to see Martha enter with Daniel beside her. The butler took her heavy cloak and the boy's jacket.

"Welcome to my home, Martha...Daniel," Trace acknowledged graciously. He was amused to see Daniel's hair washed and neatly trimmed. His clothes weren't of the best quality, but they were warm and clean. Martha looked stunning in her striped wool suit. Before she dropped her skirts the few inches to the floor, he saw snow still clinging to the bottom of her shoes.

Watching his arrogant perusal, Martha tilted up her chin. "Is supper ready?"

"Probably, but first I thought we would have a brandy."

"You know I don't approve of spirits."

Trace smiled. "Unless you're by yourself?"

Martha blinked. He couldn't possibly know what had happened to his bottle of whiskey!

"Please, follow me."

Trace took them into the large study with deep, leather chairs, polished tables and books on the shelves that lined two walls.

"Have you read all these books?" Daniel asked, his eyes taking in everything.

"Most of them. I like to read at night. How about you? Do you like to read?"

"I'm not very good at it yet."

"You will be." Trace went to the bookshelf and pulled out a small book. "I think you'll find this interesting," he said as he handed it to the boy.

Daniel opened it and stared in disbelief at the picture of an Indian staring back at him.

"Why don't you sit down and look through it while Martha and I have a brandy?"

Martha was about to tell Daniel to give back the book, but the boy was obviously entranced with it. He didn't even look up as he moved to one of the chairs and practically disappeared in its depths. She felt Trace's hand on her arm, starting to lead her out of the room. She tried to jerk away, but his hold was firm and he easily moved her forward.

"What do you think you're doing?" she demanded when they were outside the study.

He didn't allow her steps to falter. "Having a brandy. Surely you had brandy when you attended Iris's supper party."

"How do you know about that?"

"Reginal told me. He also warned me that Iris considers herself quite the matchmaker. You and I are her present endeavor."

No wonder she's always talking to me about Trace at the club meetings, Martha thought.

It wasn't until they entered the large parlor that Trace finally released Martha's arm. She stared in awe at the beautiful Chippendale furniture with its graceful outlines and rococo ornamentation. She moved forward, trying to estimate where Trace had been sitting when she shot the chair out from under him. She wanted to see if there were still bullet holes in the floor.

"I had new floorboards put in."

Martha looked up. Trace was holding out a snifter of brandy. She debated whether to take it. It was true that Iris had served brandy, but she'd refused.

Trace grinned at seeing Martha's hesitation. "Come, come, Martha. It's not as if we're going to become drunken sots. I assure you, it's excellent brandy."

"Well, perhaps a sip wouldn't be too sinful." To put some space between them, she moved away, trying to make it appear that she was looking around the room. In reality, she felt jelly-legged at just being alone with Trace. This was going to be more difficult than she had anticipated. She took a sip of brandy, enjoying the smooth taste. "Don't you think we should rejoin Daniel?"

"He's probably welcoming the opportunity to spend some time alone."

She turned and look at him. "He might get into something."

"I doubt it." He went to a side table and removed a slender cigar from a burgundy leather box.

"Trace, I only came tonight because of what you said about Orvil."

"I'm aware of that," he replied before lighting the cigar.

"You can't expect me to come here every night."

"Oh, but I do."

"Were you serious about firing Orvil?"

"Uh-huh."

"Why are you doing this? What purpose does it serve?"

"It serves my purpose. Here I am, trying to be the perfect host, and I already see anger flashing in your eyes. Having company for supper isn't much to ask, Martha. I could have made the price higher."

Martha tipped her glass and took a drink, trying to calm her nerves. He was right. She certainly ought to be able to handle a few nights, and after all, there would be a child with her. Child? "Why did you want a child each night?" she asked out of curiosity.

Trace sent a slow trail of smoke into the air. "It's easier to teach manners to one child at a time. Now if you'll excuse me, I'll tell the cook we're ready to eat."

"By all means, don't let me detain you. The sooner we eat, the sooner we leave." She walked back to him, a sweet smile forming on her full lips. "In fact, give me your cigar and I'll put it out for you."

Trace frowned. "For some reason, I don't trust you when you suddenly become so congenial." Nevertheless, he handed her the cigar, then strolled out of the room.

Martha took several puffs. Trace certainly did have good cigars. Maybe she should go to a tobacco shop after all. She could say she was buying the cigars as a gift. She had just taken another appreciative draw when she heard the click of approaching footsteps on the hardwood floor. Seeing no other recourse, she tossed the cigar into the spittoon and swallowed the smoke. The smoke caught in her throat, throwing her into a coughing spell that quickly brought tears to her eyes. Trace rushed in. She tried to wave him away but the coughing continued. Next thing she knew, he was striking her between the shoulder blades.

"Are . . . you trying . . . to kill me?" she sputtered between coughs. Then of all things, he grabbed her wrists and held her arms up! Finally she began pulling more air into her lungs and the coughing slowly subsided. Still gasping for breath, she pulled a scented handkerchief from her sleeve to mop her red eyes.

"What happened?" Trace asked worriedly.

"I have no idea." She blew her nose. "I just suddenly started coughing."

"Are you all right?"

Martha managed another smile. "Yes, I'm fine. I'll go get Daniel."

Trace glanced suspiciously at the snifter she'd left on the low table, thinking she might have swallowed wrong. But there was as much in it as when he had left. He was shaking his head as he followed her.

When they all entered the dining room, Martha was surprised by the formality of the occasion. A lovely damask tablecloth covered the long table, and the silver bowls and dinnerware were polished to perfection. There were three settings of fine china and crystal. Daniel started to pull a chair out to sit down when Trace stopped him.

"Gentlemen always let the ladies be seated first," Trace gently reprimanded. "It is also proper to pull a lady's chair out for her." He demonstrated how it was done. "If you want to make something of yourself, Daniel, you'd best start learning manners early."

As the meal progressed, Martha was amazed at the infinite patience Trace showed as he guided Daniel through each step—everything from which pieces of tableware to use to how to set his glass on the table properly. He also joked with the boy so he wouldn't feel ill at ease. Every time Daniel looked at Trace, it was with adoring eyes.

"I want you to know, Martha, that I've hired men to watch over Orvil's land as well as mine," Trace commented as the servant poured coffee.

"I told you, it's none of your affair." She didn't want to admit it, but hearing there would be guards alleviated her concern considerably.

"I've made it my affair. As soon as Orvil's leg heals, it will be safe for the family to return home."

Martha shook her head when the maid offered cream for her coffee. "And will Orvil have a job waiting for him?"

"I thought Pa already had a job," Daniel spoke up.

Martha bit her lip. She shouldn't have said anything around the boy. She glanced at Trace, but he was no help. He just sat there, glaring at her. "Of course he will, Daniel," Martha assured him. She gave Trace a hard stare, which he answered with a faint smile.

"I'm glad you've come to see things my way," he said softly.

"Mr. Lockhart," Daniel said, "can I take that book home with me? I'd sure like to try to read it. I never knew there was so much to learn about Indians."

Martha was about to tell the boy he'd have to leave it behind, when Trace spoke up.

"Only if you promise that when you return it, it will be in as good a condition as when I gave it to you."

"I promise I'll take real good care of it."

By the time Martha climbed into bed that night, she had to admit that her evening with Trace had been most enjoyable. Still, she'd never known Trace to do anything without a purpose, and his purpose now wasn't just to teach children table manners. Eddie was right. Trace was stalking her. She'd seen that determined glint in his eyes more than once tonight. She also knew he wasn't going to back down on his threat about Orvil. She gnawed at her inner lip.

At least some good things had come out of tonight's supper. Daniel had returned home on a cloud, telling everyone about how the servants brought the bowl around and placed the food on their plates instead of their having to dish it out for themselves. Also, Orvil and Eddie were ecstatic to learn that they could soon return home safely.

The next day Martha took the small farm wagon to town. She'd told Eddie that she was going to the ladies' club meeting and to buy supplies. Which was true, but actually she needed to get away from the constant demands of a large family. She wanted some peace and quiet. She also needed to think of a plan to divert Trace. Though it was cold enough to see her breath, and the roads were muddy, at least there were no clouds in the sky.

Deep in thought, Martha took the most direct route to the feed store. It was too late to turn around when she realized she would be passing Josh's office. All she could do was hope he didn't see her. Those hopes were dashed when she saw him standing on the walk, talking to a tall, lanky man. She knew the exact minute he saw her because he started crossing the street, going in the very direction she was heading. She didn't have to stop the horses; he did it for her.

"I don't want to talk to you, Josh," she said as he came around the side, still holding on to the reins. She didn't like the hard, set look on his face.

"I've been waiting for you to come see me about our getting married."

"There's not going to be any marriage, Josh, so you might as well make your mind up to it." She tried yanking the reins from his hand, but he had too tight a grip.

"Hear your neighbors got roughed up a bit."

"How did you find out about that?"

"Word gets around."

"Well, it's not going to avail those crooks anything. The land is in my name."

Josh's eyes narrowed. "I didn't know that. I also heard Lockhart is back in town." He curled his lip in disgust. "You haven't forgotten my warning, have you?"

Martha pulled the revolver from her holster, then rested it on her lap, the barrel pointed at Josh. "I haven't forgotten your warning. Trace and I are good friends and neighbors. Nothing more. But I warn you, if you do one thing to him, I'll kill you. Now turn those reins loose."

"You think that gun's going to stop me? Think again, Martha. Before I finish, you're going to be begging me to marry you."

"I said, turn my horses loose."

"How are you going to stop me from taking care of Lockhart? You going to be around him all the time, protecting his cowardly ass? And what about those neighbors of yours? Be a shame to see them get roughed up again, or killed. Did she have any trouble bearing her babe?"

Martha was horrified. How would Josh know Eddie had gone into labor when those crooks arrived unless he was involved? "What are you talking about?" she whispered.

"I think you know exactly what I'm talking about." He released the reins and backed away. "Let me know when you're ready to marry. A fine lady like you should have a big, proper wedding."

"There are guards now to protect them!"

Josh smiled, shrugged his shoulders and went back across the street.

In a daze, Martha flicked the reins. She was horrified to think Josh could have had something to do with what happened to the Grahams.

"Well, I'll be damned!" Vern uttered when Josh rejoined him.

"You'll be damned about what?" Josh snapped. His gaze followed Martha down the street, his irritation at her lack of compliance eating away at him. Couldn't she see how much he loved her?

"Blossom."

Josh turned and looked at Vern. "What did you say?"

"I said Blossom. Everyone in Missouri was wonderin' what happened to her. I sure as hell never thought I'd find her here. How did you get to know her? You gonna introduce me?"

Josh glanced back down the street, then returned his attention to Vern. "Are you sure that's Blossom?"

"Hell, yes. As much money as I lost to her, I'd know her when I saw her. That paint she wore didn't hide her face that much. Damn, she's a beauty. What saloon is she working at?"

Josh still didn't believe him. "Maybe it's just someone who looks like her."

"Dammit, I'm telling you that's her! Hell, that little mole just above her left lip is a dead giveaway. She used to keep it painted black all the time."

Josh suddenly realized Vern was right. From the very beginning something about Martha had suggested to him she was Blossom. He'd forgotten all about the mole. Though it was hardly noticeable now, it was definitely there. "That damn little bitch. And to think all this time I've been treating her like some highfalutin lady."

"Blossom? Hell, she's probably slept with most of the men that came to the Spur Saloon."

Yet I wasn't good enough for her, Josh thought angrily. She probably planned on sinking her claws into Lockhart because he had so much money, but she sure as hell wouldn't want him to know about her past. Well, her plans weren't going to happen. But first he was going to take care of a few things.

"Vern, don't waste any more time on that Graham property. They don't own the land. Here's what I want you boys to do."

Panicked, Martha hurriedly bought her supplies, then headed straight home, forgetting all about the Albatross

Club meeting. Josh was in on the land robbing! She'd
known for some time that he was dangerous, but until
now, she hadn't known just how dangerous! He'd forced
people off their land, and possibly even killed them. The
realization of what he'd done to Orvil and Eddie made her
nauseated. Maybe he hadn't done it himself, but he certainly knew the men who had. He had a perfect setup. As
a real estate dealer, he could tell the men just where to at-
tack. Even Trace had once said that he didn't know where
Josh's money came from.

Oh, God! Trace! Whether or not they saw each other
again was of no importance. In Josh's mind, Trace was
the man standing in his way. Josh was obsessed, and there
seemed to be nothing he would stop at until she agreed to
marry him. But even if she did marry him, that didn't
mean he still wouldn't kill Trace.

By the time she reached home, Martha's head was
pounding unmercifully. There seemed to be nowhere for
her to turn. She couldn't even leave. Other than the men
he'd hired, she was Trace's only protection, for what little that was worth.

To Martha, the next few days seemed to pass in an im-
penetrable haze. She tried to remain cheery during the
day, not to worry Eddie and Orvil. They had enough
problems without her adding to them. Each evening she
took a child to Trace's house for supper. Having brandy
before the meal became a routine. Though Trace treated
her with perfect respect, she avoided looking at him as
much as possible. But even without direct eye contact, she
could feel those crystal-blue eyes constantly on her, boring into her very soul.

By the time she made it back to her bedroom each
night, her body and mind were pulsating with raw desire,
just from being around him, listening to him talk in the

deep, velvety voice that always seemed like a caress, remembering the strong, naked body lying next to hers. To make matters even worse, her resolve to have nothing more to do with him after this supper episode was finished was wearing thin. She loved him more than she thought humanly possible, and her desire to have him make love to her was so overpowering that she thought of little else. It was even beginning to transcend her concern about Josh, something she could ill afford to let happen. She tried telling herself that everything was going to turn out all right, and that Trace was quite capable of taking care of himself. But she knew he couldn't. Not against a man like Josh.

As Martha and Edwina rode the short distance in the carriage toward Trace's home, Martha was convinced that tonight Trace would make his move. After all, he certainly hadn't insisted she come to his house each night just to feed her. Tonight was the last visit by the children, and the fidgety two-year-old sitting beside her was going to be Trace's biggest challenge. After the final meal with the entire family, there would be no reason for her to see him again. She needed time to herself. She *needed* to mend her frayed nerves.

When the carriage stopped and the driver opened the door, Martha felt the cold air rush in. Thick snow was falling, so as soon as the driver helped them down, Martha picked up Edwina, and hurried to the porch. The front door immediately swung open, but it was the butler who greeted them. On the previous visits, Trace had opened the door. Had the supper been called off? Martha had to fight her disappointment. *You don't know what you want,* she scolded herself.

"Mr. Lockhart will be right down," the butler informed Martha as he took her wraps. "He only arrived home a few minutes ago. He asked that you and the little girl make yourselves comfortable in the parlor.''

"Thank you," Martha replied. Seeing Edwina eyeing everything and her small hands opening and closing by her sides, Martha immediately grabbed one of them. As they entered the large room, Martha kept a firm grip on the child's hand, mentally picturing the lovely vase sitting on the marble-topped table crashing to the floor, or the ceramic eagle on yet another table suddenly taking flight with Edwina's help. Martha sat on the far side of the room, as far from temptation as possible, then had Edwina sit beside her.

"I want up!" Edwina insisted a moment later. She began struggling to free herself from Martha's grip.

"No," Martha said patiently, "we'll sit right here and wait."

"I'm hungry!"

"We'll eat shortly."

Edwina leaned forward and sank her sharp teeth into Martha's hand.

"Ouch!" Martha groaned.

The moment she felt her hand released, Edwina slid off the sofa, heading straight for the eagle.

"I believe Miss Jackson told you to remain seated!"

The booming voice stopped Edwina in her tracks. Her eyes traveled all the way up to the stern face of the giant looking down at her. She ran back to Martha as fast as her feet could carry her.

While rubbing her sore hand, Martha stared at Trace. On past nights, he'd worn starched shirts, trousers of fine wool and even a frock coat. Tonight, however, he had on jeans and a plaid shirt. Even his hair looked tousled, as if he'd been in bed. Did he have a woman upstairs?

"I hope we haven't interrupted anything. I'll feed Edwina when we get home." Angry, she stood, ready to leave.

"Supper is ready. Come here, Edwina."

Edwina hesitated, but the minute Trace smiled, she ran straight to him. She giggled when he swung her up in his arms.

He has an effect on all women, no matter what their age, Martha thought bitterly. Martha was about to insist that they leave, when Trace walked out of the room, still carrying Edwina. Refusing to follow, Martha stood her ground. After five minutes of not seeing a soul, she was about to begin searching for them when Trace reappeared through the parlor archway. The little girl wasn't with him.

"What have you done with Edwina?" Martha demanded. "I'm ready to leave."

"Edwina is eating her supper in the kitchen. She'll eventually learn how to act from observing the other children. If you'd be so kind as to follow me, our supper is waiting."

"I'm not hungry. I'll wait here until Edwina is finished."

Trace straightened his hair back with his fingers. "*I'm* hungry. If you don't want to eat, you can sit and keep me company."

Martha's chin jutted forward in defiance. "I said I would wait here!"

"You've picked the wrong day to get stubborn, Martha. I am in just the right mood to have one hell of a fight. Now, are you coming peacefully, or do I have to carry you?"

"I'll scream."

"Scream all you like. Now, are we going peacefully or not?"

Throwing back her shoulders, Martha marched past him.

"We're not eating in the dining room."

Martha stopped and turned. "Where then? The kitchen?"

"Not likely."

Martha balked as he took her by the arm, leading her down one hallway, then another. But each time she attempted to pull away, his hand tightened on her arm, and she continued on. Trace wasn't in a congenial mood tonight, and she definitely felt it would be ill-advised to thwart him. She could only hope that she wouldn't end up regretting it.

When Trace finally ushered her through a wide doorway, Martha gasped with delight. The room was a large greenhouse with all sorts of growing plants. She could even smell herbs. Though humid, it was quite comfortable. There were a few chairs, a beautiful water fountain that wasn't running—probably because it was winter—and a round table with lit candles, places set for two and steaming bowls of food. She looked up and saw that the glass walls and ceiling curved into a dome overhead. Though it was nighttime, the heavy snow falling made it look almost light outside.

"It's beautiful," Martha whispered as she moved toward the table. It's also terribly romantic, she thought nervously.

"I eat here often," Trace said, pulling out a chair for her. As soon as she was settled, he circled around to his side of the table. "There won't be any servants tonight, so you'll have to help yourself to the food."

Though Martha had claimed she wasn't hungry, she quickly discovered that the venison was cooked to perfection and the green beans excellently seasoned.

Trace was amused to see Martha devour everything she'd put on her plate. For such a little woman, she certainly had a big appetite. Over the course of four nights now, he'd watched that barrier she persisted in throwing in front of him gradually dissolve. And when she'd thought his attention was centered on one of the children, he'd clearly seen desire in those magnificent brown eyes. He knew she wanted him, but he didn't know why she'd put a stop to any more lovemaking, especially when she'd derived sheer, uninhibited pleasure from it. But nothing about the woman had ever made any sense, so why should this be any different?

"Haven't you been getting much sleep?" he asked casually.

"Of course I have. Why would you ask?"

"You have dark circles under your eyes and your cheeks are becoming quite hollow."

"Oh. Well . . . that's probably because having so many people in my house keeps me hopping." She took the last bite of food, then set down her fork. The meal she'd cooked for him so long ago had been nothing compared to the meals she enjoyed at his house. She glanced at his plate, suddenly realizing he'd eaten very little.

A servant came in, whispered something in Trace's ear, then left.

"I thought you were hungry," Martha commented, feeling satisfied after eating such wonderful food.

"I am."

Martha glanced up, then immediately looked away. His steadfast gaze made it very clear he wasn't talking about food. "I'm sure Edwina is ready to leave by now."

"Has your lack of sleep had anything to do with me?"

"No! Absolutely not!" Suddenly she desperately needed to get away, but for the life of her she couldn't remember what halls they'd taken to get here.

"I think your denial comes too quickly. Why do you fight it, Martha? You know you want me every bit as much as I want you."

"That's foolish. How do I find Edwina?"

"Right now, she's on her way home."

"What?" Martha rose, so fast that she tipped over her chair. "I'll walk home!" She threw her napkin onto the table. "Staying here by myself was not part of our agreement!"

"What's wrong, Martha?"

"I don't trust you. Now how do I get out of here?"

"You don't trust me, or is it you don't trust yourself?" he asked as he slowly stood.

"Stay away from me, Trace. I swear I'll scream, bite and kick until there's no breath left in me."

"You make it sound exciting."

"What will your servants think? Don't you dare take another step." She grabbed a fork from the table and pointed it at him. She was about to run for the doorway when he broke out laughing.

"What do you think I'm going to do to you, Martha? If I was interested in rape, I could have done that a long time ago."

Again there was that silken tone in his voice that always sent a thrill up her spine. Danger signals were going off in her head. She couldn't afford to let him have any effect on her. Yet, as he slowly moved forward, her feet seemed rooted to the floor.

"I want you, Martha. Fight it all you like, but you know you feel the same way about me."

Martha kept trying to tell herself that if she went to him, he would be murdered, but she was mesmerized by his voice and eyes.

"Do you really want to use that fork on me?" Trace asked as he stopped in front of her. "Do you really want to go home?" He took her face in his hands, then traced his thumb across her lips. "You have such a wonderful, desirable mouth." He heard the fork hit the floor before he claimed his kiss. When he felt her tongue caressing his, he knew she was finally his for the taking. He lifted her in his arms, drawing pleasure from her face nuzzling his neck, then headed for the back stairs.

"We shouldn't be doing this," Martha whispered, making one last effort, even though she knew it was too late.

"Not one damn thing is going to stop me, short of death! I've waited too long."

To Martha the word *death* was like having ice water splashed in her face. "You have to let me down," she demanded as she began to struggle, but Trace continued up the stairs. "Trace, listen to me! We can't do this. You'll be killed." Suddenly she went flying through the air, landing on a bed large enough for three people. She tried to scramble off but he reached out and shoved her back down.

"What the hell are you trying to pull now?"

Martha raised herself into a sitting position, never taking her eyes off Trace who was still standing beside the bed, hands on hips. His nostrils were flared, his eyes dark with anger.

"There's no way in hell that you're going to get away with acting full of fire one minute, then cold as ice the next. Now you'd better come up with some good answers, or so help me God, I'm going to claim you, whether you like it or not."

Martha bowed her head. She didn't blame Trace for being so angry. Everything he said was true. She needed to warn him instead of keeping Josh's threat a secret. "You're going to be—"

"Speak up. I don't want to miss a word of the excuse you're fixing to come up with. Now pray tell, how am I going to be killed? Are you planning on doing it?"

His biting words caused Martha to flinch. "No, Josh is."

"Come on, Martha. You can find a better excuse than that."

"Trace, you have to listen to me! When we came back from the opera, Josh was waiting in my house. He said he loved me and wanted us to get married."

"Your voice is fading again."

"You don't believe me!" she gasped.

"What are you trying to say? That you shared his bed while I was gone, that you've agreed to marry him and now you feel guilty because I ignite your desire?"

"No! He never laid a hand on me. I told him I wouldn't marry him, then he demanded to know if it was because of you."

"And what did you say to that?" Trace pulled his shirt from his jeans, then began to slowly unbutton it, watching Martha's eyes growing larger by the moment.

"I told him no, but he didn't believe me. Trace, he swears he'll kill you."

"I'm *not* afraid of Josh, Martha."

Martha leaped forward, delivering a fist to Trace's chest. "Then you're a fool, Trace Lockhart!"

Furious, Trace was about to throw Martha back down on the bed, until he saw the tears building in her eyes.

Though he didn't want to let her get by with yet another stunt, he'd never seen her cry, except when she'd had the snake on top of her. Suddenly he began to give some credence to what she was saying. "Martha, why should I worry about Josh's threats? They were probably only made to scare you."

"No, that's what I'm trying to tell you!" She angrily brushed the tears from her cheeks. "He's dangerous. I saw him again in town the day after Daniel came to supper here. He knew about what happened to Orvil and Eddie. I hadn't told anyone. Trace, I know he's involved in the land grabbing."

Trace sat on the edge of the bed and gathered her in his arms. "Martha, I saw the marshal that morning. It was probably through him that Josh heard about what happened to Orvil and his family. Is it because of Josh's threats that you don't want me to make love to you?" Martha looked up, and he couldn't resist kissing her tears away.

"Trace, I'd never forgive myself if something happened to you because of me."

He kissed her moist lips. "Why don't you let me worry about that."

"But I—"

"Shh, my love, let the devil take tonight. I have a far more urgent matter to take care of, and it definitely involves you."

"Eddie and Orvil—"

"Will be told that the snow and ice made it too dangerous for another trip. Now are you going to kiss me or leave a hungry man starving for your love?"

Martha smiled and placed her arms around his neck. "I could never be so cruel. You were right, you know."

"About what?" He nibbled her neck, delighting in the smell of her perfume and the taste of her smooth skin.

"I suffered terribly while you were gone. Oh, Trace, I wanted you so badly."

"I'll try to make sure it doesn't happen again anytime soon." He drew her to her feet, then began removing the pins from her hair. "You're beautiful," he whispered, feeling her hand caressing his chest.

"So are you," she replied huskily, her need for him already pounding in her ears.

At ten the next morning, Trace sat atop his horse, glaring at the Whitten Real Estate sign. The office had been vacated. Of course, Josh could have decided to leave town permanently, but Trace doubted that. Josh had to be in hiding. During his night of carnal bliss with Martha, Trace had asked her seemingly unimportant questions about what exactly Josh had said. He'd then proceeded to convince her it was all a bluff. Trace knew better. The former real estate man wasn't making idle threats.

Trace was now convinced that Curly's death wasn't just related to the seizure of his land. Curly had been showing interest in Martha. Trace had also come to realize that Josh had something to do with the men who had tried to burn down Trace's lumberyard yesterday. He'd just returned home from fighting the fire when Martha and Edwina had arrived last night. No, Josh was out to get him, and he was just taking his time. Toying with Trace. Since Josh was so determined to make Martha his wife, it didn't make sense for him to leave without at least one more try.

Trace turned his horse around and looked up and down the street. Somewhere along the line, Josh would make a mistake. Trace could only wait until it happened. At least

Martha would be safe while the Grahams stayed at her house, and he'd taken the precaution of posting a guard in his own barn to watch both places. Willard Hawkins was a crack shot.

Chapter Fourteen

"Orvil, please reconsider returning home," Martha pleaded. "What if those men come back?"

Orvil shifted his crutch to a more comfortable position. "If they do, this time we'll be ready for them." He patted Martha's shoulder fondly. "You've already done more than a soul could ask for, Martha. You're a good woman, but it's time I started lookin' out for my own family. I wouldn't feel much of a man if I couldn't do that."

Martha nodded. She understood what Orvil was saying, but it didn't alleviate her anxiety. Hearing noise behind her, she turned and watched Eddie come down the stairs, the children laughing and following behind. The baby was tucked in the crook of Eddie's arm, warmly wrapped and ready to travel. "I shall miss all of you."

"It's not as if we're goin' to the end of the earth," Eddie said cheerfully. "And you're not to worry about us. We'll be just fine. Now, you children gather around and kiss Aunt Martha goodbye so we can be on our way."

Martha bent over, returning each child's hug and kiss. "Keep your coats pulled tightly around you," she said as she straightened up. "It's terribly cold out." She pulled their hats down firmly on their heads, giving Edwina a special smile. "I must say, Orvil, when your boys are full-grown, you're going to have all the help you'll need on the farm."

Orvil smiled proudly.

Eddie gave Martha a firm hug, then they all went outside. Not until their farm wagon was headed home did Martha allow her smile to sag. Having so many people living in her house had been a bit of a strain, but she already missed them. Orvil was right, though, she thought as she entered the house, they did have to take care of themselves.

Martha wandered through the parlor and the kitchen, and finally ended up in her bedroom. For the life of her, she couldn't think of what she'd done to keep busy before the Grahams moved in. Embroidery, she suddenly thought. She had never finished that piece Iris had given her. She went back downstairs.

After thirty minutes of trying to concentrate on her stitches, Martha gave up and set the work aside. The house was too quiet, too empty. At least there was one consolation, she thought. With the Grahams gone, she and Trace could spend time together.

She relaxed against the back of the chair, her pink lips spreading into a smile as she relived her night with Trace. Had it been only a week ago? It seemed more like a month. How she longed to have his hands creating magic on her flesh again as he sent her spiraling to heights she had never known existed. After a night of practically endless bliss, she'd been exhausted when she returned home. She'd told Eddie that Trace had arranged a special supper for her, and that by the time they finished their meal, Trace felt the snowstorm was too bad for her to return. She'd assured Eddie that she'd stayed in a separate bedroom, had a good night's sleep and felt quite refreshed. Martha laughed. That statement had proved hard to stand by come five that evening.

Martha glanced toward the window, surprised to see it was already turning dark outside. She decided that tomorrow, after her meeting with the Albatross Club women, she'd pay Trace a call at the lumberyard. Never again would she try holding him at a distance—it wasn't worth the sleepless nights. Even the week since he'd made love to her was far too long to suppress the appetite he'd ignited in her. When he'd come by the other day to ask Orvil if he could work in the office until his leg healed, it was all she could do to keep from touching him. If sharing his bed was the only way she could be with him, then so be it.

But it was his love she so desperately needed. She wanted to be his wife, bear his children, soothe away any disappointments. A dream that didn't show much promise of coming true. She wished she had someone she could talk to. Even though Eddie had made comments in the past about enjoying Trace's pleasures, Martha didn't want her friend to think she was promiscuous. No matter what Eddie said, the woman was a firm believer in marriage being the basis of all romance. Of course there was Iris, but Martha dismissed that possibility as fast as it had entered her mind.

Martha picked up her embroidery again. Though she hadn't let it show, for nearly a month she'd worried herself sick that Josh would make good his threat. But surely if Josh was going to do anything it would have already happened. And Trace did have armed men keeping an eye on everything. She looked down at her work and sighed. She'd never finish the tablecloth. She reached for her shears to clip the threads that were going in the wrong direction.

* * *

Though the snow was deep and the weather chilling, Martha enjoyed the fresh air as she rode to town. She'd spent entirely too much time in the house. She saw a few rabbit tracks in the snow, but Trace's prediction had been right. Game was becoming nonexistent.

As Martha dismounted in front of Iris's big brick house, a livery boy came running forth to take her horse. One rap of the knocker, and the door opened.

"Martha, dear," Iris greeted her guest as she walked into the parlor, "we weren't sure you'd want to ride in today."

Martha smiled. "I needed to get out of the house. Besides, you know I always enjoy these meetings. How else would I be able to keep up with what's happening in town?"

"That's so true."

Before taking a seat, Martha acknowledged the other women seated about, sipping hot cider.

"How is Trace, Martha? Reginal says he hasn't been by the bank lately."

Martha accepted a cup of cider from the maid. "He was at the house the other day asking Orvil Graham to go back to work."

"How are those people doing now?" Adaline Foster asked, concern showing in her round eyes.

"They moved back to their home a couple of days ago. I'm going to see them on my way home. I can only hope those robbers don't come around again."

"I certainly hope Marshal Huggens will soon put a stop to such goings-on." Myrtle Smith patted the back of her gray hair. "How are we going to keep the town civilized and respectable if such crimes go unchecked?"

The other women nodded their heads in agreement.

"The men who started the fire at the Lockhart Lumber Company haven't even been arrested," Iris added.

Flooded with concern, Martha turned to her hostess. "What fire?"

"Didn't Trace tell you?"

"No, he didn't. When did it happen?"

"Let me think." Iris placed a long finger over her lips. "A week ago Tuesday? Yes, that's about right. I heard the fire was put out before it did much damage. Still, those men should have been caught." Iris glanced at Martha, disappointed that the younger woman showed no apparent interest. As attentive to Martha as Trace had seemed at the opera, Iris had been sure there was a romance budding between them. She'd even told Reginal that a wedding would soon be forthcoming. Perhaps the problem was Martha. Iris considered the advisability of having another small supper party and inviting the two of them.

Though Martha managed to maintain a serene outer appearance, she felt as if she'd just had her windpipe cut. She knew exactly why Trace hadn't told her about the fire. He didn't want her to think Josh had his hand in any of it. She knew differently. Josh was keeping his promise. What did she have to do to make Trace realize his life was in danger? she wondered desperately.

As the meeting progressed, somehow Martha managed to paste a smile on her face at the appropriate times, but she added little to the conversation. Finally unable to sit still a moment longer, she stood. "Iris, please forgive me, but I must leave early. I have an appointment at the dressmaker's."

"Of course, my dear." Iris escorted her to the door. "I'm planning another supper party next week. I would like you and Trace to come."

"Thank you, Iris, but with the weather so cold I don't like to go out at night. I haven't seen Trace in days, so I'm afraid you'll have to ask him personally." Martha felt guilty when she saw Iris's obvious disappointment.

"Then perhaps soon."

Martha flashed a bright smile. "I'll keep it in mind. Now I really must be on my way."

As soon as Martha had mounted her gray, she headed straight for Josh's office. When she discovered the place empty, she prayed Josh had left permanently, while knowing deep down that he hadn't.

Trace was in his office talking to Colbert when Martha barged through the open doorway, the angry look on her face immediately alerting him to trouble.

"Colbert," he said casually as Martha came to a halt in front of his desk, "we'll discuss this later. Oh, and please close the door behind you." His eyes remained on Martha. "Has something happened?" he asked as soon as Colbert had left.

"Why didn't you tell me about the fire?"

"I considered it of little consequence."

"Of little consequence? I warned you about Josh, yet you calmly sit there and tell me it's of little consequence?"

"All right, suppose Josh *was* behind it. What would you have me do?"

"Get a gun!"

"Martha, respectable men don't go around town toting a gun."

"Trace, I know that! But we know Josh doesn't fall into the respectable category. I think—"

"I'm honored by such concern." He rose from his chair and went to her.

"Naturally I'm concerned. You're . . . you're my neighbor."

Trace crooked a finger under her chin and gently lifted it. "And you enjoy having me make love to you."

"Well, yes. That, too." Their close proximity was making it difficult for Martha to concentrate. Then his arms encircled her, drawing her tightly against him. His kiss was soft and coaxing. Delicious sensations crept up her spine as their tongues met.

"Orvil told me they had moved back home. I would have come by, but my manager was here from Oklahoma City and I had to stay in town to attend to business. Do you have any idea how I've yearned to have you in my arms again?" When he spoke, his moist lips teasingly brushed against hers.

"Trace, you're trying to avoid the issue."

"Very well," he said softly, refusing to let her leave the harbor of his arms. "If we must pursue this, then let's look at some facts. To begin with, the fire was almost two weeks ago, and nothing has happened since. Nor is there any evidence that Josh was behind it. He's left town, Martha. His office is vacant. Can you produce any arguments to what I've just said?"

Martha lowered her lashes. "No, but you didn't see his face when he said he'd kill you." She looked up at him with pleading eyes. "Trace, why don't you at least let me teach you how to shoot a revolver? Or even a rifle. I'd feel so much better knowing you could protect yourself."

"I have no desire to learn to shoot a gun, and I haven't sloughed off your warning. I told you that I hired men to protect everything. I even have someone in my barn to watch over both our places."

"Your men didn't stop someone from starting the fire." His hands were gently kneading the tight muscles in her back, and she was having a hard time fighting the quickly building desire that threatened to destroy all rational thought.

"Believe me, I'll be all right. It's you I'm worried about, especially since you're now alone. Martha, I want you to keep your eyes open for any trouble."

Martha looked up, longing for another kiss, when the door suddenly swung open. Turning, Martha watched Hazel Carpenter glide in. Colbert was right behind her.

"I tried to stop her," Colbert said apologetically.

"That's all right," Trace replied. "Do come in, Hazel."

Embarrassed at being caught in Trace's arms, Martha quickly stepped away. Though it went against the grain, she considered letting Trace and Hazel have their conversation in private, until she saw the smug look on Hazel's face. Martha wasn't about to let the auburn-haired witch think she had succeeded in making her leave.

"What is it that's so important, Hazel?"

"Trace," Hazel purred, "don't sound so angry. I didn't know you had . . . company." She walked up to him, then tenderly ran a finger across the scar on his jaw. "If you prefer, I'll go back out and wait until you and Martha finish your little . . . discussion."

Martha's jealousy boiled. Trace had just kissed *her,* yet he was making no effort to move away from Hazel! "Please don't let me interrupt," she said flippantly. She circled around the desk and sat in Trace's deep leather chair, making it clear she had no intention of going anywhere. "Trace and I can continue our discussion after *you've* left."

Realizing she wouldn't get anywhere with Trace as long as Martha was in the room, Hazel changed tactics. "Actually, Martha, I'm glad you're here. I know it's well past due, but I want to apologize for the way I've acted toward you. You're such a lovely young woman, and I'm afraid I was terribly jealous." She glanced at Trace, then returned her attention to Martha. "I'm sure you've found out what a charmer Trace can be. He had me convinced that I was someone special to him. I hope he hasn't done the same thing with you."

"What is it you wanted to talk about, Hazel?" Trace interjected.

"Don't be so rude, Trace," Hazel gently scolded, "and wipe that scowl from your face. I'm talking to Martha. However, I did come by for a reason. Josh Whitten told me about the little fire you had, and I wanted to be sure you were all right. See, I'm not still angry at you for the way you acted at my house last week."

Martha slowly rose from the chair, devastated that Trace had visited Hazel so recently. She'd thought... But, as Hazel said, Trace was quite good at making a woman feel she was someone special.

"You've seen Josh?" Trace asked nonchalantly, deliberately letting Hazel think he was uninterested so she wouldn't hold back any information.

Hazel strolled over to the desk, picked up the silver letter opener, then studied the lion's head carved on the end. "I thought you might be jealous. He has shown me a lot of attention lately. Papa is interested in buying some land from him, so he asked Josh over for supper last night."

"I thought he'd left town. His office is vacant," Trace commented.

"Heavens, no. He's been much too busy traveling around, looking personally for land to buy." Hazel put the letter opener back down. "After all, according to Josh, he has to, what with you grabbing up so much land. But he's doing extremely well. He plans on opening a much larger office in the near future. He's asked me to marry him."

"I think you two will make a perfect couple." Trace glanced at Martha, who was making her way to the door, the skirts of her forest-green velvet suit rustling along the floor behind her.

"Do be careful going home," Hazel called. "The ice is terrible."

Martha ignored her and left the office.

Hazel looked up at Trace. "Did I say something wrong?"

"Don't try playing the innocent, Hazel. I know you too well. Where's Josh staying?"

"He was staying at Papa's hotel, but he's out of town for the next week. Well, I really must be on my way." She walked up to Trace, stood on tiptoe and kissed him on the lips. "I don't suppose you'd like to take me to the theater tonight?"

"Hazel," Trace said, feigning shock. "Whatever would Josh think?"

Hazel's smile broadened. "He wouldn't have to know." She turned to leave.

As Hazel went through the doorway, Trace heard a loud smack. Looking up, he not only saw a shocked Hazel, but also a vivid red welt on the side of her cheek.

"That's for spilling the wine on me!" he heard Martha say. By the time Trace reached Hazel, he saw a forest-green skirt pass through the outer office door.

"The nerve of that woman!" Hazel screeched.

Trace's deep, hearty laughter burst forth. "You can't say you didn't ask for it," he finally managed to say.

"Oh!" Hazel lifted her skirts and hightailed it out of there.

"Mr. Lockhart?" Colbert asked sheepishly. "I hope you're not angry because Miss Carpenter barged into your office."

Still laughing, Trace shook his head. "Not in the least."

By the time Trace was again seated behind his desk, his humor over Martha's retaliation had faded. Hazel had said Josh would be gone for a week. What was he up to?

Martha kept the gray gelding moving through the snow and away from the icy road. After talking to Trace, she'd stopped for a short visit at the Graham cabin. Martha had enjoyed holding the baby, who was growing faster than a weed. He was such a happy child. When she told Eddie about slapping Hazel's face, they had both laughed until their sides ached. Pride swelled in her just knowing that she'd played a small part in the family's growing prosperity. There was no doubt in her mind that they would be just fine as long as those raiders didn't return. The Grahams still had a long row to hoe, but they'd make it.

The gelding's ears kept flicking back and forth, and Martha reached down and stroked the horse's thick neck, letting him know he was doing just fine. She wished she could say the same for herself. She'd darted out of the lumber office for fear Trace would be angry with her for what she'd pulled, and also because she didn't want him to see the tears that had been threatening since she discovered he'd been seeing Hazel. But she knew that if she had it to do over again, she wouldn't change a thing. If ever a woman needed to be slapped in the face, it was Hazel. Martha's big worry was still that Trace refused to protect himself.

As she neared home, Martha was surprised to see Trace's black stallion tethered in front of her house. He'd obviously started a fire, because thick smoke was rising from the chimney.

By the time Martha reached the house, Trace had stepped outside, making her realize he'd been watching for her.

"You go inside and get warm," Trace said as he lifted her from the saddle. "I'll put your horse away."

Chilled to the bone, Martha wasn't about to argue. As she hurried into the house, she realized she was tired of arguing. Tired of arguing, tired of worrying and tired of the unfulfilled dream of spending a lifetime with Trace.

Martha felt a cold draft as the door opened and closed. Then Trace walked into the parlor, tall, broad-shouldered and so handsome he made her knees weak. "Trace, I—"

"Your hands are still red." He took her hand and gently started rubbing it. "I've missed you, Martha."

Martha drew her hand away and faced the crackling fire. "Trace, I'm not going to apologize for what I did."

Trace stepped up behind her, placing his arms around her tiny waist, and gave in to the temptation to kiss her creamy white neck, luxuriating in the smoothness of her skin. "I don't expect an apology," he whispered as his head moved up to nibble at her delicate earlobe. "You were more than justified."

Martha closed her eyes, her breathing becoming shallow as his hands cupped her breasts, his tongue trailing a path along her ear. "Trace, I can't accept you seeing another woman. I—"

Trace turned her around so that she was facing him and smiled. "There are no other women, Martha. I already have more than I can handle with the vixen in my arms."

"But Hazel said—"

"You should know by now that Hazel does nothing but stir up trouble. I haven't been with her since the night of my ball. The only reason I was at her father's house a couple of days ago was because Albert wants me to put up some money to build another hotel. I turned him down not only because I don't believe another hotel would be profitable, but also because I don't want to give Hazel any more ammunition for gossip. I've never forgiven her for what she did to you."

"You knew she spilled the wine on purpose?"

"Uh-huh. I saw the whole thing."

"Trace, I'm so worried that Josh—"

"Shh," he murmured, "I don't want to hear another word about Josh Whitten." He trailed his tongue along the outline of her lips and felt her body start to quiver with desire. "Would it be terribly ungentlemanly if I carried you to the bedroom?" he asked, his voice husky with desire.

Martha smiled. "I would die if you didn't."

Chuckling with pleasure, he lifted her up in his arms. "So would I, my love. So would I." He headed for the stairs.

For the next three days, Martha lived in a shell of happiness, the like of which she had never before known. She idolized Trace more than words could ever say, and for the first time, she truly believed that her love was returned. Every night she anxiously waited for Trace to arrive for supper, which she always had ready. They ate and talked, then made wonderful, glorious love. The soft-spoken words they exchanged were like sweet frosting on an already delicious cake.

Finally, Trace belonged to her. Lying in his arms, she told him about Lawrence and how she wished she knew where her brother was. Of course she left out the part about the saloon. Unfortunately, she was finding it more and more difficult to discuss her past, especially since she sometimes had trouble remembering what she'd told Trace before. She was becoming worried that she might contradict herself. Though she felt guilty about the lies, she refused to let anything interfere with her happiness. She had even convinced herself that Josh was indeed just bluffing. Nevertheless, she felt considerably better knowing Trace would be with her. She could protect him if Josh should happen to show up. *She* certainly wasn't averse to using a gun.

It was on the fourth day that Martha heard gunshots. Terrified that Trace might have gone home early and run into a trap, she grabbed her revolver and flew out the door.

Having circled the house, Martha scanned the area, but could see no one. Heedless of the cold, she began making her way through the snow toward Trace's house. She hadn't gone far when she saw a man come staggering out of the barn. His hand clutched at his chest, blood seeping through his fingers. By the time she reached him, he'd already fallen, facedown. The servants also came running out.

"Miss Jackson," Trace's housekeeper gasped, "why did you kill him? He was here to guard everyone."

Martha leaned down and turned the big man over. He was dead. "I didn't shoot him," she replied, realizing that her holding a gun made it appear that she had. "Did anyone see strangers about?"

The servants shook their heads.

Martha motioned to the butler. "Have someone take him to the marshal in town, then go straight to Trace. He needs to know what happened. The rest of you get back inside before you catch your death of cold."

Wilma, the housekeeper, removed her shawl and handed it to Martha. "You'd best be worrying about yourself, as well."

Martha looked at the elderly woman and smiled. "Thank you. I'll see that it's returned."

Not sure there was anything else she could do, Martha again glanced around, then went inside the barn to see if someone might still be in there. She hadn't gone far when she discovered a note nailed to the wall. She pulled it loose and read it.

This is just a reminder that I keep my promises. You're next, Lockhart.

Martha's hand began to shake. She wanted to scream. Even with his guards, her beloved Trace wasn't safe.

Martha's nerves were nearly at the breaking point by the time Trace arrived at her house. She ran into his arms, needing his strength to help calm her. "Oh, Trace," she murmured, "I've been worried senseless that something might have happened to you on the way here."

He stroked her hair and kissed the top of her head. "As you can see, I'm fine."

Martha couldn't believe that after all that had happened, he seemed so calm. He still didn't realize the danger he was in. Frantically she led him into the parlor, then handed him the note. "I found this in the barn."

Trace read it, then wadded it up in his fist.

"Aren't you going to say anything?" Martha asked worriedly.

"There's nothing to say."

"You can't just—"

They both heard the front door open and close. A moment later, Josh stepped into the room.

"I see you got my note, Lockhart." He glanced at Martha. "My note and my woman."

"Get out of my house," Martha ordered him.

"I have a right to visit the woman I love."

Clutched with fear, Martha stepped in front of Trace. Josh's black beard, rough clothing and gun belt made him look like the criminal he was. She had vowed to protect Trace, yet she'd foolishly left her gun in the kitchen. She didn't dare leave for fear Josh would kill him.

Josh moved to the side and picked up a candle holder, pretending to examine it, waiting for Lockhart to make some kind of move. But the big man continued to stand perfectly still. "How do you want to die, Lockhart?" he finally asked. "Personally, I prefer making it slow and easy."

"I've got no quarrel with you, Whitten, so why don't you just drop the matter?"

"Drop the matter? You've been sleeping with my woman and I'm supposed to drop the matter?"

"I'm not your woman."

"The hell you're not! Do you know any other man who's willing to kill for you? Sure as hell not that namby-pamby you're standing in front of, who thinks all he has to do is sit around and give orders. He makes a good show, but I know he's quivering in his boots. He's a coward." Josh pulled out the revolver wedged in the waistband of his pants, placed it on the sideboard and stepped away. "Why don't you go for it, Lockhart? Scared? Or is it that you don't even know how to shoot the damn thing? You haven't got the guts of a chicken."

Trace had been watching Josh's eyes closely, waiting for that certain glint that meant he was ready to gun someone down. But it wasn't there. No, Josh was here for only one reason. To taunt. To prove to Martha that he was a man.

Though Martha would rather have died than let something happen to Trace, she still felt sick to her stomach. For so many years, Lawrence had been her idol. Brave and powerful. Until now, she hadn't realized how important those two words were to her. But until now, she hadn't suspected Trace was a coward. He didn't even try defending himself against Josh's demeaning accusations. It was probably from fear of being killed. Well, she wasn't afraid to go for the gun!

She dashed forward, and snatched it up off the sideboard. "Now get out of my house," she warned, pointing it at Josh, "or so help me God, I'll pull the trigger."

Josh broke out laughing. "Go ahead. You don't think I'd be foolish enough to give the man a loaded gun?"

Martha looked down at the cylinder. There were no bullets. She threw it at Josh, who easily dodged it.

"See why I want her, Lockhart? She's like me. Not afraid of anything. She's got more guts in her little finger than you possess in your entire body. You're a dead man, Lockhart. I want you to think and worry about that. You can hire all the men you want, but it's not going to do you any good. I want you to sweat and wonder just when and where it's going to happen. Decide whether taking my woman was worth it." He picked the revolver off the floor as he left the room.

"If you ever come to my house again, Josh Whitten, I'll kill you!" Martha yelled.

When Martha heard Josh's horse galloping away, she turned to Trace. "You have to leave for Oklahoma City immediately. We'll go to your house, and I'll help you pack."

"I'm not going anywhere, Martha."

"This is the wrong time to act brave, Trace. Do you think Josh was joking about killing you? Think about the other men he's already taken care of. Now, come on. We can't waste time."

"I said I'm not going anywhere."

"What are you going to do? Hire more men? Lock yourself in your house?" Martha placed a hand on her pounding forehead and began pacing. She had to find a way to make Trace understand. "Don't you realize why Josh is doing all this? He knows I care about you, and just killing you would only make me hate him. But if he can run you down in front of me, proving you're not the man he is, then he thinks I won't be upset by your death. And believe me, he is going to kill you. There's no doubt in my mind."

"How much do you care for me, Martha?"

The words were spoken so softly, it took a moment for Martha to realize what he'd said. She stopped pacing and looked at the handsome man still standing in the same spot. "Too much to see you dead." She went to him, but this time she didn't feel safe in his arms. "Trace, I beg of you. Please leave."

"You think I'm a coward, don't you?"

"I think you're a fool."

Trace gently pushed her away. Seeing the disappointment in her brown eyes twisted his gut. "I'm not a coward."

"Fine!" Martha spit out at him. "You're not a coward. Now, are you going to leave or not?"

"I've already told you I'm not."

"So you're going to stay and get yourself killed, just to prove you're brave? Somehow that doesn't make a hell of a lot of sense to me."

Trace was quickly becoming every bit as angry as Martha. "I'm afraid I'm not that noble, my dear. My life happens to mean a great deal to me, and by God, no man or woman has ever called me a coward!" He raked his fingers through his hair. "And just what makes you think I can't protect myself? You've already made up your mind I'm a dead man!"

Martha poked a finger in his chest. "Why? I'll tell you why. Because you can't move faster than a bullet!"

"I've told you, I don't like guns!"

"I'm happy to hear that. I once saw a man who claimed he could catch bullets with his teeth. Is that what you plan on doing?"

"Dammit, Martha, I'm not running from Whitten!"

"Then there's nothing more I can do. Go ahead! Get yourself killed! I don't care! And don't think I'm going to feel responsible when it happens!"

"Well, you'll have one consolation, Miss Jackson. You'll finally have the land to yourself!"

Martha watched him leave, then collapsed on the sofa, her head pounding and tears streaming down her cheeks. "Why, why, why won't he listen to me?" she sobbed.

Chapter Fifteen

Worried and exhausted, Martha finished washing the few dishes, then dried her hands on a cup towel. She felt as if she were standing in a heavy gray cloud, unable to see which direction to turn. Ever since last night's argument with Trace, she'd racked her brain trying to figure out how to get Trace out of town.

"Blossom!"

Martha's heart stopped upon hearing that name called out loud. She had no trouble recognizing Josh's voice. Her hand shook as she picked up the revolver from the counter and left the kitchen. Josh had made a mistake. He'd returned. For the first time in her life, she was going to kill a man.

"Blossom, get out here now!"

Martha opened the front door and stepped out into the thin layer of snow. There were at least ten grubby-looking men on horses gathered in front of her house, but her eyes focused on Josh. He wore a black, wide-brimmed hat. His duster was pulled back, exposing the revolver resting in his holster. "What do you want, Josh?"

Josh laughed, relishing the defiant look on Martha's face. "What are you aiming to do with that gun, *Blossom?* You planning on shooting me?"

"If I have to."

The other men chuckled, well aware that she couldn't even raise her hand before Josh could draw.

"Since you didn't come to me, I've come to you, my sweet. Aren't you going to deny that you're the famous Blossom?"

Suddenly Martha's anxiety disappeared and was replaced with an odd calmness. "Why should I? You seem already convinced who I am."

"Well, I'll be damned. Did you hear that, boys? She still won't admit it."

Again the men laughed.

"What do you want, Josh?"

"I came to fetch you. Like I've said before, you're my woman."

Martha raised the gun and pointed it at him. "Fetch me? I'm not going anywhere with you. I told you that if I ever saw your face again, I'd kill you."

The other men shifted nervously in their saddles, wondering why Josh had let her get the drop on him.

"What good is killing me going to do?" He slowly slipped the toe of his boot from the stirrup. With one swift kick, he could knock the steel from her hand. "These men will kill you. Word will spread all over town that you weren't the lady you pretended to be, but a whore who owned a saloon. Those people don't take kindly to having the wool pulled over their eyes. Your death would be a blessing. After all, it's better than having to admit they were wrong about you. But me? I like you just the way you are."

He watched her glance at his foot, then step out of kicking range. It delighted him to see that she wasn't easily fooled. What a pair they were going to make. His manhood was already hard just thinking about how it was going to feel to be deep inside her.

At a wave of his hand, his men began circling their horses around her. "Now drop that gun," he demanded, his words clipped.

"I'd rather die. But first I'm going to take you with me." Just as she pulled the trigger, a rope circled Martha's wrist and her hand was jerked away. The bullet went harmlessly into the air. Martha struggled to get her hand back down, only to feel the rope pulled tighter, cutting off her circulation. Josh had already moved his horse forward, and pain shot through her hand as he wrenched the gun away. Accepting her failure, she stood still, allowing him to remove the rope.

"What fun I'm going to have taming you, my beauty." Josh grabbed her around the waist, lifting her off the ground onto his horse.

"We'll both be dead first," Martha said venomously. She could smell cheap liquor on his breath, and when his lips crushed hers, his mouth tasted rank. She jerked her head away.

Another man rode up and joined them.

"Well?" Josh demanded of the sandy-haired cowpoke.

"Lockhart hasn't returned yet."

"Then we'll just have to wait," he replied, angry at feeling Martha stiffen from the news.

With Josh's attention on the other rider, Martha managed to twist free and fall to the ground. Frantic with concern for Trace's safety, she tried scrambling to her feet, only to get caught up in her long skirts. She looked up, seeing a cruel smile stretched across Josh's lips.

"Hide the horses in the trees," Josh ordered as he dismounted. "We'll be in the house. Let me know when

Lockhart arrives." He grabbed Martha's arm, jerking her to her feet. "Now we wait, Blossom. I want you to see me kill Lockhart so you'll know what'll happen if you ever try flirting with another man." He dragged her forward. "I took care of Curly Roberts. Now I'll take care of Lockhart."

"You killed Curly?" Martha gasped as they entered the house.

Josh guided Martha into the parlor. "Have a seat. I hope we won't have long to wait."

"I asked you a question! Did you kill Curly?"

Josh settled himself in the large, red chair. "No, I had one of my men do it, but I intend to handle Lockhart myself. I figure he's had enough time to squirm. Besides, I've waited too long to have you all to myself."

Martha was numb, and heartsick for having failed to kill Josh. Sweet, gentle Curly had been killed because of her, and now Trace was next. She loved Trace, even if he was a coward. But didn't it take more strength to stand by one's values?

She glanced toward the window, worry tearing at her heart. It was already starting to get dark. How much longer would it be before Trace came home? She sat on the sofa, twisting her hands. *Think, Martha, think! There has to be a way of turning this to your advantage.*

She forced herself to concentrate on what had happened between her and Josh, wishing she had never agreed to go to lunch with him that first time, so many months ago. But throughout the boggled mess, two things were consistent. Josh had never harmed her, and he wanted her for himself. It was an obsession.

Slowly she began to wonder that if Josh was obsessed, wouldn't he prefer her to go to him willingly? If that were the case, she had the very tool she needed to save Trace's life.

"What do you plan on doing with me after you kill Trace?" Martha asked cautiously, detesting the smug look on his face.

"I don't plan on getting rid of him until he's signed over everything."

"After all that. What then?"

"Then you and I go to San Francisco. I have it all planned. I can get a good price for his land holdings, plus the lumber and brick businesses." He leaned forward. "Then once we reach California, I'll open a saloon and gambling hall, with you as the dealer, of course. You'll become the queen of California."

"And your lover."

Josh looked shocked. "We'll marry."

"How do you plan to make me go along with your plans? Beat me? Kill me?"

"I love you, dammit! You belong to me!"

"I don't belong to anyone unless it's my choice!" Martha barked back at him. "Beating or killing isn't going to make one bit of difference. I care about Trace, but that doesn't mean I love him or that we've bedded, which you keep accusing me of. It means that he's been a good neighbor. Nothing more."

Josh leaned back in his chair. "Real soon, it's not going to make any difference who is right."

Martha was now convinced that she did indeed have the ammunition to save Trace's life. She took several deep breaths. "You say you love me," she said softly, looking at him straight in the eye. "Prove it."

"I've already proved it. There's soon going to be two dead men because of you."

"But they're not the first men you've killed, are they?"

"Hell, no."

"So that's really no proof."

Josh's eyes probed hers. "What are you getting at?"

Needing to gather her wits, Martha took her time smoothing out the skirt of her flannel dress, then brushed back the blond tendrils that had worked their way loose from her hair ribbon during her struggle. "I've thought of a real test," she said evenly. "It will prove you love me as much as you say you do."

"And just what is the test?"

"You and your men leave with a promise to do nothing to Trace. Killing him is the easy way. Letting him go unharmed proves to me that your love is true. When you return at ten tonight, I'll be all yours and gladly go with you to San Francisco."

"And just what guarantee do I have that you won't up and take off, or have a posse waiting?"

"Leave a man here to make sure I don't. I'll even tell you exactly what I'm going to do. As I said, Trace has been good to me. He's furnished beef for my table and fenced in my land, to mention but a few things. He's also asked me to marry him. Don't go getting upset. I never would have accepted. He's nothing like you," she said with a hint of a smile. "I couldn't live with a coward. Nevertheless, I think it only proper that I turn down his proposal to his face. Once I tell him who I really am, I doubt that he'll want anything more to do with me." Nor will he do something foolish enough to get himself killed, she thought. She waited anxiously for Josh's reply.

His elbows resting on the chair arms, Josh steepled his fingers. If that was all it took to make her willing, why not let Martha think she was having her way? After all, she didn't know he had two men trailing Trace, and if she tried anything, they'd put a halt to it fast. All he had to do was tell them to stay out of sight, and Martha would be convinced he'd kept his word. It would also let him see how good she was at keeping her word. He'd tell Vern to let her think she was being trusted.

Of course, as soon as he and Martha were away from here, the two men watching Lockhart could take care of what needed to be done. Martha would never know the bastard was dead.

"Very well," he finally said, "I'm willing to prove my love. I'll do what you ask."

"I have your word that nothing will happen to Trace?"

"Absolutely. And you? Do I have your word not to try to escape?"

Martha had to draw on every ounce of willpower to smile and say yes. She steeled herself to do what she knew had to follow. "Oh, Josh, I really do believe you love me." She stood, went over and sat on his lap, then sealed the bargain with a full kiss on his lips. "We're going to have such fun," she crooned. "I've always wanted to see San Francisco." Feeling his arm start to tighten around her, she quickly slid from his lap. "We'll have plenty of time for that later." She gave him a seductive smile. "Now you have to leave before Trace comes home so he won't become suspicious."

Due to Martha's welcome change of attitude, Josh felt like a man who could conquer anything. But if she was trying to hoodwink him, he'd beat the hell out of her. He rose to his feet and pulled her into his arms, feeling her soft body pressed against his. Yes, he decided, having her come to him willingly was even better than he'd dreamed. He kissed her warm, full lips, then drew away. "Until ten tonight."

As soon as she heard the men ride away, Martha rushed to the kitchen and rinsed her mouth with saltwater in an effort to erase Josh's kiss.

"Is something wrong?"

Martha spun around and saw a tall, lanky man standing only a few feet away. He had small beady eyes, and due to the lines on his face, she guessed his age to be around forty. She remembered seeing him talking to Josh on several occasions. "No. Why do you ask?"

"I saw you rinsing your mouth, and thought maybe you were sick."

"It's just a habit of mine." Martha brushed past him and returned to the parlor.

"Name's Vern. I know you don't remember me, but I played poker with you on a good many occasions at the Spur Saloon."

"Oh, really?" Martha went to the window, pulling the curtain back in an effort to see Trace's castle. If she could rebuild her house, she'd put it at a different angle so the trees wouldn't block her view. She released a heavy sigh. What difference did it make? After tonight she'd never see this place again. But at least Trace would be safe, and that was all that really mattered.

"I always thought you were the most beautiful woman I ever laid eyes on."

"How nice of you to say so."

"I'm the one who told Josh who you were," Vern bragged. "Hell, I would've known you anywhere."

"You'll never know how much that means to me." Seeing movement near the castle, Martha stood on tiptoes so she could look between the tree branches. Even though it was practically dark, she could tell it was Trace by the way he sat in the saddle. Tall and straight.

Martha let the curtain fall back into place, then glanced at the clock on the fireplace mantel. Five forty-five. In four hours and fifteen minutes, her life would cease to exist. She'd dealt her cards, now she had to play them. "Trace Lockhart has arrived home. I might as well go over there and get this over with."

"Josh sure is a lucky man to have a woman like you."

Martha hesitated to leave. Perhaps Vern could tell her more about Josh. Something she could use to her advantage. Convinced she should have been an actress, she gave Vern a broad smile. "You boys have done pretty well around here, haven't you?"

"Yep." Vern tucked his thumbs under his gun belt. "It started out with Josh, me and a couple of others, but the taking was so good, Josh decided to quit actin' like a real estate man and ride with us. Then he realized we could double our take and hired some more men."

"Did you and Josh ride together before coming here?"

"Naw. Josh was always a loner. We just happen to know each other."

"I guess he's a pretty famous outlaw."

"I wouldn't say that. He robbed trains and banks, but nothing real big. He's best known for being fast with a gun. I have known other famous gunmen. Especially around Dodge City, Kansas, and Texas."

Martha was quickly losing interest. Vern wasn't telling her anything she hadn't already suspected, and she had a more important matter to take care of. She headed for the hall tree to get her cape.

"Did you hear about the gunfight between Luke Shor and Sam Coffee?"

"Who didn't?" She draped the cape over her shoulders, then pulled the hood up. "It was even in the news paper."

"I saw the fight," Vern said proudly. "It weren't no contest. Coffee didn't even clear leather before Short shot him. They buried Coffee right outside of town with nothin' more than a little cross. Didn't even have his name on it. When I die, I want a tombstone with my name on it."

Martha stared at the hard-faced man. "Tell me, Vern, the people that you took land from, did you kill them?"

"Most of them," he stated matter-of-factly. "Hell, we couldn't very well leave anyone to identify us."

"Vern, I hope you get that tombstone."

"What do you mean by that?"

"Nothing." She tugged her leather gloves on. "I know Josh had you stay to keep an eye on me, so he probably also told you I'm going for a short visit with Trace Lockhart. I'll walk over. You can watch through the window to make sure I'm not up to anything. That way you won't have to stand out in the cold."

Vern nodded. "You got any whiskey?"

"There's a little left in the kitchen cupboard."

Vern opened the door for her.

The cold air sapped Martha's breath, but she felt the need for it. She needed to clear her head before facing Trace. She had to create a convincing performance that would make him believe she wanted nothing more to do with him. It wasn't going to be easy. Even though they had argued, she knew he still wanted her, and for as long as she'd known him, he'd never backed down when something he wanted was at stake. It was too bad he didn't have that same drive when it came to handling Josh.

The snow was deeper than Martha had thought. With each step, a little more found its way into the tops of her boots. She slipped several times on ice, causing her hood to fall back, but still she trudged on, her dress getting weighed down with the snow that collected on the hem. The sooner she got this over with, the sooner she'd be able to determine when she could kill Josh.

It seemed like an eternity before Martha reached the porch and lifted the brass knocker, and another eternity before someone answered.

"Miss Jackson!" The maid opened the door wider. "Come in. My goodness, you shouldn't be out in such weather. Here, let me take your wrap. You go right into the parlor and warm up by the fireplace while I tell Mr. Lockhart you're here."

Martha was starting to get feeling back into her hands when she heard the click of heels on the hardwood floor behind her. Bracing herself, she slowly turned to face the one man she was willing to die for.

"Pearl told me you walked here," Trace said as he stopped in the entryway. "Whatever your reason for coming, it must have been important."

He wore jeans with his wool shirt hanging out, and his thick black hair was tousled. He looked as if he hadn't slept in days. His stern, ungiving face hurt Martha deeply. That he was still angry over their argument last night was obvious. "I came to tell you I'm leaving."

"Couldn't that have waited until tomorrow?"

"No, I'm leaving tonight. Permanently. I'd have brought the deed to the land with me, but as luck would have it, it slipped my mind. You'll find the papers in the drawer of my dressing table. They'll be signed."

"You're not taking your furniture?"

"No, I'm traveling by train. Hazel had a good idea about using my place to house servants. You might want to give it some thought."

Pearl entered, carrying a silver coffee service. After placing it on one of the small tables, she poured two cups full of the steaming, dark liquid, then handed one to Martha, the other to Trace. "Will there be anything else, sir?" she asked.

"That will be all," Trace replied.

The chubby maid scurried out of the room.

Martha was grateful for the coffee. It helped thaw her innards.

Trace set down his full cup. He'd already ascertained that Josh wasn't going to hurt Martha. All night and day he'd fought with himself over what he should do about Josh. He was still mad as hell that Martha thought of him as a coward. His knowing he loved her didn't help matters. Before Josh had barged in last night, he'd been ready to ask her to marry him. "Why the haste to leave, Martha?"

"I decided to go look for my brother Lawrence, and I've come to the conclusion that I hate the winters here. So there's no reason for me to delay."

"Will you marry me?"

Martha almost dropped her cup. How she'd prayed to hear those words. She bit her lip to keep from showing the momentary excitement that surged through her. He loved her! He had to love her or he would never have asked her to marry him. But it was too late. Maybe some things were just never meant to be. Now, even more than before, she had to convince him there could never be any future for them.

"Marry you?" she said scornfully. "Heavens, no. I have to admit that at one time I wanted you to marry me for your money, but I've lost interest now. There's someone else I find far more exciting."

"And just who might that be?" he asked in a danger-ously soft voice.

Martha took a deep breath. "Josh. Josh Whitten."

"I don't believe you! He's forced you into this. You know as well as I do the kind of man he is. He even had his men beat up Orvil!"

It was all Martha could do to force out the next words. "Yes, but then he left Orvil alone. What you don't un-derstand is that Josh is rich and exciting. The type of man I like." She walked over to the side table and set down her cup. "Would you care to join me?" she asked as she held up the whiskey decanter. "After that cold walk, I could use a stiff shot. No? Fine. I'll drink by myself." She poured a hefty amount into a glass and downed it.

"Now it makes sense," Trace scoffed.

"What makes sense?"

"Why you insisted I leave my bottle of whiskey at your house."

Martha shrugged her shoulders. Seeing a box of ci-gars, she opened it, pulled one out, then ran it beneath her nose, inhaling deeply. "You do smoke good cigars, Trace. I always appreciated it when you left a long butt be-hind."

"You smoked my cigars, too?" Trace demanded, his eyes growing narrower with each passing minute.

"You see, Trace—" Martha bit off the end of the cigar and lit it "—there are a few things I failed to tell you." She took several long puffs. "In fact, the few things I did tell you were lies, with the exception of my brother." She blew two perfect smoke rings. "One of those lies was about why I came to the Oklahoma Territory. True, I did want the land, but you see, I had just been run out of town by the social biddies in Bickerton, Missouri. That's where I owned the Spur Saloon. I was known as Blossom. In fact,

I lived in that saloon for practically ten years. Perhaps you've heard of me?''

"I don't believe you. You were a virgin.''

"Yes, well, even that can be faked if you know the right tricks. So you see, I'm actually doing you a favor. I would never have made you a good wife. I never could abide a coward.''

"A coward?'' Trace stormed.

"Don't take it so hard. I've duped better men than you.''

"Then, by God, if you're a whore, I see no reason why I can't treat you like one!''

Seeing him marching toward her, Martha became frantic. Never had she seen such fury on a man's face. Not even Josh's. His crystal-blue eyes now looked as black as his hair, and they were boring right through her. "You lay one hand on me and I'll scream so loud every servant in the place will come running. Then I'll tell them you wanted to marry a whore. I'll even remain long enough to inform the whole town. What will your precious reputation be then?''

"I don't give a damn about my reputation. You've pushed me too far this time.''

Martha was about to scream at the top of her lungs when Trace came to a sudden halt.

"Get out of my house,'' he sneered.

Martha ran as fast as her feet could carry her. She snatched up her coat by the door, not bothering to put it on until she was outside. Realizing she still held the cigar, she let it fall in the snow. The moment she heard the door slam behind her, the sobs began. She'd seen the anger on Trace's face, but she'd also seen the hurt. It was that hurt that caused something inside her to die. Life no longer had any meaning.

Martha continued to run, fall, run and fall again until she neared the house. The sobbing had stopped, but she couldn't afford to let anyone know she'd been crying. Grabbing a handful of snow, she washed her face, then continued on, her efforts causing her to gasp for breath.

Consumed with fury, Trace went back into the parlor, slamming his big fist onto the first table he came to. The glass Martha had drunk from went flying across the room, crashing against the far wall. Hands on hips, he remained still, trying to get his temper back under control. He'd stopped himself just in time to keep from raping Martha right on this very floor, just to get even with her. He thought of all the times he'd gone out of his way to treat her like a lady, and all the times she'd been making a fool of him. Dammit, he should have realized what was going on right from the beginning. He'd seen all the signs staring him in the face. But no, like an ass, he had to go fall in love. And what made him even more furious was that he still loved her.

He began pacing the floor, and slowly some other realizations came into focus. When he was younger, he'd slept with the best whores in the business, and there was a hell of a lot of difference between them and Martha. Especially that first time. No, it didn't add up. He truly believed she had been a saloon girl, but how could she have been a virgin? Then he remembered her telling him how overly protective her brother had been. And didn't she say he'd left only about a year before she came out here?

He stopped and glanced at the grandfather clock. The same one Martha kept looking at before she left. The gnawing in his gut was telling him something wasn't right. Two and two might not add up, but he was positive of the love he'd seen shining in her eyes so many times. He'd known too many other women who'd tried faking love. Martha wasn't one of them. So if she truly loved him, why would she run off with Josh?

Thinking of Josh reminded him of the two rough-looking gunslingers that had been following him all day. He'd deliberately acted as if he didn't notice. It was time he got some honest answers.

His anger only partially under control, Trace left the parlor and bounded up the long staircase, two steps at a time. No man, or woman, had ever called him a coward, and by damn, he wasn't going to take it. There would be no more vacillating. Maybe some vows were only made to be broken.

With cold-blooded determination, Martha sat quietly in the parlor, listening to the clock tick. Earlier Vern had tried to get her to play poker, but she'd flatly refused. All she wanted to do was to get Josh and his men away from here. She glanced over at Vern, sound asleep on the sofa, the empty bottle of whiskey still in his hand. Martha's smile was venomous. She'd already sneaked upstairs to get the derringer that was presently tucked safely in her stocking.

Suddenly, she heard a sound and jumped.

Were those gunshots? No, it couldn't have been. She was just jittery, and her imagination was running away with itself. To make the time pass, she decided to choose a time to kill Josh. She finally settled on the first night they were alone. She'd wait until he was undressed.

Her gaze snapped toward the window, convinced she'd seen something move out of the corner of her eye. Nothing. She sneered at herself. Now she was seeing things. Yet she couldn't get rid of the feeling that something was about to happen.

Then, as quiet as a cat, Trace stepped into the parlor. Martha was too dumbstruck to speak. A gun belt rode low on his narrow hips, the holster tied around his thigh, and an ivory-handled revolver was nestled inside. He looked toward Vern, and raw fear raced through her veins. Trace was fixing to get himself killed! He didn't even know how to shoot a gun! He started to move forward, and without considering the ramifications, she yelled, "No!"

Vern jerked to his feet, the bottle falling to the floor as his hand went for his gun.

Martha also rose in an effort to prevent what was about to happen, knowing it was already too late. She heard a shot fired, then watched in disbelief as Vern slumped to the floor. She looked back at Trace, but his gun was still in its holster. In a daze, she ran to him. "Darling, are you all right?" She looked him over, checking for blood. "Did he..." Suddenly she stopped and backed away. "You killed him!" she accused.

"Better him than me," he stated in a chilling voice.

"You killed him!" Martha repeated. "Of all the..." She felt her temper rising in her throat. "Where did you learn to draw like that?"

"You weren't the only one keeping secrets, my love."

"You mean to tell me that you've known how to shoot all along," she questioned slowly and deliberately, "yet you let me worry myself sick that you might get killed? Do you have any idea what I've gone through? You worthless ... underhanded ... uncaring ... conniving ... bastard!" She reached back and grabbed the first thing her hand connected with. A candlestick holder fit her hand perfectly. But before she could throw it, Trace grabbed her wrist. "Don't you touch me!" she warned, but dropped the silver holder. "I hate you! I deserve an explanation!"

"Dammit, Martha, I just killed three men. Now I want to know what the hell is going on here!"

"Three men? Holy Mother! What three men?"

"I'll tell you about it later. Now answer my question!"

His words snapped Martha back to reality. "Trace, you have to get out of here." She tried shoving him toward the door, but it was like trying to push a wagon single-handedly. "At ten, or maybe even sooner, Josh will be returning with his men. They'll kill you."

"Is that one of them?" He nodded his head toward Vern.

"Yes."

"What was he doing here?"

"Guarding me. Now you must—"

"Why was he guarding you?"

"Stop asking questions and get out of here!"

"Not until I have some answers, lady."

"All right." Martha started wringing her hands. "You really are a glutton for punishment. Josh and I are leaving together, and Vern was here to make sure you didn't try to interfere."

Trace glared down at her, noting how nervous she was and how she refused to look him in the eye. If she didn't give a damn about him, why did she just call him darling? And why was she so concerned about him being killed? "I'm going to put a stop to Josh and his men once and for all."

"How? There are too many of them."

"You said he was going to return at ten. I don't have time to get the marshal, but I sure as hell have time to round up the homesteaders." Trace turned to leave, then stopped and looked back at Martha. "It's all in your hands now. You can either warn Josh and his men when they come riding back, or you can be rid of him. But if you choose the latter, you'd damn well better be ready to give me some straight answers about what you're trying to pull!''

"What about Vern?"

Trace came back and picked up the dead man as if he weighed no more than a feather, then slung him over his shoulder. "Wipe the blood off the floor. If Whitten comes early, you can tell him the last time you saw Vern he was headed for the outhouse. Like I said, it's your choice."

Martha shuddered. Trace's voice was devoid of any warmth.

For nearly an hour, Martha sat or paced the floor, worrying, wondering, clinging to the desperate hope that everything would turn out all right. But even as much as she loved Trace, she came to realize she couldn't forgive him for all the worry and unnecessary heartache he'd put her through. She had no idea how many other things he'd kept from her, or if she could ever trust him again. She also wanted to know where he had learned to draw like that—an ability one didn't acquire without years of practice. He was certainly no Easterner. One thing was for certain. He'd have to have a mighty good explanation, or, as devastating as the thought was, there would be no wedding. On the other hand, marriage might not be an issue anymore. Tonight she'd probably killed what love he'd felt for her. She went to get a rag and water to clean up the blood.

By ten to ten, Martha felt like a spider dangling from a single web that could be severed by little more than a breeze. Her thoughts darted in a dozen different directions. Where were the homesteaders? How close was Josh? Why hadn't she heard any noise outside? Surely if the homesteaders were gathering she'd be able to hear them. What if they refused to come? Had Trace returned? If so, why hadn't he let her know?

Perhaps she'd been wrong about his draw, she mused. Maybe he'd already had the gun drawn when he entered the parlor and she just hadn't noticed. She didn't know. She didn't know anything anymore. She stopped breathing. Were those hoofbeats she heard?

Her hand flew to her mouth as bile rose in her throat. Could she delay Josh? Could she once again force herself to act as if he were the only man she cared for, when she couldn't bear having him touch her? She forced her arms down to her sides and squared her shoulders. There was no choice. She had to do it. She had just reached the front door and was about to open it when the silent night was suddenly filled with an explosion of gunshots, seeming to come from all directions. In a stupor, Martha continued staring at the doorknob, expecting it to turn at any moment, and Josh to come walking in.

The door suddenly flew open, and Martha fainted.

Martha had a hard time pulling herself out of the thick fog that imprisoned her. Then something cold was placed on her forehead. Her eyelids snapped open, and she was looking directly into a pair of blue eyes.

"Are you all right?" Trace asked, concern threading his words.

Remembering the horror of waiting for the door to open, Martha called out, "Josh!"

Trace straightened, a bitter taste invading his mouth at hearing that name and seeing the concern etched across Martha's face. "Josh and his men are dead," he stated coldly. "Eddie," he called over his shoulder, "you can come in now. Martha is fine." He left the bedroom.

Martha was flooded with relief, but her exhaustion was overpowering. Seeing Eddie's gentle, round face helped ease her mind. "What are you doing here?"

"Oh, Martha, you look like death." She tenderly removed the cloth from her friend's head and dunked it into the bowl of water sitting by the bed. Her heart ached at seeing the dark circles beneath Martha's lovely eyes. "Thanks to you and Trace, everything is just fine. Now you get some rest. There will be plenty of time for explanations in the morning. I'll be right here by your bed."

Martha raised up on an elbow. "Eddie, I have to know. What about Josh and his men?"

"They're all dead."

"I didn't get a chance to see. Is Trace hurt?"

"Like you, I think he just needs a good night's rest."

Martha managed a smile. "He got the homesteaders."

"That he did. Now you rest."

"How did I get up here?"

"Trace carried you. Oh, Martha, he was so concerned, he wouldn't even let me take care of you. He insisted on doing it himself."

Martha settled back down on her bed, knowing everything was going to be all right. At least she could go on with her life, standing by Trace's side. She closed her eyes, allowing her exhaustion to take over. "I love him," she whispered before dropping off to sleep.

Chapter Sixteen

Martha awoke feeling rested and lazy. It had to be nearly noon. The sun shone brightly through the window, fluffy white clouds were floating against a cornflower-blue sky, and she felt as if the weight of the world had been lifted from her shoulders. Trace was safe.

A frown suddenly creased her forehead as the joyous mood vanished. Trace. After everything she'd told him last night, would he still want her? She could always lie, saying Josh had forced her to make up the story, but what purpose would it serve? What if someone else rode into town and recognized her?

The delicious aroma of frying bacon drifted in through the open door, making her realize how hungry she was. She climbed out of bed. She hadn't eaten in two days. Strange, she thought as she slipped on her robe and slippers. How could she be hungry when she had lost the man she loved? She suddenly broke out laughing. She couldn't believe Trace would have asked her to marry him if he didn't love her in return. Surely there was a way for them to get back together; she just needed time to figure it out. Even the fact that he hadn't told her he could shoot a gun no longer seemed important enough for her not to want to marry him.

"Eddie?" she called as she went down the stairs. "I'm starving."

Eddie poked her head out of the kitchen, her face beaming with delight. "It will only take me a minute to fix the biggest breakfast you've ever set your eyes on."

"Has Trace been back?"

"No, I haven't seen hide nor hair of him." Eddie giggled as she returned to the stove. "Is there going to be a wedding?"

Discovering that Trace hadn't even been over to see how she was faring caused Martha's happy mood to wane. "If I have anything to do with it, there will. It just depends on how forgiving Trace can be," she said sadly. "You see, I told him last night that I owned a saloon, then proceeded to drink his whiskey and smoke his cigar."

"Oh, my. You could lie about it."

"I thought about that," Martha said as she sat at the round table, "but the time has come for truths. Tell me what happened last night." As hungry as she'd been when she came downstairs, she could now only pick at the plate of biscuits, gravy, eggs and bacon that Eddie set in front of her.

"There's not much to tell." Eddie sat across from Martha. "Trace must have ridden like the devil to get to so many homesteaders, and each one branched out to tell others. I came with Orvil and saw it all. Oh, Martha, it was a sight to behold," Eddie said excitedly. "Trace had the men well hidden in the snow and trees, and when them crooks rode in, they were surrounded. Trace hollered for them to drop their guns, but Josh and his men started firing and trying to escape. Our men returned the fire, and within minutes they were all dead. I can't tell you how good it made me feel."

Martha placed her fork on the plate, her appetite completely gone. So many men had been killed. But thank God it was them, not Trace, and that the raids on the homesteaders had come to an end. "Where are the children?"

"Trace told Orvil to stay home and take care of them so I could watch after you."

He still cares, Martha thought, I know he does! "Thank you for the breakfast, Eddie. I'm sure you're anxious to get back."

"Well, I am a bit concerned about the baby."

Martha gave Eddie an endearing smile. "You've been a good friend. Now you go along. I'll be just fine."

By the time Martha had attended to her toilet, she was ready to face Trace. She had to keep clinging to the belief that there was still a chance for them.

Outfitted in her royal-blue satin dress, devoid of corset and bustle, Martha left the house. Norman Jordan, who was busily cleaning out the chicken coop, waved when she passed by. Even the gelding tossed his head up and down, offering a friendly nicker.

As she made her way across the field, Martha saw slivers of green grass sticking their heads up through the melting snow. Spring was going to arrive early, she decided. Nearing the castle, she crossed her fingers. After all she and Trace had been through, it couldn't end here.

Wilma, the housekeeper, answered Martha's knock. "Hello, Miss Jackson. Isn't it wonderful that those terrible men are finally taken care of? At least we can all breathe safely now."

"Yes, it is. Is Mr. Lockhart in?"

"I'm afraid not. He left early this morning for town. He had to talk to the marshal."

"I see," Martha said with disappointment. "When h
returns, please tell him I want to see him."

"I'll certainly do that."

Martha made her way back to the house, not feeling
nearly as hopeful as she had when she'd left.

As the day passed, her spirits and determination to win
Trace back continually plummeted. She tried fortifying
herself by remembering that she wasn't the only one who
hadn't told the truth. Trace was awfully handy with a gun
for a man who had claimed he didn't believe in them.

Martha had just lit the candles in the parlor when she
heard the hard knock. Cupping one of them with her
hand to keep the flame from going out, she made her way
to the door. At first she hesitated to turn the knob, sud
denly remembering her fear last night. Annoyed with
herself, she reached out a shaky hand and opened the
door. Trace's jaw was set, his eyes cold. "Please," she said
softly, her heart fluttering, "come in."

Trace stepped inside, closing the door behind him.
"Wilma said you wanted to see me."

"Yes. Could we go into the parlor and talk?"

"I'll follow."

All day Martha had planned what she was going to say,
but once they were seated on either side of the room
words failed her. Trace's silence and stern look weren't
helping matters one bit. "I think I deserve an explana
tion," she finally managed to say.

"About what?"

Martha was rapidly becoming angry. He was acting as
if everything that had happened was her fault. "To begin
with, how about telling me how you became so good with
a gun."

"What difference does it make?"

"Because I have a right to know. Don't you have any idea of the hell I've gone through worrying about your safety?"

"I would think you'd be more concerned at having lost Josh."

"What is that supposed to mean?"

"That was the first name you called out when you came to."

"I'm not surprised. I was scared to death that he was the one who had banged the door open!"

Trace wanted to believe her, but could he afford that luxury, especially after all her lies? This was probably just another one of her tricks. She didn't get Josh, so now she was turning back to him.

"You don't believe me, do you?" Martha gasped. "Or is it because you now know I owned a saloon, and want nothing more to do with me?" Martha stood, all her past insecurities crushing down on her. "Trace, I thought when you asked me to marry you that it was because you loved me. Was I wrong?"

Seeing the hurt in her eyes was more than Trace could handle. Martha Jackson was the only woman he'd ever loved, and he'd be a fool to let her slip from his hands. She could have warned Josh, but she hadn't, and if he couldn't believe her now, he never would. He studied Martha for a moment, his need for her becoming all-consuming. Damn, if she wasn't a handful! But in all truthfulness, he wouldn't want her any other way.

"So when do you want to get married?"

Martha was both laughing and crying as she ran into his arms. "I love you...I love you," she said, in between kissing his face and neck. When his lips captured hers, she knew this had to be heaven.

* * *

Martha lay languid in her lover's arms, her need for him temporarily sated. "Trace," she said lovingly, "I want to tell you about my past. I don't want any more secrets between us."

"It's not necessary, Martha."

She rolled over and faced him. "No, you need to know. When I was little, my mother died. . . ."

For an hour, Trace listened as Martha revealed her past. He laughed at times, was saddened at others. By the time she finished, all his confusion about the things she'd done since they had first met was answered. His anger flared when he heard about her last talk with Josh, and he wished he'd been the one to kill the bastard.

"Now," Martha said quietly, "do you still want to marry me?"

Trace leaned forward and kissed her lips. "More than ever. You're the only woman I know who had all the experience of a prostitute and was still a virgin."

They both broke out laughing.

The big wedding was held at Trace's castle, with hundreds attending. Eddie cried as Trace took his place beside Martha. The bride wore a white wedding gown with yards of material splashed with hundreds of hand-sewn pearls, and Edwina restlessly stood behind her, holding the end of the long train. Iris sat next to her husband, her hand tucked in his. She watched smugly, convinced she was the one who had gotten the couple together.

After the wedding vows, Trace kissed Martha and everyone cheered.

At the reception, Trace's wedding gift proved to be the most precious of all. It was a letter from Lawrence. Trace escorted her to the library, then closed the doors so she would be left alone.

Slowly Martha opened the letter and read.

Dear Sis,

I am so pleased that your future husband hired someone to find me. I have wondered and worried about you often. Ruth and I are doing fine, and own a big and successful ranch. You're an aunt. I'll tell you all about it when you arrive here for your honeymoon.

Lawrence

Martha dropped the letter and rushed to the door. When she swung it open, she found Trace still standing on the other side. "Trace Lockhart," she accused. "How long have you planned on marrying me?"

"I'd say for about two months."

Martha laughed. "Is there anything else you've kept from me?" She was surprised to see his expression become serious.

"Let's go back inside."

Martha started to remind him of their guests, then thought better of it. "Very well." She sat in one of the deep leather chairs, then watched Trace make sure the heavy doors were securely closed. "Is something wrong?" she asked, her concern quickly growing. "Has something happened to Lawrence?"

"No, Lawrence is fine." Trace leaned against the floor-to-ceiling bookcase, studying his wife. "I had thought it best to let a sleeping dog lie, but I've come to the conclusion that it wouldn't be fair to you. I even considered telling you on the train ride to California."

Martha held her breath, already afraid of what Trace was about to tell her.

"There used to be an outlaw in New Mexico by the name of Sam Coffee, and a year or so ago, because there were Wanted posters all over and a big reward on his head, he decided it would be in his best interest to get out of the territory. On his way to Texas, he saw a coach being attacked by four men. Coffee rode forward, killing the bandits. As it turned out, it was the coach of the governor of New Mexico. When the governor and his secretary climbed out, the secretary recognized Coffee. The governor, convinced they had stepped from one bad situation into another, offered Coffee amnesty in return for his life. The governor was clever enough to add that should Coffee ever return to New Mexico and continue his robbing he would be a dead man. Coffee was more than happy to accept, considering he was leaving the state, anyway. He was tired of being on the run and wanted to start a new life."

"Trace, this is all very interesting, but what does it have to do with us?"

"Let me finish." He walked over, sat in one of the chairs, stretching his legs out. "But Coffee still had one problem. He had a reputation for being a fast gun. Others could make a name for themselves if they could out-draw him."

"Trace—"

"Martha, I'm Sam Coffee."

In shock, Martha fell against the back of her chair. "But...but that's impossible. Everyone knows Sam Coffee is dead. He died in a gunfight with Luke Short."

"Everyone *thought* Coffee was dead."

"There were witnesses, a picture," Martha persisted.

He pulled up his knees and leaned forward. "Luke Short is a friend of mine. It was all set up. Even the sheriff had been paid off to run out and throw a coat over me so no one would discover the truth. Then all it took was to bury an empty coffin while I rode out of town by the back road. No one ever suspected, and no one's ever come looking for me."

"Did you really live in Boston?"

"Uh-huh. But we moved, and I became Coffee. Trace Lockhart is my real name. Luke, Sheriff Cooper and now you are the only ones who know the truth." He watched her closely for some kind of a reaction, but she continued sitting there in a daze. "I won't give you a divorce."

Martha snapped out of her stupor. "A divorce? Why would I want a divorce?"

"Well, I thought—"

"Trace, do you realize the marvelous skeletons we're going to have in our closet? Sam Coffee and Blossom. And since the homesteaders took care of Josh and his men, no one will ever suspect. Do you think we should tell our children?"

Trace laughed at the excitement dancing in her eyes. "Martha, my love, what a challenge it's going to be trying to figure out what goes on in that mind of yours."

"There is one other thing. I can understand why you wouldn't want anyone to know how fast a draw you are, but how could you allow Josh to threaten you?"

Trace saw no reason to tell her about his vow to never pick up a gun again. Enough had already been said. "I knew my time would come." He stood and pulled Martha to her feet. "How long do you think these people are going to hang around here?" He leaned down and gave her a lingering kiss.

"Isn't there a back staircase?"

Trace chuckled. "I can even do better than that. I might not be a wanted man, but the need for a quick escape always remains." He twisted one of the lion's heads on the bookcase, and it slowly swung open. Taking Martha's hand, he led her through the wide opening.

Martha gladly followed. *And to think I thought he was a coward!* So much for her being a good judge of character. She could hardly believe her fortune—she was actually married to Sam Coffee!

They made it as far as the barn, but neither was able to sustain their desire for a moment longer. They ducked inside and climbed up to the hayloft.

"Trace," Martha said as he began undoing the many tiny pearl buttons, "my dress will be ruined."

"I'll buy you a hundred more if you want them."

Martha laughed. "What if someone comes in?"

"Then they're going to be in for one hell of a shock if they climb up here. Nothing is going to stop me from claiming my love."

Martha smiled. "My love. What wonderful words." She lay down beside him in the bed of hay, her life just beginning.

*   *   *   *   *

COMING NEXT MONTH

#127   THE LADY AND THE LAIRD—Maura Seger
Forced by her grandfather's will to live in an eerie Scottish castle
for six months or lose the crumbling keep to rogue Angus Wyndham,
beautiful Katlin Sinclair discovered a tormented ghost, hidden
treasure and burning passion in the arms of the one man she could
not trust.

#128   SWEET SUSPICIONS—Julie Tetel
Intent on reentering society, Richard Worth planned to find a well-
connected wife. But he hadn't expected the murder of a stranger to
revive his scandalous past—or that his marriage of convenience to
lovely Caroline Hutton would awaken his passion and heal his
anguished soul.

#129   THE CLAIM—Lucy Elliot
A confrontation was inevitable when determined Sarah Meade and
formidable mountain man Zeke Brownell both claimed ownership of
the same land. Yet underneath their stubborn facades and cultural
differences there lay a mutual attraction neither could deny.

#130   PIRATE BRIDE—Elizabeth August
Pirate captive Kathleen James impetuously married prisoner
John Ashford to save him from certain death. But although
freedom and happiness were only a breath away, a daring escape
brought them further danger in the New World.

AVAILABLE NOW:

® *Harlequin*®

JANELLE TAYLOR

Valley of Fire

HARLEQUIN IS PROUD TO PRESENT *VALLEY OF FIRE* BY JANELLE TAYLOR—AUTHOR OF TWENTY-TWO BOOKS, INCLUDING SIX *NEW YORK TIMES* BESTSELLERS

VALLEY OF FIRE—the warm and passionate story of Kathy Alexander, a famous romance author, and Steven Winngate, entrepreneur and owner of the magazine that intended to expose the real Kathy "Brandy" Alexander to her fans.

Don't miss VALLEY OF FIRE, available in May.

Summer Reading At Its Best

In July, Harlequin and Silhouette bring readers the Big Summer Read Program. Heat up your summer with these four exciting new novels by top Harlequin and Silhouette authors.

SOMEWHERE IN TIME by Barbara Bretton
YESTERDAY COMES TOMORROW by Rebecca Flanders
A DAY IN APRIL by Mary Lynn Baxter
LOVE CHILD by Patricia Coughlin

From time travel to fame and fortune, this program offers something for everyone.

Available at your favorite retail outlet.

BSR

H A R L E Q U I N
American Romance®

Be a part of American Romance's year-long celebration of love and the holidays of 1992. Celebrate those special times each month with your favorite authors.

Next month, we pay tribute to the *first* man in your life—your father—with a special Father's Day romance:

JUNE

S	M	T			S
	1			4	
7	8				13
14					20
21	22				27
28	29				

**#441
DADDY'S GIRL
by Barbara Bretton**

FATHER'S DAY

Read all the books in *A Calendar of Romance*, coming to you one per month all year, only in American Romance.